In Pursuit of Slave-hunters

By

Henry Wermuth

*To Daniel
with best wishes*

Henry Wermuth

17-05-2015

 New Generation **Publishing**

Contents

Chapter 1

A meeting in the desert

The widow of the late banker Jonathan Ellman looked out of the window of her elegant villa in a prosperous area of a London suburb. Her daughter-in-law, Esther, spoke to her:

"Why are you looking so glum? It is two years since your husband died and he would certainly not want you to be miserable all your life. Think of your two loving sons and your daughter-in-law, who loves you no less; then your outlook will be happier."

"You may be right. Jeremy has taken over my late husband's business and handles it capably. You, his wife, are with me and you help me over my depression. If only Leopold had not gone to Africa, looking for adventure. He is my greatest worry. Our people don't usually crave such things."

"Nonsense! His yearning for distant lands and adventure is no different from that of other young men. He has inherited enough to indulge in such whims."

"You are forgetting that he is engaged and should prefer to be with his betrothed," intervened another voice in the room. It belonged to a lovely young girl of about seventeen. "My parents find his behaviour irresponsible."

"This is my opinion too," said her prospective mother-in-law. "He is my beloved son and I hope he will come to his senses soon."

"It is better he follows his urges before marriage than after," opined the daughter-in-law, Esther.

There was a knock at the door. A girl with a white apron entered. "A letter from your son," she beamed. "I can see an African stamp."

The older woman took it and opened it hastily. The letter was dated 24th August, 1862. "Oh," she exclaimed, "It was written almost two months ago."

"That is not the most important thing. What does he write?"

"I will read it aloud.

"Dearest Mum!

"Knowing you, I am sure you worry about me. Let me tell you that there is no reason. I am happy and I had a great adventure and success recently. I became friends with the famous Reis Effendina, who is the

most feared hunter of slave-traders. We, he and I, had many successes and liberated many slaves. I managed to play the biggest role in this. We have freed over 400 female and about the same amount of male slaves from the hands of these inhuman fellows. Unfortunately, we did not manage to catch the big villains, but we are not finished with them yet. As we have learned, they are planning some more raids on Negro villages, and we will try to prevent them. The slaves we freed were taken back to their village. You would have loved to see the way they feted your son. But there was sadness too, as there were many deaths when the village was originally raided.

"I trust you and the family are keeping well. With hugs and kisses from your loving son,

"Leopold.

"P.S. A letter to my beloved Sarah is on the way. Meanwhile give her a kiss from me!"

Rifka, the mother, put the letter down with a sigh. "I still wish to have him here, out of danger."

"Youth is youth," answered Sarah, her prospective daughter-in-law. "He is clever and will succeed were many others wouldn't."

As said, the letter was nearly two months old and Leopold had left the village with twenty asakers, soldiers in uniform. They were between Es Safih and Kordofān in the Sudan. Their camels had to take a rest. When they reached a well, they could let them graze and refill their own water hoses. They were given a guide to take them to Khartoum where Leopold, after successfully ending his task of taking the freed slaves of the Es Fessarah tribe back to their village, had to hand the asakers back to their commanding officer, the Reis Effendina.

The guide, Abdullah, had a great sorrow. His rifle did not shoot straight, but he loved it and liked to talk about it. He showed it to Leopold and asked him whether he had ever seen such an admirable rifle. The butt displayed an inlay of ivory in such a shape that it was impossible to discern what it was meant to represent.

"Very nice, but what does it mean?"

"What a question! Can't you see?"

He held the butt near Leopold's nose. Leopold tried hard to solve the riddle, but there was nothing to help him.

"You are blind," said Abdullah. "May Allah enlighten your eyes. As you are a disbeliever, it is no miracle that you don't recognise whose head it is."

"A head?" Leopold shook his own.

"Allah, Wallah, Tallah! It is the head of the prophet who sits with Allah."

"Impossible! There is nothing of a head. Where is the nose?"

"The prophet needs no nose. He consists of ten thousand sweet scents."

"Where is the mouth?"

"The prophet needs no mouth. He talks to us through the Koran."

"I can see no eyes and no ears."

"You can't find them because they are not there. Mohammed doesn't need eyes because Allah knows everything and the prophet needs no ears because he prescribed the prayers himself."

"Where is the beard?"

"You cannot see it. One cannot desecrate it through ivory. An oath on the beard of the prophet is the highest and holiest."

"There is only the forehead to see."

"No. It is the seat of the spirit. One cannot make a likeness of it."

"So there is nothing to see of a head?"

"Nothing," confirmed Abdullah, "but I recognise every feature of his face."

"But it is forbidden in your religion to portray a human face; how much more the face of the prophet."

"The artist who made the portrait didn't know this."

"But he must have seen the prophet and known his teachings?"

"He has seen him, but only in his mind. The rifle is ancient. The man who made it lived before the prophet."

"That is impossible. At that time powder was not invented."

"Effendi, please do not rob me of the happiness of possessing such a costly rifle. When Allah wills it, the rifle will shoot without powder."

"I agree that Allah does perform miracles. Here we have two at once. Firstly, a rifle from a time when there was no powder, and secondly a picture of the prophet who wasn't born yet. How did you get it?"

"Through inheritance. I am a descendant of the artist and will pass it on to my son."

"So you are the most famous man of your tribe; it is an honour to know you."

"Yes," said Abdullah seriously. "It is an honour to know the descendant of the artist and I am known in all of the Sudan..." He interrupted himself and shaded his eyes with his hand. "I can see a rider

7

approaching."

When the man on a camel saw the group he stopped. Then he came closer and greeted them: "Salām alźik! Will you permit my camel to graze here, and me to drink from this well?"

"Alźik es salām! I cannot hinder you from doing what you like." Leopold gave him a cool answer without adding a welcome. The stranger had made a bad impression on him. His face had no repellent features, but the sharp and piercing glance with which he examined the group was not to Leopold's liking. He had learned to observe everything and it struck him as odd that the stranger did not address the soldiers in the uniforms of the Viceroy. In these circumstances, he should have asked them. All of this created a slight mistrust that later developed further.

The rider dismounted, let his camel graze after giving it water from the well and sat down opposite Leopold. He filled his pipe and passed his tobacco bag to him.

"Take some, Effendi, it is the pipe of greeting which I offer you."

"Thank you for your kindness, but I won't make use of it," Leopold answered.

"You don't smoke? Do you belong to the strictly religious sect that forbids its followers to smoke?"

His tone was that of a man who knew the answer in advance. It made Leopold even more reserved. "I do smoke, but not your tobacco. The one present has first to receive the newcomer. That is the rule, especially in the desert."

"I know, but I have my heart on my tongue. I liked you at the first glance and I wanted to show this by offering you tobacco. May I ask where you come from?"

"May I first ask, why do you ask me and not those in uniform?"

"I assumed they belong to you."

"Then your perception is admirable."

"So you do not know the desert, while I ride through it often."

"As I was here before you, may I ask where you started your journey?"

"I have no reason to conceal it. In the desert, every man must know who the other is and what he does. I come from El Feky Ibrahim and want to go to El Fasher."

"Between those two places is a well used caravan route. Why have you made such a detour?"

"Because I am a trader and want to know the requirements of the area. I want to make my purchases in El Fasher and sell on the way back."

"You seem to be a beginner in trading."

"Why, Effendi?"

"An experienced trader would not make such a journey empty. He would have carried goods on the way to El Fasher. You lose half your profits. An experienced dealer would not do this."

"I wanted to reach my destination fast and did not want to burden my animal with weight."

"A trader has but one aim – profit. By the way, you are riding an expensive camel. A trader uses a donkey."

"Everybody according to his riches, Effendi. I am not poor. You have heard my answers. May I now ask where you are coming from?"

From Leopold's questions the 'trader' should have felt his distrust. They were, for an honest man, even insulting. Leopold noticed an angry light in the trader's eyes, but he controlled himself and answered politely. The difference between his glance and his speech gave Leopold reason for caution. He didn't believe the stranger to be a trader. Because of the stranger's lies, Leopold decided not to tell the truth.

"I come from Badjaruga," he answered.

"The asakers as well?"

"No, I met them here and they allowed me to use this well."

There was a sly twitch around his mouth but he pretended to believe Leopold's answer and carried on asking:

"And where do they come from?"

"I don't know."

"In the desert curiosity is a duty. I therefore request your permission to ask you about the destination of your journey."

"I am going to Kamlin at the Blue Nile."

"And where do the asakers go?"

"I don't know this either."

He turned quickly to Abdullah who was sitting next to Leopold. "Who are you? I am sure a ben Arab?"

Leopold hoped that Abdullah had noticed his mistrust, but he was disappointed.

"I belong to the Beni Fessarah."

"You come here straight from your homestead?"

"Yes."

"I have heard about the Beni Fessarah. They are valiant and happiness dwells in their tents."

The stranger wanted to sound out the guide; Abdullah was careless and told the stranger to what tribe he belonged. Now it was irrelevant what other information he would divulge. Leopold pretended to be

9

uninterested and stretched himself out on the ground, resting his head on his upright arm but really listening to every word.

"Yes, happiness lived with us but, unfortunately, has left us."

"Allah will bring it back. What happened?"

"Ben Mubarek has robbed our women and daughters. Do you know this infamous slave-hunter?"

"Certainly! His deeds are such that everybody knows him. But you are strict Moslems and he wouldn't take slaves from you. It must have been a pagan tribe who did this."

"I am not mistaken. If you don't believe me, I can easily prove it to you…" Leopold saw that Abdullah was going to point at him. Luckily he looked at him and Leopold gave him a warning sign. He stopped for a moment and then pointed to the asakers. "They were there and know everything."

Abdullah started his report, but was careful enough to call Leopold the foreign Effendi. When he ended the stranger seemed amazed.

"Such infamy! What execrable crime. Allah will punish him!"

"Yes. And the Reis Effendina and the foreign Effendi will find him for sure. He won't escape them."

"Oh, Ben Mubarek is not only audacious, he is also cunning. They will not get him."

"I don't believe that. The foreign Effendi is a man who finds everybody he seeks."

"Then he would be all-knowing. Only Allah is that."

"That is not necessary, his eyes and his mind perceive everything. What he sees connects his sagacity to fruitful results. He did not know the way the slave robbers went, but he calculated it exactly and we have our women back."

"Where is he now?"

"He is – is – is still in our village," answered Abdullah hesitatingly.

"Still in your village?" repeated the stranger with a hidden smile, while looking at Leopold. "I would have liked to meet this man, but my time is short – I have to be off now." With this he went to his camel, saddled it and mounted. Then he turned toward Leopold: "You have told me where you have come from and where you are going, but I don't believe you. I guess who you are. You will soon get to know me."

"What was that?" asked Abdullah. "What did he mean? That was an insult and almost sounded like a threat. He doesn't believe you. He guesses who you are. Do you know what he wants?"

"Probably my life."

"Allah, Allah!"

"And those of the asakers."

"Effendi, you give me a shock."

"So get on your camel and ride home. There will probably be a battle soon and as your rifle does not do what you want, you had better save yourself."

"Effendi, do not shame me. I should take you to Khartoum and I will not leave you until we are there. Where do you get the idea of hostility? The tribes around here live in peace."

"The 'trader' told me."

"I haven't heard a word about it."

"He did not tell me in words, but in his behaviour. Did you believe him to be a trader?"

"Why would he tell us a lie?"

"To deceive us. A spy has every cause to do so."

"A spy? You think he is a spy? Who would have sent him?"

"Maybe Ben Mubarek, to revenge himself."

"How would he know where you are?"

"That is not too difficult. He will have learned that I took the freed slaves back to their home. It is easy to guess that I will go to Khartoum. I must, therefore, be found somewhere in between."

"If you talk like that, I begin to understand. Ben Mubarek wishes to take vengeance on you. If he wants to attack you, he has enough people to do so. I will show you a way where an encounter is avoidable."

"I thank you very much, but I can't accept. How can I avoid a man who I want to apprehend if I go out of his way? I leave it to you whether you accept the danger."

"I am staying with you. How could I leave a man to whom we have so much to be thankful for? But where will you find them?"

"You have said yourself that I found the way of the slave-hunters without knowing their whereabouts. This one is easier, I have a guide."

"Do you mean me? In this case I could be of no use to you."

"I don't mean you. The 'trader' is my guide."

"How could that be? He went west to El Fasher and we're going east."

"The man lied. He is not going to El Fasher. As soon as we no longer see him, he will turn back to those who have sent him. There will be no danger in open spaces. We must expect them in a wood, a bushy or rocky area where we would fall into their hands unexpectedly. The question is, whether there is such a place in our direction. You, our guide, must know."

"I know the stretch exactly. It is noon; if we start now, we will be at a wood one and a half hours before sunset."

"And I can give you my word that the enemy is in this wood."

Abdullah looked at Leopold with amazement and shook his head. "How can you be sure?"

"You will learn that I am not mistaken. When we reach the tracks of the returning false trader, we will follow them until we reach the point where he meets the sentry or sentries who were on the lookout for us. By the way, how big is that wood?"

"It is as long as it is wide. One needs an hour to get through it. In its midst is a well with a lot of water."

"Can we go through it on camels?"

"Yes, there are places with sparsely planted trees."

"I know enough for the moment – let's go."

Chapter 2

A battle against larger odds

"Don't we ride to the west first to find out whether the trader has turned back?" asked Abdulla.

"That is superfluous," answered Leopold. "I am convinced that he has and we will soon find his tracks."

They went east. Leopold, his friend and servant, Ben Nil, and their guide, Abdullah, in front of the asakers. The soldiers were curious about whether Leopold's predictions would come true. They would welcome a battle.

After only half an hour they saw the tracks coming from the west. "How do you know these tracks are from the trader?"

Leopold, who observed the tracks were skewed, answered: "I observed before that one of his camel's hoofs pulls up the grass. This track shows the same pulling. These tracks also show me that he is in a hurry." He mounted again; now they doubled their speed. After another hour they reached a place where the grass was trodden down in a wide circle. These were the tracks from three of his comrades who were stationed here to observe Leopold's and the asakers' arrival.

"We have to make a detour and we will enter the wood from the other side where they don't expect us." They rode on. When they entered the wood from the rear, Leopold asked the asakers to dismount and wait for him while he found out where the enemies were and how many of them were there.

"We will surround them and shoot them down," Abdullah suggested.

"We will probably overpower them, but we are not going to kill them. We will hand them over to the Reis Effendina for punishment."

"That's a pity," said the Fessarah. "We have to listen to you, but when I think what happened in our village, I am enraged and would not spare them."

"The ones who did the robbing have been punished. They are dead. The people before us are not the robbers of your people."

"Very well, but I have to bring to your attention that you endanger us and many of us will be killed or wounded."

"I don't know yet what I will decide. I will have to adjust my plans according to circumstances. You know that I caught the slave-robbers of your people without anyone being wounded."

Abdullah shook his head but made no further remarks.

There was still a good half hour to sunset. The well, according to Abdullah, was in the middle of the wood. As he was on foot now, there was no danger that Leopold would reach the enemy before dark and risk discovery. His loyal companion, Ben Nil, wanted to accompany him, but Leopold declined. Abdullah wanted to come too. When he was declined as well, he told Leopold he would not find the way to the well. Leopold told him not to worry. "By the way," he said, "the enemy expects us to go to the well, they will surely hide some distance away from it." He told them to observe silence until he returned.

"What should we do if you don't return?"

"I will return."

"You speak with confidence. May Allah be with you."

Leopold left his light upper garment behind. His dark grey suit did not contrast so much with the surrounding bushes and underwood. After a quarter of an hour it was as if he heard someone speaking. He went on all fours and crawled carefully closer to the sound. The voices became more distinguishable. One of these seemed familiar. By the time he reached near enough to hear what they were saying, the sun had gone down. He recognised the 'trader' among sixty enemies. This man reported to Abd Mubarek, the father of the infamous slave trader and biggest enemy.

"They have all to go to hell except this Englishman, Poldi Ben Anglesi. I want him for my son, who will let him die of a long torture."

"Then you must expect that he will escape."

"I know he is a devil, but I have ways and means to tame even such a Satan. I will treat him like a ravenous animal. No, he won't escape. If it was up to me, I would torture the asakers as well. They killed our comrades and robbed us of a big profit."

"Yes, we would have received a lot of money for the Fessarah slaves. One should cut off this man's hands and tongue and sell him to the cruellest Negro ruler."

"This thought is not bad. Maybe we will do that. This foreign son of a dog deserves it. He guesses all our plans and, with the help of the devil, escapes us when we were sure we had him."

"Then we have to use the greatest care, otherwise he will escape us again."

"Not to worry. My orders are well thought out; a failure is impossible. I will shoot first. I will aim at the Englishman's leg. Once he is wounded he won't escape us. After my shot, sixty bullets should be enough to mow down all our enemies."

"One would think so. Actually it is a shame to use sixty men to conquer twenty asakers."

"That is not because of the asakers, but for the English Effendi. Under his leadership twenty are as good as a hundred. Were it not for this unexpected attack, success would be doubtful."

Leopold laughed secretly. Neither the 'trader' nor Abd Mubarek had the necessary brains for such an undertaking. They didn't even put out guards to report the arrival of the asakers. From further conversation, Leopold learned that Ben Mubarek had arranged for a trap for the Reis Effendina. This worried Leopold. He decided to act quickly and reach Khartoum to warn the threatened Reis. He had to judge the situation. He crawled further to the left, where he could see better, and found the necessary information. He saw a place where there were no trees. Sixty men were well armed. There were faces from light brown to the deepest black. Abd Mubarek, the Fakir and holy man of the group, sat with the trader a little away from the others. They were near Leopold and it was favourable that he hit the right spot.

The others were sitting in groups of three or four; not closely together. This would make an attack easier. There was room for his asakers near where he stood and he could direct every one of them in which group to attack. Leopold returned to his men.

He led them quietly to the place, where he showed each one the group he should attack. The raid was more likely to succeed if done in complete silence. They would hit three or four of the enemy on the head with the flat side of the butt of their rifle. He did not want them killed. As soon as he broke through the bushes, the others should follow.

They did it quickly. Their silent attack was a shock, the enemy were transfixed; shouting would have made them more liable to move. It was over in less than a minute. Leopold asked the asakers to tie them up before they regained consciousness. So great was their surprise, not a single shot was fired by the adversaries. To Leopold's regret, some of the asakers did their job too vigorously. Ten enemies lost their lives.

Leopold turned to Abd Mubarek and the trader. They were tied up, hands and feet, but had their eyes wide open and looked with horror at the surrounding scene. Leopold sat down next to them. They closed their eyes, whether because of weakness or anger was immaterial to him.

He greeted the older: "Salām, ja Weli el mashhūr – be greeted, oh great and famous holy man. I am delighted to find you here and I hope that you are happy to see my face."

"Be cursed," he answered in a subdued voice without opening his eyes.

"You wanted to say 'be blessed'. I know how much you were longing to meet me. This longing, unfortunately, would have been fatal for me. You wanted to kill the asakers of the Reis Effendina and cut off my tongue and my hands before selling me to the cruellest Negro ruler."

"He knows everything," the words escaped Abd Mubarek as he opened his eyes and directed this exclamation to his comrade, who looked at Leopold with deadly hate.

Leopold turned to him. "You were right when you said that we will meet again soon, although you wanted to go to El Fasher. I am delighted about that. It is proof that I judged you rightly. You had the idea to cut off my tongue and my hands and you are not mistaken if you have the joyous conviction that I am not going to withhold my thanks."

"I don't understand you. Why did you attack us? What evidence do you have? I demand you untie me."

"This wish will be complied with the moment we hand you to your executioner. You are too stupid to deceive me. I knew what type you were before you dismounted."

The trader answered angrily: "How can a giour be so presumptuous against a true believer? If you were clever, you would have left your false belief long ago. Take off our fetters, which are dirtied by your hands, otherwise…"

"Be quiet," Leopold interrupted. "Don't dare to threaten me. I would answer you with the whip."

"You will not dare to do that. I am a Sheik."

"You told us you are a trader. You are a member of a group of murderers and will be treated accordingly."

"Then woe to you. My tribe would kill you all."

"This man is impudent. He threatened you. Should I stop his evil mouth?"

"Do that!"

Ben Nil turned the 'trader' over with his foot. Leopold moved away. He did not want to witness such punishment, but soon heard that Ben Nil gave air to his anger.

Leopold ordered that the prisoners be taken to the well. The asakers were in a good mood. They had the camels, weapons and other things from at least three captives. Leopold took nothing and Ben Nil followed his example. He sent people out to gather wood, needed for several fires. One of the wood gatherers brought him some bones.

"They seem to be the remains of a calf. Nobody takes a calf into the desert. Thieves must have rested here."

"These are not calf's bones. They come from a human being,"

declared Leopold.

"Allah! So it was a human who was killed here!"

"Not killed, but torn apart and eaten." Leopold, who said this, was surrounded immediately. They all called out that he must be mistaken.

"I am not mistaken. I know the difference between human bones and those of an animal. This is a shoulder from a human being who was crushed by a strong animal – maybe a lion."

"Allah save us," shouted the Fessarah guide. "It must have been the lion from El Teitel."

"Why is he called after this place?"

"Because it visits all the wells between El Teitel and the Nile. This lion has been more than a year in this area."

"Did nobody hunt him down?"

"Hunt him down? What do you think? May Allah protect every human from this voracious eater, bigger than an ox and stronger than an elephant!"

"Has anyone seen him with a lioness or cubs?"

"No, he possesses no dwelling place. He is constantly on the way from one well to another."

"A hermit. They are even hostile to their own. They are the worst. Once they have tasted human flesh, they stick to this type of nourishment. They kill animals only from great hunger."

"That's right, Effendi, such a tramp is the one from El Teitel. When do you think he was here?"

"From the condition of these bones, I calculate he was here four or five days ago."

"Oh, Allah, that is bad. If it had been yesterday or the day before, he would have been somewhere else. After this time he may have made his round already."

"A lion, like any other beast of prey, prefers the place where it has found food before. We have to be careful."

"May the caliphs prevent that," shouted the Fessarah. "Maybe he is already here and ready for an ambush!"

"In this case I would have noticed his tracks. We still have to be careful. These hermits are cunning. They don't announce themselves by roaring like other lions. They sneak silently upon their victim, like a panther. I once shot such a sinner who only roared once when he saw our tracks. Then he became completely noiseless."

"Effendi, you have shot a lion?"

"Yes, more than one."

"Oh, Effendi, how well you can lie."

Leopold took no umbrage at the guide's disbelief. He knew the way the natives hunt a lion. Every man of the tribe participates. If the lion really dies, it is from the loss of blood from the many bullets that have hit him and not before he has torn apart several members of the group. That a single European kills a lion with only one shot was for these people an impossible thing. He didn't blame Abdullah for believing that he only wanted to entertain him.

Abdullah kept on laughing. "He killed a lion with only one shot and he was alone. Oh Allah, oh Mohamed, what a great hero is Poldi Ben Anglesi. I wish I could see him do it."

"Don't wish for that," Leopold warned. "Your wish can only come true if the lion came here. I don't think you would like that."

"I would even enjoy it," Abdullah still laughed. What a stranger can do, I, a son of this country, will do the same. I offer to bet you that I will do the same as you."

"As an exception I agree. What is the bet?"

"Your watch and your telescope against my valuable rifle."

"All right, but should a lion come I will not await him at a large fire. I will go toward him."

The Fessarah looked down for a while, then he said: "I don't want to insult you, but I don't believe you."

"So ask your prophet to keep the lion away. If he doesn't fulfil your wish, you will lose your famous rifle. But now let's talk about our…"

He was interrupted. A rider appeared from the west side of the clearing. When he saw the group, he seemed confounded. He looked doubtful whether to carry on or stop at the well. Finally he came closer and dismounted. He asked immediately: "Who is the leader here?"

"I am," answered Leopold.

"Your group are asakers. Why aren't you in uniform?"

"Does the uniform make an askari?"

"No! Why are the people on the ground tied up?"

"They are slave-hunters."

"But that is not a crime."

"Well, then, robbers of human beings."

"Black slaves are not human beings. You will free these people."

The stranger was about thirty years old, lean, with a full beard. His attire was white, though not very clean. He stood proud and erect, staring at Leopold, threatening as if he were the one to give orders. Leopold had no idea that this man would play a role in history as the Mahdi – the Islamic Messiah.

"Will I?" asked Leopold. "What right have you to demand things here?"

"Because I said so, I, Mohammed Achmed, the Fakir el Fakura."

18

"Very well! And I am the askari el asaker and I do what I like."

Fakir el Fakura is the highest and most prominent of the Fakirs: Hence Leopold called himself the most prominent of soldiers. Mohammed Achmed did not expect this answer.

"Don't you know me? Did you never hear of the Fakir el Fakura?"

As he said this, Leopold noticed him exchanging a look of agreement with the 'honourable' Fakir who lay on the ground: They knew each other. Leopold answered accordingly: "I don't know you but my prisoners do."

"How do you know that?"

"Your eyes told me. You made a promise to Abd Mubarek that you will not be able to keep."

"I will keep it. Ask your prisoners about me."

"Who and what you are is immaterial to me. I am here to represent the Reis Effendina and the Khedive. That will be sufficient."

"By no means is that sufficient. The Viceroy and the Rei Effendina are nothing in my eyes. Don't think that I will conform to their rules."

"You will conform because I give the orders here."

"You will see at once how I respect your orders." With this he pulled his knife and bent down to Abd Mubarek to cut his ties.

"Stop!" ordered Leopold. "What are you going to do?"

"I am freeing my friend from his fetters."

"I don't permit that."

"I don't care about your permission." Mohammed Achmed put his knife to Abd Mubarek's straps.

Leopold put both of his hands on his hips, lifted him up and threw him several steps away from the prisoners. He recovered quickly, lifted his knife and headed for him. "You dare to lay hands on the Fakir el Fakura? Here, take that."

The asakers didn't move. They knew that Leopold could handle the attacker. Only Ben Nil put his hand on the whip but stood still. Leopold's fist hit the armpit of his lifted arm, which was strong enough for the attacker to drop his knife. He then pulled his revolver and threatened to use it.

"Stay still, he will use it. He is a giour," warned Abd Mubarek.

"And this son of a dog dares to…"

Ben Nil stood behind him with his whip. "Effendi – should I?"

"No, not this time. He spoke in excitement. Should he insult me again, he will get the bastinado that he won't get up any more."

"The bastinado from a disbeliever!" grated the man. "What an outrage, what boldness. The others are Moslemin. How can a Moslem suffer that a believer be threatened with the bastinado?"

Ben Nil answered in Leopold's stead: "Listen, Mohammed Achmed. We like our Poldi Ben Anglesi Effendi and are prepared to fight for him against a hundred Fakir el Fakuras. You would not be the first to taste my whip. Take care, one more insult and the bastinado waits for you."

"Boy!" raged the Fakir. "Watch your tongue. What are you and twenty asakers against my followers, who would rush to me if I raise my voice!"

"Well, raise your voice. We will see whether the wood becomes alive."

"You can talk like that because there is no one with me. Later I will quash you like a worm which I step on with my foot."

From the asakers, an angry murmur was heard. The fanatic didn't care and continued: "As you serve an unbeliever against these Moslemin, you deny the prophet. You have no right to imprison believers. Where in the Koran is it forbidden to deal in slaves?"

His intention was to incite the asakers against Leopold and he believed he might succeed. There was no need for Leopold to take the word again. Ben Nil, who took the word for others, replied: "You don't know the situation. Abd Mubarek's son has attacked the Beni Fessarah, killed many people and taken the women and young men for slaves. We have rescued them and led them back home. In revenge he has sent his father and many men to attack and kill us. Is it allowed to make slaves from believers?"

"No," confessed Mohammed Achmed.

"Are the Beni Fessarah believers or not?"

"They are believers."

"So Ben Mubarek has committed a deadly sin, besides the intention to kill us, and these people are his accomplices."

This information made an impression on the Fakir el Fakura. He turned to Abd Mubarek: "Is this true?"

"They should prove that we intended to kill the asakers." The old man was defiant. "It is a shameful lie."

Leopold answered impetuously: "Don't deny what I have heard myself when I eavesdropped on you behind the bushes, where you and the pretended trader were sitting."

"You are mistaken," said the Fakir el Fakura to him.

"I have heard properly and I have other evidence."

"What other evidence? I must hear it."

"You must? Who has made you a judge over me? You have burned your fingers in this matter and I advise you to stay away from the fire. You may go or stay at the well with the asakers, but keep away from the prisoners."

Mohammed Achmed saw that Leopold would suffer no more contradiction. He took the saddle of his camel and sat down to eat and drink. There still was a bad weather cloud on his face.

Chapter 3

An encounter with the king of animals

Many fires were lit to in order that every prisoner could be observed. They were surrounded by the asakers who, in turn, were surrounded by the camels. Leopold was also sitting at the well, eating his food. He had hardly swallowed the last bite when Ben Nil accosted him with the question: "Effendi, I have to honour your meal, but now, as you have ended, I must again bring up the subject of my revenge against Abd Mubarek. You know why and promised me, when the time comes, I could take it."

"You know I want to learn something from him first. Your time hasn't come yet."

"I know you don't want his death, but you are sinning against your God if you let this murderer live."

"That is right," the Fessarah agreed with him. "He was the leader of those who killed my people, he escaped death at the time, but now he wants to kill us all."

"That is exactly it," the voices came from the asakers.

"Did you hear, Effendi?" asked Abdullah. "Do you want to rob us of our right? You must expect that we will take it."

Leopold had thought about this. In their views and by their laws, they were right. It was better to sacrifice one and keep their respect, especially as Leopold could not give them any assurance that they would get real punishment in Khartoum. He had already half decided to give in, when the eldest of the asakers stepped in front of him.

"Effendi, I am asked by my comrades to utter a plea."

"Well, speak."

"Tell me first ask whether you were satisfied with us?"

"I can give a good report to the Reis Effendina about everyone of you."

"I thank you. Your orders were sometimes inconceivable to us. But you were always right. You have gained our respect. But we have to censure one thing, if you permit. You as a Jew are much too indulgent to our enemies; enemies we have to destroy to keep ourselves alive. We will still listen to you and take the prisoners to Khartoum, except for one. Abd Mubarek must die. If you don't agree to this, you must expect that one or the other knife will find the heart of our enemies. And of those you want to save, many will no longer be alive in the morning.

Please decide!"

That was clear enough. What could Leopold answer? Was it really his duty to keep that monster Abd Mubarek alive and bring others into danger? Leopold apparently yielded by saying: "According to your views you are right. But I cannot decide about his life. It is Ben Nil who has the first right for revenge. Will you agree to that?"

"Yes, we agree." The askari went away satisfied.

"Thank you, Effendi," declared the youngster eagerly. "Now I will deal with this murderer of my family according to the law of the desert. There will be no more infamous action from this monster."

"Then go and push a knife into a tied up old man. That deed would be worthy of a hero." Leopold reckoned with Ben Nil's pride.

Ben Nil dropped his head for a while. Leopold saw that he fought with himself, but then he jumped up and pulled his knife. The Fakir el Fakura jumped up too and grabbed Ben Nil by his arm.

"Stop! That would be murder. I can't allow that."

Ben Nil shook him off with a strength no one expected of him. "Be quiet, you have nothing to say here. I care about your words like I care about the buzzing of a fly."

"Be quiet yourself, you wretched boy. If I want to, I squash you with my fingers."

"You may try." Ben Nil stood with the knife in his hand and now the Fakir el Fakura pulled his own knife. Leopold jumped up as well, tore the weapon off Mohammed Achmed and ordered him:

"Back, or you have me to deal with."

"I do not fear you. Do you think a Fakir el Fakura fears any enemy? Not even the strongest!"

Before Leopold could answer, a noise came from the distance which sounded like thunder. Leopold knew this sound. He had heard it repeatedly and it always became a matter of life or death with the king of the animals, the lion. "Don't you fear this one either?" Leopold pointed in the direction from which the sound came.

"No enemy at all."

"And are you ready to tackle him?'

"Yes," he laughed, "provided you take me to him."

"Well then, come!" Leopold picked up his rifle and checked its charge.

"What a hero you are," Mohammed Achmed laughed mockingly, "to fight a hyena."

"Are you deaf or didn't you recognise the king of the animals?"

"The king of the animals? You mean…"

He stopped. The rolling sound was repeated, but only a little louder.

A sign that the lion neared slowly. The camels began to pant and Abdullah called with shock: "Allah kerīm – God is merciful! That was the big lion from El Teitel. He will devour us."

"Yes, he found our tracks and then those of the Fakir el Fakura. That's why he roared twice. He will, from now on, come silently to collect his meal," explained Leopold.

"Allah save us from the tricks of this tailed devil."

"Are you afraid, Abdullah. How about our bet?"

"Oh Effendi, this bet!"

"You wanted to do what I do."

"Yes, I will." Abdullah pulled himself together, but Leopold noticed that the rifle trembled in his hands.

"Well, come, we will go toward the lion."

"Are you mad?"

"No, if I go toward him, I will find and kill him. If I stay here, the beast will find a human for his food."

"But not just you or me. I beg you to stay here and hide behind a camel."

"The lion will get his victim from behind the camel. I am going and this excellent Fakir el Fakura will accompany me."

"Are you serious, Effendi?" asked Mohammed Achmed.

"You wanted to come with me to the lion. Should I believe that I possess more courage and dexterity than you? Every coward can brag but a Fakir el Fakura…"

"Be silent," he interrupted. "I am coming."

"And you, Abdullah?"

"I am staying here."

"I knew that. You are only heroic with your mouth. I am going to win your costly rifle."

"Oh Allah, oh Mohammed, oh Abu Bakre and Osman, my famous rifle," he lamented.

"If you stay here, you have lost the bet, hand me your rifle."

"So – so – I am coming. Go ahead, I will be behind you." Abdullah's body trembled, but he kept exactly behind Leopold to make sure the lion would attack him first. Leopold felt sorry, but Abdullah deserved a punishment. Besides, Leopold was convinced that he would get lost after a few more steps.

No sound came from the asakers and the prisoners. Fear numbed them. They tried to find safety behind the bodies of camels. Leopold was the calmest inwardly. At the moment of danger any anxiety has to disappear. The Fakir el Fakura was driven by the fear of being thought a coward and walked behind Leopold. Abdullah, now, had made room for him. He walked last in the row.

They had half stepped over a clearing, Abdullah noticed a movement in the near bushes. Frightened, he hid himself behind another shrub and shouted: "There he is – there! Oh merciful Allah. Run away, save yourselves."

Yes, they should run to be seen by the lion, while he hid courageously behind the bushes. Leopold had also noticed the movement which shocked Abdullah so much. Whatever it was, it couldn't possibly be the lion. "Come on. Do what I do, otherwise you lose your rifle."

"No, no. I will stay here and shoot him. Run away and shout, so he will be frightened of you."

Abdullah asked them to shout to direct the lion's attention to them. The carnivorous animal could not be here yet. When the lion roared for the first time, he was about three kilometres away. That's why Leopold took the time for his mocking challenges. The animal by now had probably advanced three quarters of the way. The pair walked on. When they reached big trees Leopold sat down. The Fakir el Fakura did the same and whispered, "Why here?"

"Because the lion should break through about ten steps from here."

"Allah kerim! Why so near? We must go back fifty or sixty steps."

"No. The nearer we are, the surer the shot."

"Effendi, you have lost your mind!"

"No, but I have more courage than you. I can hear the chatter of your teeth."

"I can't help it, my chin got suddenly quite loose."

"Does your hand tremble as well?"

"Yes, a great chill goes through my arms."

"So don't shoot, leave it to me. A bad shot increases the danger."

"Would Allah that I hadn't come. I am undaunted, but to draw the attention of the lion intentionally to yourself is too bold. Don't let us talk any more, he might hear it."

"But we are only whispering and the lion is not here yet."

The Fakir el Fakura was in great fear. When Leopold put a hand on his arm, he uttered a terribly cry. He thought the hand was a lion's claw.

Leopold saw Abdullah pointing his rifle in the direction of the bush where the movement had previously been seen. Did he want to shoot? Leopold thought to hinder him through a warning call. But it was too late. Abdullah had already shot whatever it was he thought was the lion. He jumped up and shouted in jubilation. "Hamdulillah! I have shot and hit him. There he lies, the devourer of humans, the murderer and killer of herds. Rejoice with me, you men. Shout and sing to his end. An end without fame and honour. Come, Effendi, that I can show him to you."

The careless man had jumped out of his skin. He gestured like a madman. The asaker believed him and came forward slowly. What did he shoot? It could not be the lion. Just now, the air carried the infallible, sharp and stinging smell of the large carnivores, which is ten times stronger than of those in a zoo.

"He has killed him. We have to go to him, Effendi," said Mohammed Achmed.

"Nonsense! The lion comes from the opposite direction. He is almost here. I can smell him already."

"Oh merciful Allah, oh refuge and consolation of the believers. You are mistaken. Abdullah is the victor and I am going to him." He rushed away. Leopold could not hold him. There was no time – the lion was there.

He appeared at the outer trees of the clearing, lit by the light of the fires. Over a metre high and two and a half metres long.

Leopold had his rifle at the ready. The lion stood badly for a sure shot. He didn't dare to fail and there was no time for long consideration because the animal saw the running Fakir el Fakura and made a turn to jump at him. Leopold shouted with all his bodily strength to direct the attention of the lion to himself. If the lion would do that, Leopold would have a better aim. But the lion paid no attention. It was two or three jumps away from the Fakir. The asakers cried out in horror. Abdullah clamoured as if in hell. The Fakir el Fakura looked around. When he saw the animal, he broke down, unable to utter a sound. Two more jumps and the lion would have reached him. Leopold had a rifle in his right hand and a revolver in his left. Running after the lion he shot six times into the air while roaring too. The lion heard the shots and turned around. He would throw himself on his attacker.

The giant beast measured the distance with his eyes. To reach Leopold it would have to make two jumps. When the lion touched ground after the first jump, Leopold gave it the first bullet in the eye. The second shot went into its heart while it was in the air in its second jump. Leopold threw himself sideways and pulled his knife. But there was no need – the lion fell to the ground, dead. Leopold reloaded his rifle and touched the lion with its barrel. The animal stretched its four claws and no longer moved. Leopold went to the Fakir el Fakura, who was still kneeling down. He lifted him up.

"Why are you still praying? The man-eater is dead."

"Dead." The Fakir imitated the last word absent-mindedly.

"Yes, dead. You have nothing to fear any more.

"Hamdulillah." Mohammed Achmed uttered this praise of Allah, stood up and went into the wood, without concerning himself with the lion and without saying a word of thanks to his life saver. Abdullah asked:

"Are you sure he is dead?"

"Quite sure."

"So we can look at it and touch it?"

"Why not."

"So I will call the asakers to praise our victories."

Leopold was curious to see the other 'lion'. First they wanted to see the lion shot by Leopold. They did not come hurriedly, but hesitatingly. The size of the lion's body inspired respect even in death. Only after repeated assurances by Leopold did an asaker touch the lion's head. But then the mood changed into frolicsome liveliness. Abdullah stepped on the dead animal and began to speak: "Praise be Allah and hail to the prophets! This day is a day of victory. Confirm it, believers."

"Yes, hail, praise, victory," shouted the asakers. Only Ben Nil, the dutiful, stayed to guard the prisoners.

"Listen," continued the speaker. "The lion from El Teitel devoured every week a follower of the prophet. Confirm it, friends and comrades of the two heroes of the day."

"We confirm it," was the answer.

He continued. "In the belly of this male with a thick head are buried many hundreds of Moslems. Today he came to this well to continue his crimes. He inflamed the anger of the fighters and the fury of the biggest heroes in Africa, namely Poldi Ben Anglesi and I, Abdullah Ben Kalaun es Ssaijad. They opposed the devourers. Raise your voice and exclaim hail and fame, you witnesses to their deeds."

"Hail, fame, hail," resounded all around.

"The murderer did not come alone, he brought a comrade whose soul Allah may put in a lame dog. It had the audacity to oppose me. An heroic eagerness befell me to exterminate this monster and drive it out of the land of the living. There it lies, lit up by the beam of my heroism. I will show it to you later for you to be able to shout disgrace and shame over it. Me, the victor, you will praise with a triumphal shout."

His invitation was obeyed, after which the braggart turned to Leopold. "As I have killed the grave of so many believers, the watch and the telescope are mine now. I have won the bet and you will not cheat me. I wouldn't have cheated you if you would have won. And now let's go to the other beast. I will go ahead and you are to follow me."

They all started moving in the direction of Abdullah's heroic deed.

27

The nearer they went the slower were Abdullah's steps. Until he finally stopped and turned to Leopold. "Effendi, you are convinced about my heroic deed?"

"Completely. You have shot the biggest and most famous animal in the desert. But I am afraid that Mohamed Achmed will not thank you."

"I don't expect that. He was not attacked by my lion, but by yours. Now you walk in front, your eyes are better than mine."

"You are mistaken, at the moment they are so bad that I might think a lion is a camel. That would be an insult to you. You are the victor. You go ahead." Abdulla had to accommodate this. His courage seemed at a very low ebb. He moved as if walking on eggs. After six or seven steps he stopped again. "Effendi, I saw a movement. What should I do?"

"Well, finish him."

"But he is only wounded. He may bite."

"Give him another bullet. Although this will minimise your fame of killing the animal with only one bullet, whereas I needed two."

"I don't mind this fame, but you have a double barrelled rifle and I have only one shot in my rifle."

"My modesty doesn't allow me to fulfil your wish."

"That is very nice of you, Effendi, but – oh Allah, he moved his legs again, and can you hear his panting. He is angry. I am going to the back of the line." The 'hero of the day' sought safety from the supposed lion. The panting he had heard was the sound of pain. Not from a lion, but from a camel. The asakers had also fallen back with shock.

Leopold told Abdullah that the movement he saw was from the legs of a camel.

"You are mistaken, Effendi. You yourself have said that your eyes sometimes take a lion for a camel."

"And you take a camel for a lion." Leopold went to the bush where the animal had been shot and pulled the twigs apart. The asaker could see a camel whose back leg had been hit by the bullet. Their fear had gone and they broke out in a resounding laughter. "What a lion, what gruesome monster," called one of them. "Abdullah has saved us from a terrible danger. He is the most famous lion hunter in the country. Raise your voices, men, and call three times hail to him."

"Hail, hail, hail," they all laughed and rejoiced.

The so praised didn't answer, but ran away and hid in the bushes. The camel couldn't get up; its shank was shattered. Then its owner returned from the woods and said for all to hear:

"Effendi, forgive that I let you stand here without thanking you. It was too terrible. The man-eater aimed for me. Without you I would have been torn to bits. Horror had robbed me of my speech. Now I can talk again I give you my thanks. Any hostility has gone. You are my friend and brother. Will you forgive me?"

"With pleasure," said Leopold and offered his hand.

"Tell me, how can I serve you? How can I pay my debt to you, at least in some measure?"

"You owe me nothing. I will take the skin of the lion and I am satisfied."

"I understand. You scorn the thanks of a man who had insulted you. But I also have my honour and will think of an opportunity to be of service to you. Later, when you hear about me, you will recognise that all Islam and the whole orient is beholden to you. Here is my camel. What happened to it?"

"Abdullah thought it was a lion and shot at it."

"What a blockhead! Fear has made him blind. What am I going to do without a camel?"

"I will present you with one of the captured camels. Do you allow me to kill and redeem it from its pain?"

"I don't mind."

It took eight asakers to take the heavy body of the lion to the camping place. Abdullah returned with downcast appearance. He ignored the mocking praise. Sighing, he put his rifle down. "Here it is. I cannot hand it to you. It would be sinning against my ancestor. If you are really so unfeeling – take it."

"Yes, I take it. It is my rightful, well earned possession."

Abdullah had hoped for Leopold's indulgence. It was not Leopold's intention to keep the rifle, but he wanted to punish Abdullah for his boasting. When Abdullah saw Leopold taking it, he clapped his hands over his head. "Oh Allah, oh heaven, oh heartache. Now I have been robbed of the fame of my ancestors, the legacy of my forefathers, I cannot be seen in my village any more. There is nothing left for me but to melt away in tears. My life dives under the waters of the pain of my soul. Oh Allah, Allah!"

Chapter 4

The Mahdi

When at midnight the camp became quiet, Ben Nil asked again for the punishment of Abd Mubarek which had been interrupted by the appearance of the lion. When Mohammed Achmed heard this, he stood up and said: "I owe you thanks and won't mix in these matters again. But my eyes cannot look at the death of a friend. I will withdraw until it is over." He went beyond the circle of the camels and sat down, turning his back toward the rest.

Ben Nil stood there with his knife in his hand.

"So I have your permission now, to take my revenge, Effendi?"

"Do what you like," answered Leopold. "As I said before, if it suits your honour to stab an old man in fetters, go ahead, but I would like to have a word with him regarding the danger to Reis Effendina."

Abd Mubarek had heard everything. Leopold accompanied Ben Nil to the old criminal and said: "You have heard what your fate will be. Make your reckoning with Allah."

"Who kills me is a murderer," he answered.

"Think and say what you like. In a few moments you will go over Es Ssiret, the bridge of death. Lighten your conscience. Maybe Allah will be merciful."

"I don't need his mercy. It is no sin to exterminate unbelievers and their followers, but a merit that Allah rewards."

"When you think that death by knife is a reward – I don't care. You did not seek only my life, but also those of my companions. They are Moslems. Further, you also know about the attack on the Reis Effendina. You cannot justify that before Allah. I give you the opportunity to avoid this extra guilt if you tell me the danger he is in."

A mocking grin appeared on his face. He spat before Leopold. "I spit on you and death. My days are calculated by Allah and you can't rob me of a minute of my life without His will. I wouldn't think of telling you what you ask. Kill me, you sons of dogs. I will be silent."

"Good. Abd Mubarek shall have his will. We will find out without him. Let him go to hell." The youngster knelt next to him, opened the front of his attire and put the point of his knife on his chest. Abd Mubarek did not seem to expect this and cried out.

"Hold it! Think that I am a holy Fakir who cannot be touched! Allah would punish this murder with a thousand torments in hell."

"You want to be a holy man," mocked Ben Nil. "You are a monster a thousand times worse than the lion. Go to hell, where you will be received with joy by millions of devils." Ben Nil held the point of his knife over Abd Mubarek's chest and slowly, very slowly, pricked the skin. The old one rolled to his side, cried out and revealed the hitherto concealed fear of death.

"No, no, I don't want to die, I will tell you what you want."

"Tell me the danger that threatens the Reis Effendina."

"He will be poisoned in Khartoum."

"By whom?"

"By – one of his servants."

"How will it be done?"

"His baker is bribed to put poison in his rolls."

"Will you put it on oath that you are telling the truth?"

"By Allah, by the prophet and by all the teaching of the caliphs."

"See how quickly we learn what we want to know, but to your annoyance, I will tell you that I would not kill a tethered old man and soil my honour. Choose one of your men to fight with me to the death. If he wins, you are saved. If he dies, you will both die. Effendi, I hope you will give me permission for this fight."

This was brave of the gallant youngster. But Leopold did not like the whole thing. Ben Nil had courage and was agile, but whether Leopold could trust him to be victorious against the best fighter among the prisoners, he was doubtful. But could he withhold his consent? Hardly.

"Do not worry about me," Ben Nil interrupted Leopold's thoughts. "I know what I am capable of and I do not fear."

"But he will give you the strongest opponent."

"I prefer that to a weakling."

"It is your life you are risking. Do not rush it. Look your opponent in the eyes, not his knife. Try to stand with the light behind you."

Leopold did not expect the old man to choose the false trader. There were taller and stronger people among the prisoners. Perhaps he was chosen because he was good in single combat. Or maybe they had planned some trick? They were next to each other and could have done so. Leopold was prepared for whatever that would be.

"We will take off our upper garments and fight with only our trousers on," said Ben Nil.

"Why? let us stay as we are."

"No, it will be done as I say."

The trader opposed this, but had to give in in the end. Why? thought Leopold, did he want to keep on his garment? Without it, it was easier

31

to fight. Maybe he wants to flee?

"Are you ready?" asked Ben Nil.

"I am ready. Let us start."

There were no rules, but Leopold gave the trader a short warning.

"Take care of your legs!"

"That is superfluous," he laughed, "Ben Nil will not stab my legs."

He did not see Leopold taking his rifle into his hands for any action, should it be necessary.

"Now!" said Ben Nil, "Come on."

Neither of the combatants tried the first hit. They moved about in circles, keeping the other in their sight. Suddenly, the 'trader' jumped on Ben Nil. But it was only a feint attack. Hardly had Ben Nil eluded him by jumping aside, when the 'trader' rushed past him and jumped over the head of two asakers who were sitting in his way – and made for the woods. It was what Leopold expected. He aimed and shot him in the leg. Before the 'trader' had reached safety, he broke down.

Three asakers, with Ben Nil in front, run after him. They brought him back, taking into consideration his condition. He was dropped before Leopold, who told him: "You laughed when I advised you to take care of your legs. You recognise again that it is not easy to outwit a foreign Effendi."

Leopold examined the leg. The bullet was not in the wound and he made him a provisional bandage. He asked Ben Nil to take him to the two trees standing near each other outside the clearing and to tie him with his back against them, but so that he wouldn't be able to move his head. When he was asked why he told them that the 'trader' would soon get wound-fever and would disturb others in their sleep. Leopold found his flight comprehensible. He should tell Abd Mubarek's son, Ben Mubarek, that their attack had failed and that he should come and free them.

Abd Mubarek grew angry about the failure of his plans and chose another one for the fight. The present opponent had a wide chest and a much stronger build. Ben Nil was not disturbed by this. They stood about five steps away from each other, motionless. There, suddenly, the opponent made a tiger-jump to Ben Nil, to take him by surprise. The youngster made a lightning jump aside and then jumped back before his opponent turned around. He pushed his knife to the hilt into the opponent's back. The strong man fell to the ground where he stood.

"Afārim 'alźk – bravo, bravo!" shouted the asakers loudly. "The first hit felled him. Who would have thought you, Ben Nil, son of valour, would be able to do this?"

The youngster turned calmly to Leopold. "Effendi, you see now that you didn't have to worry about me. I would have won if he were twice as strong. My eyes are sharp, my hand is sure and my heart knows no unrest or anxiety. Does Abd Mubarek belong to me now?"

"Yes," answered Leopold. He was eager to know what Ben Nil would do. In case he wanted to kill him, Leopold would have to ask him to delay. But Ben Nil looked at his bloody knife, shook his head and said:

"You are right, Effendi. It is a great responsibility to kill a man. This blood is unpleasant and disgusting. Are you sure the Reis Effendina will really punish him?"

"As heavily as possible."

"He deserves to die. His life belongs to me, but I am not taking it. His man died for him and I will be satisfied with that."

Leopold liked what he heard. "Your decision gives you more honour than if you had killed the old man."

"But I insist that he later be given the heaviest punishment..."

"I will see to that and, in order to stop another attempt to escape, take him next to the 'trader' and tie him to the tree."

Ben Nil asked: "Why do you do that? Here we have them safely."

"That is true and I will bring them back later, but first I want to learn their real intention against the Reis Effendina."

"But you know that already."

"No. The story of the poison was a lie. Go there now and stand guard over them. I will sneak behind them. When you see me, you will casually move away. When they think you are out of earshot, they will talk."

Ben Nil went to sit next to the two prisoners, who faced the camp and could see if anybody was missing; but not if people were sitting down. The asakers built a wall behind which Leopold disappeared into the woods. Then they sat down. When Ben Nil saw Leopold creeping up behind the prisoners, he stood up and walked away, casually. This ruse had the desired effect The 'trader' spoke to Abd Mubarek:

"Quickly, before he comes back. Do we have anything to talk about?"

"Nothing," snarled the old one, furiously.

"But we have to make a plan!"

"I know none. Allah curse this damned Effendi to the lowest abyss of hell. If only you had succeeded in escaping, you could have been at the isle of Hassanieh and told my son about us. He and his people would have freed us. This opportunity has passed."

"Is there no other way of rescue? Think of Mohammed Achmed, the Fakir el Fakura. He had large profits because of you. He would do his best to help us."

"This is over now. Poldi Ben Anglesi, the dog, has saved his life."

"Perhaps he would do nothing directly, but he could go to the isle Hassanieh and inform your son. You should speak to him."

"They wouldn't allow this and if they did, the Effendi would be present and hear every word."

"So what? Two or three words in the Shilluk language are quickly said to save us. The Effendi probably doesn't know this language. But the Fakir el Fakura does. He would then know what to do."

"That is right. If it succeeds, rescue is possible, but my son has plans to destroy the Reis Effendina and his ship. He lured him to a place near the island where he will destroy them all with fire. Once their leaders have gone, we will be able to continue our trade unhindered as before. We have to fear the leaders, not the asakers."

"If there is no way of rescue for us, what will happen in Khartoum?"

"It will not be too bad. With the Reis Effendina gone, we don't have to expect strong judgement. Especially as the main accuser is an unbeliever. If we deny everything, the judges will believe us more than him."

The two kept talking, but Leopold had heard enough. He withdrew. When Ben Nil saw this, he went back to his post. The asakers stood up again to cover Leopold's return. He reached his place without the prisoners realising their secret was known. A short time later, Ben Nil came to Leopold to report that Abd Mubarek wanted to talk to him. Leopold thought that he would now start trying to outwit him. He went to the old man and asked what he wanted.

"Ben Nil had my life in his hand and he refused to take it. Will I be able to keep it now?"

"The decision is with the Reis Effendina. Why do you ask?"

"Your belief is, if you prepare yourself for life after death, eternal bliss is dependent on it. There is a matter which disturbs my soul. I want to settle it and need to speak to the Fakir el Fakura about it – in your presence, of course."

"You are asking for something I shouldn't allow. All right, I will call him. I do not have to be present; my ears can hear everything you say, from a distance."

Leopold went to fetch the Fakir el Fakura. He didn't need especially good ears to hear Abd Mubarek talk to his companion:

"What luck! It will work now."

Mohammed Achmed was astonished when he was called to speak to Abd Mubarek without supervision. He went to the old man and sat next to him. Ben Nil reproached Leopold, but was told that he knew what he was doing.

The Fakir el Fakura stood up after about ten minutes and returned to his place. He had spoken to Leopold about his gratefulness. Now was the time to convince him of whether he really meant it. If he was honest, he would tell Leopold about the plot. Leopold didn't give him the opportunity to do so, he went straight to Abd Mubarek and the 'trader' without exchanging a word with the Fakir el Fakura.

"Well, did the Fakir el Fakura agree to help you?"

"Yes, Effendi. He promised me to correct the great mistake I once made. I thank you, Effendi, with all my heart."

"And now you feel better about it?"

"Much better. I haven't felt as good for a long time."

"I believe you and I also know the reason."

"How could you? You don't know the deed and what it is all about."

"Don't be mistaken. I warned you that I can hear from a distance. I know your plans against the Reis Effendina."

"There were no plans. I have already told you he will be poisoned."

"And Mohammed Achmed should help in freeing you by calling your son, Ben Mubarek."

"Nobody thought about that. He doesn't know where my son is."

"You told him where he is."

"No, we haven't talked about him."

"Also not about the Reis Effendina?"

"No."

"You are forgetting that I can hear from a distance. You told him that the Reis Effendina is being lured to near the isle of Hassanieh."

"Allah, Allah!" he called out in shock, looking at Leopold as if a lightning had suddenly struck from a blue sky.

"You are shocked? Yes, your son is at the isle of Hassanieh and the Fakir el Fakura should rush to him and tell him that your attack on us has failed and that you are in our hands."

"I – I – know – nothing about that," he stammered.

"The main thing is that I know it," Leopold smiled.

"You are a devil, yes, the real Satan," shouted the old man furiously. "I know that you couldn't have heard anything, but you know everything, because you are in alliance with hell."

"Or with Allah. You are a horrible miscreant. The power that helped me must be a good one. Your plot is discovered and I will visit your son without asking whether I am welcome. You two will be returned to the others. You have too little brain to guess why I have separated you from them."

Leopold was curious whether the Fakir el Fakura would tell him of

35

their plans. If not, Leopold would have to stop him from carrying out Abd Mubarek's instructions.

After the asakers who were not on guard went to sleep, Mohammed Achmed waved to Leopold to come to him. Leopold did so in the expectation that the Fakir el Fakura would tell him what he had talked about with Abd Mubarek. But the first words showed him that he was mistaken. He began:

"You are a Christian…"

Leopold interrupted: "I am not a Christian…"

This time Mohammed Achmed interrupted: "It doesn't matter whether you are Christian or a Jew. Do you know your bible?"

"Yes, I have studied it with diligence."

"Tell me if you consider Mohammed to be a prophet."

"According to my conviction he was no prophet but an ordinary human being."

"Are there any prophets in your religion?"

"Yes, we understand a prophet to be enlightened by God to teach the eternal truth to mankind."

"Well, Mohammed did that."

"Not to my mind. Mohammed lived among Jews and Christians. He took from their bible and mixed it with heathen views and perceptions. What he took from the testaments is right – everything else is false. Therefore, the Koran contains many things we agree with, but on the whole, we reject it."

"You make a big mistake to reject it without knowing it."

"You are wrong. I can turn around your statement with one question: Is there a single Mohammedan university where the students learn about our bible?"

"No, it is forbidden for teachers and students to engage in other people's teachings. It would be a great sin."

"But in our universities are teachers who teach and students who study the Koran. You don't know our bible and call us unbelievers or giours. But we know the Koran and are able to make a judgement about Islam. I studied the Koran as well. Do you want to test me?"

"No. You wouldn't convert anyway. It is impossible for the wisest man to make a judgement about the Koran because Mohammed only started it. Someone else will complete it."

"Who?"

"With this question you betray that you don't know the Koran."

"You are mistaken again. I know that many of you expect a Mahdi to come, but the Koran doesn't mention anything about him. He lives in the oral tradition, which I don't believe."

"But I do. Allah will send a prophet to finish Mohammed's work and will convert the disbelievers or destroy them. Their earthly possessions will be divided according to the piety of the believers."

"The 'prophetology' according to the Koran is completely settled. In Mohammed's own words, he is the last prophet whom Allah has sent or will send."

"You talk like an unbeliever."

"Not an unbeliever but one who is knowledgeable about Islam. How would a Mahdi start to fight Europe? It is ridiculous."

"With fire and sword!"

"Can a water source coming from the Nile swallow the desert? It will get lost in the sand."

"Allah will make it a thousand times bigger than the Nile."

"God is almighty, but he will not, for the presumption of a Moslem or any man, flood the desert or the mountains."

"You don't know us. We are irresistible when, in a war, we flood your countries."

"Pah, your stream would sink down miserably before it reached our borders. We would laugh and the Mahdi would run away with his heroes."

"Effendi, you talk big, but if you would see him, your teeth would chatter."

"Does he look so terrible?"

"Yes, you have no idea how terrible he can be."

"But you have. Do you know him?"

"Yes, I know the Mahdi. He is here already and has received direction from Allah to prepare for the conquest of the world and the annihilation of the disbelievers."

"Do you want to give him good advice?"

"What about?"

"The Mahdi should graze his herds in peace, but in Allah's name renounce his imaginary convocation. His followers, if he finds any, would lose their possessions and their lives."

"His mission is from Allah and he will obey the orders from heaven."

"A Mahdi would have to surpass the education and wisdom of all Europeans. Where is such a man?"

"There is one," he answered, sure of himself. "One who is ten times cleverer than all Europeans."

"Hm, do you mean yourself? It almost sounds like it."

"I will not tell you who I mean, but Allah has given him knowledge and qualities for such a holy mission. The time will come soon when

37

Emperors and Kings will beg him for peace. You can rely on it, I give you my holiest oaths."

"As to the oath of a Moslem, I have learned today what to think of it. Is that all you have to tell me?"

"Yes, I wanted to know the views of an unbeliever about the Mahdi."

"You have heard them, but now I have some questions of my own. What did you discuss with Abd Mubarek?"

"About a great mistake he once made. He asked me to correct it."

"May I know more about it?"

"Why, Effendi? It was the confession of a dying man. You showed delicacy in staying away. Do you regret it?"

"No, but I am afraid this matter can't be immaterial to me."

"It has nothing to do with you."

"There were no plans against me?"

"Why do you ask this question? You have saved my life, I owe you thanks and would warn you."

"But he is your friend!"

"My gratitude to you means more to me than this friendship. Please do trust me."

"I only trust a person I know well. You I know only for one day."

"I am sorry you have no more time to get to know me, because I have to continue my journey to Khartoum. Please select one of the camels for me."

"I will do that, but only at daybreak."

"Not now? But you promised me."

"Of course I will keep my promise."

"So it doesn't matter when you give me the camel."

"So it doesn't matter for you either."

"Yes, I have to leave immediately."

"And I am convinced that you will leave only tomorrow."

"And I tell you that…"

"And I tell you," Leopold interrupted sharply, "that I know you will stay with us until we leave here."

They both stood up. "Effendi, with what right do you treat me like a prisoner?"

"With the right of anybody who has his own security to consider."

"Do I threaten your security if I leave?"

"Yes."

"Allah, Allah! You are doing that to me, the Mahdi, before whom thousands will lie in the dust!"

"Ah, now you are admitting who you think you are. You want to remove the Khedive and depose the King. You want to conquer the world and annihilate all the unbelievers. Frankly, you don't look the man who could order ten asakers. And you want to rule over all the believers and the world?"

"Don't mock. I am enlightened and know everything that was and that will happen in the future."

"So you know the future? So we both know that you are not heading for Khartoum, but to the isle of Hassanieh to look for Ben Mubarek. Your gratitude is so great that I like you so much as to not let you go..."

Leopold could not continue because the Fakir el Fakura suddenly turned and ran away. Leopold was quickly behind him and caught him by his left arm. Mohammed Achmed had his rifle in his right hand and intended to give Leopold a blow on the chest. Leopold tore him down and knelt on him. The man foamed with rage and swore in a way not befitting a future Mahdi.

The asakers were astounded when they learned about the Fakir el Fakura's intention of betrayal. They would have liked to kill him.

After tying down the Fakir el Fakura, it was high time for Leopold to set off and warn the Reis Effendina. He returned the 'costly' rifle to a delighted Abdullah, who promised to lead the prisoners to Hegasi, where they would meet.

He then took Ben Nil as a companion on a journey fraught with danger.*

Chapter 5

Ben Mubarek the slave-hunter

Leopold and Ben Nil had a journey of thirty geographical miles to the isle of Hassanieh. With excellent camels, they made it in two days. Hegasi was near the river Nile and the isle of Hassanieh. It was a poor village with only a few huts. They took their camels to the river to let them drink. Where they rested was a man who was fully armed and better dressed than the people from the village. The man looked down the river. When Leopold asked him whether he expected a ship, he received no answer. From passers by, he learned that the stranger had a horse outside the village, ready and saddled to allow him to ride off at any time. Leopold then asked when the last ship had passed here. He was told it was the ship that had brought the stranger to the shore. "Who did this ship belong to?"

The natives didn't know. "Do you know its name?"

"Yes, its name was Hirdoun 'Lizard'."

"When did the previous ship pass by here?"

"The day before."

"Did that ship have two masts?"

"No, it was an ordinary one mast ship."

The answers quietened Leopold. The Reis Effendina had not passed this dangerous way.

Leopold found the stranger suspicious. It was clear he was on the lookout for something and would then ride off to report this. He walked slowly to him and bid him:

"Allah jimassig bilcher – God give you a happy evening."

"Misalchźr – happy evening," was the short reply, showing that the stranger was not interested in Leopold's company. Leopold pretended not to have noticed this and continued:

"I have no net to guard myself against the flies of this river. Is there a place in this village where I could stay overnight?"

"I don't know, I am not from here."

"So you are a stranger here as well? Allah be with you on your journey."

"His blessing be with you too. Where have you come from?"

"From Khartoum," answered Leopold, forced to say the untruth.

"Where is your tent?"

"I have no tent, I live in a house in Sues."

"What are you?"

Leopold made a cunning face. "I deal with everything, preferably…" He stopped, which indicated that it is better not to finish the started sentence.

"With forbidden goods?" the stranger finished the sentence.

"If it were so, could I admit it?"

"You could tell me. I would certainly not betray you."

"Silence is, in any case, better than talking."

"Not in any case. If a businessman wants to trade, he must talk."

"In such a case I would be talking. But presently, there is no business."

"If I understood you rightly, there might be business. Where are you going?

"To where I can purchase goods."

"What?"

"That," said Leopold smiling, leaving it unclear to the asker.

The stranger became friendlier. He thought Leopold a slave-dealer. It was important to strengthen his belief, without telling him directly. A slave-dealer does not tell a stranger what he is and what he does. Leopold was convinced the other was an underling of Ben Mubarek, whose task it was to look out for the Reis Effendina. The noqer Hirdoun – 'Lizard' must belong to Ben Mubarek and couldn't be far away. Most probably at the isle of Hassanieh.

"You are discreet. I like that," said the stranger. "One can do business with discreet people only."

"Ah, you are also doing things not everybody has to know about?"

"I think we suit each other," said the guard and winked at Leopold.

"Really? Do you know slavery is a dangerous business?"

"Pah! What is dangerous to surround a village of blacks, put fire to it and take the Negroes prisoners when they alight from their huts. The old and weak are shot. With the others one moves away. Where is the danger?"

"The danger starts with the conveyance. You must not let yourself be caught. It would be best to sell the slaves there and then."

"That is impossible. There is no dealer to sell them to."

"Then you take one with you. He pays and takes the dangers of transport on himself."

"Where could we find such a man?"

"Where? Hm," muttered Leopold, significantly.

"Who is it?"

"I think that wouldn't concern you."

"More than you think. Is he rich?"

41

"He has what he needs."

"He has to be valiant too?

"He has been to Abyssinia several times to buy slaves. Don't you think that this is courageous?"

"Indeed it is. Where is he now?"

"At the White Nile, perhaps not far from here."

"You are really careful. Do you mean yourself?"

"I am not telling you."

"You can tell me, because…"

"Because – ? Why do you stop?"

"Because I also have to be careful. If I am not mistaken in you, I can tell you perhaps where you can buy slaves."

"Well, from whom?"

"From Ben Mubarek."

"Allah! From the famous slave-hunter? Where is he now?"

"Where your dealer is. At the White Nile, perhaps not far from here," the stranger said smilingly as he repeated Leopold's words.

Leopold pretended happy surprise. "That is good, that is very good. I know a Turkish dealer who has bought a lot from him."

"Do you mean Murad Nasyr? Do you know him?"

"Very well, I have even bought slaves from him."

"Ah, you finally admit that you are the dealer you mentioned before."

"Allah! It just slipped out of me."

"Don't worry. No harm done, because I can now be open with you."

"Is that the truth?"

"Certainly. Tell me frankly, Do you want to buy reqiq, slaves?"

"Very well, I will trust you. I buy slaves as soon as I can get them."

"Where did you want to go from here?"

"Down the Nile, past Fashodah, until I find a seribah where I can buy slaves."

A seribah is a place for dealers and slave-hunters.

"You don't have to go that far," said the man confidingly. "Do you have any money?"

"Enough."

"Then I will take you to Ben Mubarek."

"I would be very grateful and will give you baksheesh. Has Ben Mubarek any slaves now?"

"Not yet. We are planning a journey to make reqiq. Murad Nassyr needs a quantity and there will be enough over for you."

"Is Murad Nassyr presently with Ben Mubarek?"

"No, he went ahead to Fashodah."

Leopold was pleased with this answer. He knew Murad Nassyr from the time he was first involved with the Reis Effendina. He boldly thought he would go to Ben Mubarek. He hoped there would be nobody to recognise him. "Do you know why the Turk wants to meet Ben Mubarek besides wanting to buy slaves?" asked the man, who by now was speaking quite confidingly.

"No."

"Do you know his family?"

"I only know that he has two sisters."

"That's right, and I can see that you are one of us. Murad brought his sisters, one of whom should become Ben Mubarek's wife. The marriage will take place on a seribah on the White Nile. When you come with us you will be able to participate in this festivity. Ben Mubarek is very generous, in such cases. His father will also be there."

"He has a father?" Leopold pretended ignorance.

"Yes, his father is still alive, he works up and down the Nile in the mask of a pious Fakir, to help his son in his business."

"Is he already with him?"

"Abd Mubarek is absent for a short time. He went with a group of slave-hunters to exercise judgement."

"Judgement?"

"Yes, to punish a foreign giour who has done great damage to our business."

"You make me curious."

"Ben Mubarek will tell you himself. I don't know whether I am allowed to speak about that. This unbeliever is a rogue, a devil, whom we must destroy."

If this watch only knew that he spoke to the rogue or devil.

The sun touched the western horizon and the Maghreb, the prayer at sundown, had to be said. As Leopold pretended to be a Moslem, he had to imitate the movements. Leopold went to his companion, to enlighten him about the intended visit to Ben Mubarek and about his conversation with the stranger. "I am the slave-dealer Abd Selad from Sues. You are my servant and your name is Omar. We have just come from Khartoum."

"I understand, Effendi," smiled the youth.

"For Allah's sake, don't call me Effendi, only if you are sure that we are alone. I intend to do something that requires great courage and I don't mind if you wait here for our group."

"Wherever you go, I am coming with you, even if it leads to our death. If there is danger, I am coming for sure."

"Good, you are decent and loyal. I am going to Ben Mubarek to ward off any plans against the Reis Effendina and join in a slave-hunt to buy blacks."

Leopold couldn't continue because the stranger was coming. "You have asked me for a place in this village, but you don't have to look for one. I am taking you to Ben Mubarek after evening prayers."

"Why only then?"

"Because I am waiting for a ship. You know that ships on the Nile don't journey after sunset. I have to wait until then. If it hasn't come by that time, I can leave my post."

"What kind of a ship?"

"May this young man hear everything?" he asked and pointed to Ben Nil.

"Yes, Omar is the most loyal of my servants and he can keep a secret."

"Did you hear about Reis Effendina?"

"I have even seen him in Khartoum."

"Do you know his aims?"

"Everybody knows them. He is out to catch the slave-hunters.

"Allah condemn this son of a dog and that foreign unbeliever whose name is Poldi Ben Anglesi. They have, only recently, killed many of our comrades and freed many hundreds of slaves."

If he knew, thought Leopold, that this Poldi Ben Anglesi stood before him and would shortly be introduced to Ben Mubarek by him.

"The Reis Effendina would probably not call that a killing but punishment."

"Are you perhaps defending him?"

"As a slave-dealer myself, I cannot possibly defend him, but if he continues as he did so far, there will soon no more new slaves on the market."

"This giour of which I have spoken to you before is probably in our hands already. The Reis Effendina we expect any time now."

"Does your master intend to attack his ship?"

"He wouldn't think of it. Although we have more men, why risk casualties and deaths if one can render him harmless otherwise?"

"How, for instance?"

"Easy, one takes…"

Leopold was interested for the man to continue. If he did, there would be no need to go into the lion's den. But after the third word he put his hand to his mouth, shocked. "I said almost more than I can be responsible for. Ben Mubarek should tell you himself. Please don't tell him that I was so talkative."

"Calm yourself, I don't talk." With this their conversation was at an end, at least as far as Leopold was concerned. To ask more could create suspicion. They sat together for another hour. Leopold only learned the man's name. It was Idris. The ship of the Reis Effendina, luckily, did not pass by. The time came for the Ashia, the prayer for one hour after sunset. Idris now indicated that they could start to move.

"We have horses from the Sheik who is our accomplice. You leave your camels." The Sheik refused any payment. They rode off into a dark night. The stars were not yet shining brightly. For an hour they went south into the steppe. Then a few single trees appeared, finally ending in a wood. Leopold and Ben Nil had to wait while Idris went to inform Ben Mubarek and to ask whether he could bring the guests. They dismounted.

"Are you afraid, Effendi?" whispered Ben Nil.

"No, but tense and eagerly expectant."

"I am too. If we are recognised, we are dead."

"In any case they should not part us so that we can help one another if need be."

"Is Ben Mubarek's place far from here?"

"I don't think so. We won't have to wait long." Leopold was right. Idris returned after ten minutes. He told them his master was prepared to receive them. They should take their horses and follow him carefully, because the path would lead downhill soon.

After only a few minutes they saw several fires whose flames were near the water and made it shine golden. There were no trees, but more than a hundred men. Six large barrels stood at the river bank. A little further on was a ship. There, separate, burned a smaller fire to which the guests were led. There were three people sitting there, who rose when the newcomers came nearer. One of them was of middle size but with broad shoulders and a full black beard. By his similarity to his father, Leopold recognised Ben Mubarek, who eyed Leopold and Ben Nil sharply. The other two did the same.

"Your evening be blessed," greeted Leopold and wanted to continue speaking, but the black bearded man waved his hand for silence.

"Your name?"

"Abd Selad."

"This young man?"

"Omar, my assistant." Leopold didn't want to say servant, because they might be separated.

"How many slaves do you want to buy?"

"As many as I can get."

"And where do you deliver?" Leopold did not intend to let himself to be interrogated. The more modest he appeared, the more was his safety in danger. Ben Mubarek should not think he had a submissive person to deal with. This time he gave a short, dismissive answer.

"Where I get money. Do you think I tell everybody my business secrets?"

"Abd Selad, you proceed very self-confidently."

"Did you expect anything different from a man in my profession? And how do you proceed? Does one ask a guest all these questions without offering a seat?"

"Who said that you are my guest?"

"Nobody, but I took it for granted."

"This is not understood without question. We have to be careful."

"So do I. If you don't like me I don't have to trouble either and I will leave. Come along, Omar." Leopold and Ben Nil turned to walk away.

Ben Mubarek put his arm on Leopold. "Stop, you misjudge the position you are in. Nobody leaves here without my permission."

Leopold smiled. "And if I still leave?"

"I will know how to hold you."

"Try it!" With these words, Leopold took Ben Nil by the hand and jumped between the nearby trees. Ben Mubarek didn't expect that and the two were out of reach before the others made a move to stop them. Everyone including Ben Mubarek ran after them into the wood. But Leopold made only twenty steps and ducked down in the reeds.

"Why don't we go on? They wouldn't have caught us."

"Because I didn't want to leave in the first place."

"Do you want to remain in hiding?"

"No, I only wanted to show Ben Mubarek that he can't order me about. They are all in the wood now. Come." They jumped out of the high reeds and ran to the fire where had Ben Mubarek sat. There was a vessel of clay containing tobacco. They filled their pipes and started smoking.

Behind them sounded a cry: "Here they are, sitting by the fire."

The cry went from mouth to mouth and they all returned. The men didn't know what to say. They called, shouted and laughed in confusion.

Ben Mubarek returned and called: "Allah Akbar – God is great. We are looking for you and you are sitting here?"

"I only wanted to show you that I can remove myself when I want to. I have come here for business and I will not go before it is completed."

He said it so confidently that Ben Mubarek's previous dark face showed a smile.

46

"Abd Selad, I have never met a man like you. You are extraordinarily bold. But I like it and will forgive you the trick you played on us. Return to your places!" he ordered the others, then sat on the right side of Leopold and filled a pipe. He lit it and blew the smoke into Leopold's face. "What happened today, I have never experienced. Either you are a great wag or an experienced dealer."

"The second guess is the better one," Leopold smiled. "I have been though many dangers and do not fear if someone receives me without offering a welcome."

"Can I say 'marhaba', welcome, without knowing you?"

"Yes and no. Everybody is different. I welcome everybody who comes to me."

"And if it is a bad person?"

"I still have time to chase him away."

"After he has done damage to you? No, first the test then the decision."

"Well, test then. It will be my pleasure. But please don't take all night, for we are tired."

"And we are hungry as well," added Ben Nil.

Ben Mubarek laughed loudly. "By Allah, you are unusual people, but I will act against my habit and trust you."

"Do so. You won't regret it. I was delighted when I heard that you were here. I was going to Bahr el Ghasalor or Bahr el Dshebel to buy slaves on a seribah. That would be a journey into the unknown. Now I hope to get a good business connection."

"The question is, what price do you pay?"

"The price depends on the goods. I buy the reqiq right after you have caught them and transport them myself."

"But you have no people, Abd Selad."

"I engage them later. The Shilluk or the Nuehr will provide me with enough people."

"You have to pay them with goods."

"I have enough money to buy things in Fashodah."

"You are daring a lot," smiled Ben Mubarek. "How, if I kill you to take your money?"

"You are much too clever to do that."

"Do you call it clever to leave you with the money?"

"Yes, if you would rob me now, you would have profit, but only once. If you are honest, you can have big profits more often."

"Your calculation is correct. Nothing will happen to you here."

"I am happy not to have deluded myself. About myself, Murad Nassyr will stand for me."

47

"That is the reason I let you come to me. You have bought from him and I don't mind if you come with us."

"Where are you aiming for?"

"About that later. As for now, we will get to know each other. I welcome you and your assistant. You will sleep and eat with us."

After a roast beef meal, Ben Mubarek started to tell about his past. It made Leopold shudder. This man had never had a heart or a conscience. He had a devilish lust to do evil. The more he talked, the greater the abhorrence felt by Leopold. He also questioned Leopold about his past as a slave-dealer. He had to put himself in the position of one such individual and gain the satisfaction of Ben Mubarek.

Leopold was also told about the damage and loss that had been done to his business by the 'giour'. His words of hatred and rage against this foreigner, Poldi Ben Anglesi, would have made someone weaker tremble. He told Leopold about people whom he had sent to catch him. He ended with the words: "I have sent my father as leader of that group and I am sure they have caught him already. He will suffer a hundred pains and tortures before he dies. The rest of his group will simply be shot. My father should be here soon."

Unfortunately, Leopold could not learn about what was most important to him – the attack on the Reis Effendina. It was nearly midnight when Ben Mubarek asked Leopold to accompany him to the ship, where he would be less disturbed by the flies.

"You will sleep in my cabin and I will give you a fly-net. You can see how pleased I am with you. Omar will sleep with the officers."

Leopold thought it could also be his intention to keep him under observation. He had no time to give instructions to Ben Nil, who was taken by the officers sitting with them. The 'Lizard' had cabins at the other end of the ship. There was also a kitchen, which was served by slave girls. Ben Mubarek's cabin consisted of a small and a large room. He lit a lamp and Leopold, although his time was too short to look around, noticed at the right several cushions for people to sit on, and on the left a wooden box with tools used on a vessel, a circumstance that would become important later.

Ben Mubarek asked Leopold to step into the larger room quickly so as not to allow flies to come in. Then he let the dividing mat down again. Ben Mubarek handed Leopold a net to prevent flies bothering him. When Leopold thought they were now going to sleep, he was mistaken.

"You told me that you were tired, but you can sleep as long as you want tomorrow. Now let us talk a bit more, until the oil in the lamp has burned out."

Leopold did not dislike that, as it might provide him with the information he wanted and a good excuse to bring up the subject that brought him there. "I don't mind continuing our conversation, but I can't sleep longer in the morning."

"Why?"

"Because you expect the Reis Effendina. I expect a battle and I want to participate."

"There won't be a battle. I will dispose of the whole ship without a battle."

"This seems impossible."

"You have experienced many things in your life, but you will learn here a thing or two. A slave-hunter knows no sparing. It is a matter of to be or not to be and I don't like to be the loser. With my plans, there is no possibility of anybody on that ship staying alive."

"You are right, in your place I would act the same, but I cannot imagine how you can do that without a battle."

"Actually you could guess what I intend to do. Did you see the om-sufah heaps and the six barrels which have been prepared for this purpose?"

"Yes, I have seen them, but I can't guess their purpose."

"The om-sufah burns easily. When we see the Reis Effendina's ship coming we push the om-sufah and the petroleum into the water and light it. His ship will be engulfed in flames in no time. No-one must escape."

Ben Mubarek talked with visible pride. Leopold shuddered but said admiringly: "This plan is wonderful, I would never be able to think of such ingenious tricks. Can the fire not harm your own ship?"

"No, our ship is up stream and out of danger."

"But if some of them jump the ship and reach the river banks?"

"This is most unlikely, but I thought of this possibility as well. My warriors will be stationed on both sides of the river. Anybody reaching it will be clubbed to death. I am pursued like a predatory animal. Nobody, except myself, knows where I live. A few more ghasuas* and I will withdraw. The light is going out; let's go to sleep."

There was not much oil in the small container. The flame became weaker and weaker and finally went out. They were in the dark.

*Ghasua = slave-hunt.

49

Chapter 6

Frustration of a devilish attack

Leopold thought over what he had learned. This devilish plan must be frustrated. But how? The simplest way would be to sneak off the ship, go to Hegasi and warn the Reis Effendina. But to leave Ben Nil here would be his certain death.

It was painful waiting until Leopold heard the regular breathing of the sleeping Ben Mubarek. He wound himself out of the fly net and went over to double check. Yes, it was the breathing of somebody sleeping.

Leopold went to see whether he could reach Ben Nil. There was no watch on deck and he went to the other end of the ship to the officers' cabin. He heard them talking to each other. Ben Nil, at the far end, tried to find out relevant information and thereby thwarted Leopold's plan to leave the ship with him.

Something different had to be thought of before the birds awakened anybody on board. He thought of the toolbox. Maybe he could find a suitable drill. Indeed, there were several. He chose one the size of a pencil, took it to the barrels and drilled two holes in each of them: One on top to let air in, the other hole at the bottom of the barrel.

As these vessels stood near the water, the current would, hopefully, take the liquid away. The Reis Effendina was saved, but what would happen to him and Ben Nil? Suspicion would fall on him, but he relied on the fact there was no evidence.

Going to bed, Leopold covered himself with the fly net. His excitement ebbed and he fell asleep. It was Ben Mubarek who woke him up. "Get up, Abd Selad, it is late in the morning and we will soon have a lot to do. The Reis Effendina has arrived in Hegasi."

Leopold was awake at once and jumped up. His first glance was into the face of Ben Mubarek. There was nothing to suggest that his deed had yet been discovered. His eyes looked enterprising and even friendly. Leopold was given coffee by an old Negro woman. The slave-hunters were at the shore. Leopold asked Ben Mubarek: "You said the Reis Effendina was coming. Why aren't people at their post yet?"

"There is no need yet, his ship has only landed there and we don't know for how long. Hours may pass and I have sent another man to watch when he sails again. When he returns, our time to act has come."

"I hope there won't be another ship coming."

"There is nothing coming up the Nile, my man would have seen it. And from the other direction – hell, that would be bad luck."

"Would you let it pass?"

"Certainly not. They would see us and report it to the Reis Effendina."

"That isn't for sure. They might sail by him without talking to him."

"You don't know this son of a dog. He will stop and search every ship for slaves. He would learn about the presence of our ship, conceive suspicion and could ruin our plan. No. If a vessel comes down the Nile, it will be stopped and has to wait until everything is over. To be sure, I am going to send a watch upstream. I won't let anything disturb my plan."

Ben Mubarek went ashore to send a man up river. Ben Nil joined Leopold. There was nobody near. They could talk to each other, undisturbed. "You slept very long, Effendi. Have you forgotten why we have come here? The officers have told me the ship of the Reis Effendina will be burned. I couldn't sleep all night."

"I know, with the petroleum in the barrels."

"So you know it too and you slept. The Reis Effendina is coming and there is the petroleum. What can we do?"

"It is not as bad as you think. I have drilled holes into the barrels and the oil has run out by now."

"That's why it smelled of petroleum when I got up. The people thought it was evaporation from the barrels. There were some dead fish at the river bank. "

"Was the water coloured?"

"No."

"Either the petroleum is very clear or the residuum has been swept away by the flood or the wind."

"Suspicion will fall on us anyway."

"Most probably, but who will be able to prove anything?"

"These people don't ask for proof. We have to leave immediately."

"We can't do this unnoticed, and if we are caught, we are lost."

"We managed to run away last night."

"That was different. It is daytime now and we would soon have a few bullets in our body. Besides, although they can't exterminate the Reis Effendina, they could think of another trap which we could prevent or of which we can warn him."

"How could we warn him? If we call out, we will be lost."

"The warning could happen if a rifle went off by mistake."

"But the moment they discover that the barrels are empty, it would be better to be far away."

51

"I grant you that. Let me think, perhaps I will get an idea."

"It had better be fast. There is not much time."

Ben Nil sat down next to Leopold to await the 'arrival' of the idea. But as happens so often when the need is greatest, no useful idea arrived. Five minutes passed, then ten and then fifteen. Ben Mubarek stood at the bank and spoke zealously to his people, especially to one man. It seemed as if they were often looking up to their guests. Finally Ben Mubarek came on board, his face friendly as before. He spoke to Leopold: "Abd Selad, you were right when you said the fire might endanger my own ship. I will take it a hundred metres up the river. I hope the Reis Effendina won't come until then."

So that was the reason why these people looked toward the ship. The glances were not meant for their passengers, thought Leopold. A number of men came aboard to fasten the pulling cord on the mast.

Leopold found that strange. A pulling cord could be fastened better at a different place. The men's work took them nearer to the two guests. Suddenly they threw themselves onto the passengers. This came unsuspected and fast. They were tied up before they could defend themselves.

Ben Mubarek's face suddenly become different. His people stepped back. He came nearer and said threateningly: "You didn't expect that. You seem to be cunning. I therefore had to be clever to catch you. I had to pretend to take my ship up the river to overcome you quickly."

"I am amazed," said Leopold. "What is your reason to attack us?"

"You don't know that everything you discussed was overheard."

"What we discussed could be listened to even by you, " said Leopold quickly composed. "We have not talked about anything that gives you a reason to attack us."

"You think you can deceive Ben Mubarek? You are much too stupid. This man – he pointed to the person who grabbed Leopold first – lay on the roof of the cabin where you talked. He could hear everything."

"Well, tell me what we talked about?" Leopold relied on the possibility that the man had not understood everything as they had spoken quietly.

"You spoke about the petroleum and you maintained there was no petroleum in the barrels."

Leopold was glad to be only half understood. "That was only a joke."

"You will learn that it is serious. Why did you want to flee if you have a good conscience?"

"We spoke of fleeing from the fire if it should lay hold of your ship."

"You seem to be a master of excuses. What will you answer me if I tell you that your rifle should go off when the Reis Effendina comes?"

"Should? I hoped it should not. I didn't speak about my rifle, I meant the rifles of any of us. I was afraid of incautiousness whereby the Reis Effendina could be warned. Your man has listened either incompletely or wrongly. Let him open his ears better next time."

Ben Mubarek's eyes roved from one to another. It was clear that Leopold's boldness had made an impression. It was obvious that he became confused and started to believe Leopold.

"But you were afraid for the Reis Effendina," he carried on.

"I was afraid not for but of the Reis Effendina."

"But you told me yesterday that you are not afraid."

"I am worried that matters could go wrong. That's why I was afraid. You lured him here with false information that there would be a slave caravan over the Nile here. So he knows that there are slave-hunters here. Do you think he would sail into danger in casual comfort?"

"What else?"

"I think it is quite possible that he will leave his ship in Hegasi and while you are expecting him on the river, he will sneak up on you from the steppe."

"By Allah, that is right. I never thought of that. We have to direct our attention on the steppe as well and…"

Ben Mubarek was interrupted. The sentry who was posted up the river came running and reported a ship coming from there. A boat with two officers was to meet it and make it go for anchor.

Leopold hoped to be untied when the slave-hunter asked him. "How do you know that we misinformed the Reis Effendina about our intentions?"

Unfortunately, the sentry whom Leopold had met last evening in Hegasi had made him promise not to tell Ben Mubarek about his talkativeness. He did not want to break this promise and looked for a subterfuge. "It was talked about at the next fire, that's where I heard it."

This untruth was said with good intention, but found punishment immediately. "That is a lie," declared Ben Mubarek. "There were only four people who knew about that. I myself, two officers and the man you met in Hegasi. None of these would have talked about this. How do you know it? Maybe from the Reis Effendina himself? I was going to trust you again, but everything you said was a clever excuse. I will examine this matter further. Woe to you if I find the smallest suspicion. I have no time now. For now, you will lie here under guard."

Ben Mubarek turned away, his attention drawn by two officers he had sent out to intercept the ship. They came with another man on board who was to negotiate this interception.

Leopold was shocked. He knew the man. It was the grandfather of Ben Nil, Abu en Nil. It was foreseeable that he would rush towards them and betray them. Ben Nil lay on his side and didn't see his grandfather. He had to be warned: "Don't be shocked, stay as you are, your grandfather is here."

"Oh Allah, what a joy."

"No, what a disaster for us. He will betray us."

"Heavens! That is probable. What is he doing here?"

"He comes from the ship that Ben Mubarek has forced to stop."

"Can't we give him a sign that he should not betray us?"

"If we weren't tied up, it would be possible. This way, we will have to bear our bad luck."

Leopold tried to turn on his side too and, as they were now silent, they heard what Abu en Nil said to Ben Mubarek: "I still can't see a reason why we should interrupt our journey. We are not in your way."

"But you are. Wait only a few hours to continue your journey."

"Why not now?"

"I don't have to tell you that."

"You will have to tell us or we put on sails again."

"You will not do that, I keep you here."

"You have no right to do that."

"You think so? I am the Reis Effendina. You'll have heard about me."

"No, you are not. I have seen the Reis Effendina."

"I am his lieutenant. You'll have to obey."

"That's a lie too. The Reis Effendina's people wear uniforms, your people don't."

"You are calling me a liar? Beware of insulting me. The Reis Effendina needed another ship for his purpose, so he hired mine. You will know that hired people don't wear uniform. You are the helmsman of your ship. What is your name?"

"Himjad el Bahri."

Himjad el Bahri! Why had Abu en Nil changed his name? After escaping from a slave ship where he was the helmsman, he probably changed it because he felt safer that way, Leopold thought.

He had hardly formed new hopes when their guard spoiled it. He stepped forward and exclaimed: "That is not true. I have seen him before. He is one of the best helmsmen on the Nile. His name is Abu en Nil."

"Abu en Nil?" repeated Ben Mubarek surprised. "Do you really know him?"

"Yes, and I have two witnesses to prove it." He named two people who were on board. They confirmed what our guard had said.

"You cheated us, and that deserves punishment."

"I have told you the truth and if I were this Abu en Nil, what do you have against that?"

"I have nothing against that. I would even be glad about it. Do you have a grandson by the name of Ben Nil?"

"No."

"Don't deny it, or I will force you to tell the truth. I know of a young sailor with the name of Ben Nil. Abu en Nil must therefore be his father or grandfather."

"I don't care, as I am not this Abu en Nil but Himjad el Bahri and I have neither a son nor a grandson. Leave me alone about this Ben Nil."

"Don't talk to me like that, old man; you could regret it."

"Why? I have no reason to fear you."

"That's what you think; if you knew…"

"If I knew what?"

"That I am Ben Mubarek – the slave-hunter." It slipped out.

If Ben Mubarek thought to shock Abu en Nil, he was mistaken. The old man had to fear the Reis Effendina, from whom he had escaped when the slave ship where he was the helmsman had been impounded by the Reis Effendina.

"If you really are the famous slave-hunter you have no reason to treat me as an enemy and I can tell you that I am Abu en Nil."

The old man had no idea that he was making a big mistake.

"Do you know that what you are telling me could be your death?"

"Why? I have proved that I am not your enemy but your friend."

"A friend? How?"

"Did you hear about a slave ship with the name ''Es Samak'?"

"Yes, the Reis Effendina sequestrated it."

"Well, I was the helmsman on that ship, but I escaped with the help of a foreign Effendi who helped me to flee."

"Why just you?"

"Because – I don't know."

Abu en Nil knew it well, but he couldn't tell the slave-hunter that at Leopold's request, he had made a full confession.

"At all events it happened because he was your friend – that makes you an object of suspicion."

"My friend? How could that be possible? I never saw him before."

"But you saw him later?"

"No."

"Don't lie. You have confessed that you are Abu en Nil. Where did you see your grandson last?"

"In Siut."

"That's correct. And now confess whose servant your grandson is."

"My grandson was never a servant to anybody."

"He was not? Well he is now the servant of a man who is specially important to me."

"I don't understand. Why do you sound so angry when you say that?"

Ben Mubarek was convinced that Abu en Nil knew everything. Therefore he was happy to have him in his hand. He laughed mockingly.

"Good, I will tell you. Allah has given you into my hands and you will soon see your grandson and the foreign Effendi again. The man whose every limb will rot off his body."

"Allah kerim! What has he done to you?"

"Son of a dog, don't believe that you can deceive me. You know all his deeds and you will share his fate. Should I tell you what damage this foreigner, Poldi Ben Anglesi, has done to me? I have no time for that. Tie him up and throw him with the others who lie there next to the cabins."

"What, you ask people to tie me up? I know nothing about him, I have been in Fashodah…"

"Be quiet or you get the whip," thundered Ben Mubarek. "I don't want to hear any more. You will learn later – and feel – what's going to happen."

Abu en Nil was grabbed by several men and, despite his struggling, was soon tied up. He was then dragged over to the two other prisoners. Leopold believed that the feared meeting would pass without danger, because the new prisoner was too occupied and furious with his opponents. Then his eyes fell on Leopold: "Effendi, you?" he called out loudly. "Is it possible you are also imprisoned?"

Ben Mubarek had turned away already. When he heard these words he turned round quickly. Just then Abu en Nil saw his grandson: "Ben Nil, you son of my son! Oh Allah, Allah what has happened that you are tied up too?"

The mishap had happened. At this moment Leopold regretted that he had once helped Abu en Nil to escape from the hands of the Reis Effendina. As he expected, Ben Mubarek came back with tiger-jumps. "Effendi? Ben Nil? Allah Akbar! What do I hear?"

"Be silent, babbler! You are bringing yourself and us into peril." Leopold managed to whisper to the helmsman. Then, all those on board gathered before the prisoners.

"Say it again! Repeat it," ordered Ben Mubarek. "Who are these two people?" Leopold's warning seemed to work.

"Who?" asked Abu en Nil to win time.

"Those two you just named."

"These? I don't know them."

"I heard it with my own ears. You have called one Effendi and the other one Ben Nil." Abu en Nil kept quiet.

"The devil gives you these words. How come you talked of an Effendi and a Ben Nil if you don't mean them?"

"That was because you had me tied when I mentioned their names."

"Why did you ask 'why are you imprisoned' if you don't mean them?"

"I meant myself, when I said this."

"Do you think I am mad? You son of a dog. Bring on the whip. We will open his mouth."

A loud and shocked call came at this moment from the river bank: "Oh miracle, oh shock. The barrels are empty!"

Ben Mubarek jumped to the ship's board and looked down. "Are you mad?" he shouted. "They were full."

"But they are empty now." There was a hollow sound as the barrels were turned over.

"Mashallah!" shouted Ben Mubarek. "They are really empty. Who has done that? Wait, I am coming down." He disappeared, but his head came up again to give orders to the guards of the prisoners: "Don't let these sons of dogs talk to each other. Hit them on the mouth if they do."

The man to whom these orders were given took a strong rope and swung it before their noses. They kept silent. What was there to say to undo what the old helmsman had said? After a short while Ben Mubarek returned and with him all the people at the bank. The deck was really full now. He stepped over to Leopold and gave him an angry kick. "Tell the truth, you mangy jackal or I will tear your tongue out. Where have you been during the night?"

Leopold thought: Not to answer would be stupid. If I had one hand free, I would answer with my fist. This way I will have to speak in order to avoid mistreatment. "Naturally, with you in your cabin."

"But you went away once – to the barrels."

"That could only have been in your dreams."

"But these barrels have holes."

"I know that too. I have never seen a barrel without a hole."

Ben Mubarek gave him another kick and screamed: "Do you want to make jokes! It was you who drilled the holes in the barrels. No one else. Confess it!"

Leopold thought again: It is neither a pleasant nor honourable situation to be exposed to ill-treatment in front of so many people. I wanted to catch him and now he has caught me. He was not only a criminal, but gruesome to boot. His self-reliance rebelled against the thought of saving himself by denials. Perhaps I could manage to delay matters by trickery to win some time. He should not think that I am afraid of him. My situation is bad, but in no way desperate. Even if it costs my life, I will dare to tell him the truth.

"Confess? Only criminals and sinners have to confess. What I did was no sin and no crime."

The slave-hunter stared him into the face. He hadn't expected that. "Ah, did you hear that? Do you know that you have pronounced your sentence of death? Why did you let the petroleum run out?"

"This question you can answer yourself."

"To rescue the Reis Effendina?"

"Yes, I am his friend."

"Poldi Ben Anglesi?"

"Yes."

"And your assistant Omar is Ben Nil?"

"That's right."

Ben Mubarek was confounded by such frankness. He stepped back a few steps. He was convinced that everybody else would try to safe himself with denials. He turned to his people. Ben Nil whispered:

"Oh Effendi, why have you confessed? Now everything is lost."

"Not yet. Take courage. Let me do things."

Ben Mubarek turned again and laughed mockingly. "You are a most daring individual, oh Poldi Ben Anglesi, but you don't know what it means to dare to come near me."

"Pah, nothing to it. I have dared many more dangerous things. You don't ascribe the fact that you discovered who I am to your cleverness?"

"Vermin! You dare to insult me?" He gave him another kick.

"You can kick me now as I am in fetters, but you will pay for every single blow."

"Pay you? Are you mad?"

"I am speaking with conviction. How long do you think you can hold me?

"Until you rot."

"That's a laugh. Think of the Reis Effendina."

"Do you rely on him?"

"Certainly."

"Well, hope until you die. I can't burn this son of a dog, but..."

Ben Mubarek was interrupted. A man pushed through the people. It was the sentry who had been sent to Hegasi. He was out of breath.

"Master, nothing will come of it with the petroleum fire. The Reis Effendina is not sailing here, but is coming on foot with his soldiers."

"How many people were they?"

"I don't know. They were walking two by two but in a long row."

"When will they be here?"

"In about half an hour."

"We would win in a battle, but lose many of our men. I will get the Reis Effendina into my hands another way. For the moment we will sail up the river. Get the ship ready, men. Put on the sails."

Everybody became busy now and their attention, including their guard, was directed towards the movement of the ship. The prisoners could talk to each other quietly. They had just passed the ship which had been forced by Ben Mubarek to throw anchor, when Abu en Nil turned to Leopold and asked in a subdued voice: "Effendi, should I call my people now?"

"No, you would worsen our situation without reaching your purpose."

"But I have to go back to my job, I cannot possibly stay here with this horrible Ben Mubarek."

"He won't ask you whether you want to or not. You must!"

"But what will happen to me?"

"You will have to share our fate."

"And what would that be?"

"Allah knows. I don't. You alone are guilty that you are in this situation."

"I was shocked. I couldn't know that I mustn't mention any names."

"We were tied up. That should have been enough to tell you."

They had just passed the isle of Hassanieh when Leopold saw a rider in the distance. He was on a camel and riding at a sharp speed. When he saw the ship he waved with his rifle and tried to reach the river bank as fast as possible. Ben Mubarek stood near Leopold, who heard him say: "This is Oram. He was with my father. We can't take him on board now."

Ben Mubarek held his hands like a loudhailer in front of his mouth and called to the rider: "Maijeh es Saratin, Maijeh es Saratin!"

The man seemed to understand and rode on quickly.

Chapter 7

On board the slave-ship

A Maijeh is a side-arm of a river, an inlet where the water doesn't flow. In other words, a Maijeh is also a marsh. Es Saratin is 'of the crayfish'. Leopold was happy to have saved the Reis Effendina, but now he himself was in the claws of a monster. Could he possibly expect help from his friend? Hardly likely. He will learn from the sailors of the ship that was stopped by Ben Mubarek that his vessel went up the river. He would go back to his own in Hegasi, but costly time would have been lost. The 'Hawk' of the Reis Effendina was faster than the 'Lizard', Ben Mubarek's, but if it hid in a Maijeh, the 'Hawk' would pass without noticing it.

No, Leopold couldn't rely on the Reis Effendina, he had to find a way to save them himself. He explained that to his co-prisoners. Ben Nil trusted him but Abu en Nil gave up all hope. He blamed everybody and Allah and asked why Ben Mubarek had such hatred for Poldi Ben Anglesi and his grandson. When Ben Nil told him briefly, he lamented: "Oh Allah, oh heaven, who would have thought this? Now my years nor my days are counted. Within hours we will all be murdered."

"Don't complain," requested Ben Nil, "you stop the Effendi from thinking. He will think of a way to escape. By the way, you have done nothing to Ben Mubarek. It is only us two who have to fear him."

"Haven't you heard what he said? He thinks I am your ally."

The old man seemed egotistical. He only thought of himself and not about his grandson, who was in much greater danger.

They were on their way. Ben Mubarek had time to occupy himself with his prisoners. He came with his two officers. They stood there to view the three, gazing at them mockingly. Then Ben Mubarek asked Leopold: "Was it you who pursued me at the Wadi el Berd?

"Yes, it was me."

"You? It was you? Did you catch me?"

"Don't puff yourself up. The fact that I couldn't catch you, was not thanks to the superiority of your person, but to the speed of your camel. Your Dshebel-Gerfeh-camel beat my animal."

"Do you think I couldn't beat you, you miserable worm?"

"Stand in front of me with a knife. My hands will be bound and without a knife. Then we will see who is the worm – you or I."

"Be silent. Up to now you've been lucky, and it's made you insolent. This insolence will turn now and I will show you how a believer deals with a Christian dog. It would be better if you had never been born, I will…"

"Save your threats. Firstly, I am not a Christian, secondly, I know already what you are going to do with me."

"Whether you are a Jew or a Christian is immaterial to me. You are all unbelievers. And now tell me what I am going to do with you?"

"First, you want to pull out my tongue, then my ears, the nose and all my limbs separately."

"True, who told you?"

"Somebody who knows that I know no fear, and that I know how to save myself in the worst situation."

"Who would that be?"

"Abd Mubarek, your father."

"Yes, you escaped him. The devil guarded you. But know that Heaven will collapse before I let you escape."

"Don't imagine that. If any man makes me fear him, it surely isn't you."

"Son of a dog, in a few minutes you will cry out for mercy."

"Try it!"

"You think I am joking."

"No, but you only threaten. You don't dare."

"The devil may devour you. I will show you that I dare. Come here, men. You will see how an unbeliever will be tortured."

The people on deck came closer. Ben Mubarek went into his cabin to collect a pair of pliers. Ben Nil took the opportunity to say:

"Effendi, I don't know you, the careful man, any more. You are worsening our situation."

"No, I want to show him that he has to fear me, but not me him."

Ben Mubarek returned. He held up the tool and shouted: "Who wants to tear out the fingernails from this son of a damned bitch?"

"I, I, I," several of them shouted.

One strong fellow pushed the others aside and asked: "Give it to me, oh master. It is not the first time that I made someone sing by doing it."

"Yes, do it, Tara. You have had practice in this job."

He took the pliers, stood in front of Leopold, showed his teeth and opened and shut the pliers to give a taste of pain to come. He then bent down to turn Leopold, whose hands were tied at the back. Leopold had waited for that moment. He quickly pulled his knees up and tossed Tara, with both feet in his stomach, to fly against others, who were torn

61

down, and landed with his head at the toolbox – several metres away. There he lay as if dead. Blood came out of his mouth. Leopold thought he had bitten his tongue. Everybody shouted, cursed and threatened.

Ben Mubarek ordered quiet and examined the man, who gave no sign of life. He asked Tara to be taken away, clenched his fist against Leopold and said through his teeth: "You will atone for this. Tenfold, hundredfold. Your torture shall be different now. Hold him down and pull his nails." Six, eight men threw themselves onto Leopold, who did not defend himself but called: "Halt. First one more word, Ben Mubarek. You will hear no sound of my pain. But whatever happens to me, will happen to Abd Mubarek, your father."

"To – my – father?" he drawled, astonished.

"Yes, and not only him, but all his men too."

"What do you know about my father? Where is he?"

"He tried to catch me."

"That's right, he didn't meet you."

"That's right, he didn't meet me, but I met him in a way he did not wish."

"The devil! Are you telling the truth?"

"It is immaterial to me whether you believe it or not."

"Where did you meet him?"

"At a well."

"Which one?"

"I won't tell you."

"I have to know that."

"I wouldn't dream of telling you. For the moment it is my secret. Untie me and we will lead you to your father. Otherwise you have him and your whole troop on your conscience."

"I don't mind that," Ben Mubarek laughed. "You want to save yourself by lying."

"Lying? How do I know that they went out to catch me?"

Ben Mubarek realised that this answer was not without reason.

"Were they on foot?"

"No, they had camels."

"How many of them were they?"

"Do you think you can question me like a child? We have taken them prisoners and they will suffer exactly what you are intending to do to us."

"So they are near now?"

"No, we have taken the fastest camels."

"Why didn't you stay with them?"

"They are in secure hands. Do you know the Fakir el Fakura?"

"Of course I know him. We talked about him yesterday."

"Mohammed Achmed came afterwards and wanted to save them."

"Did he succeed?

"Stupid question. Would I be here if he had succeeded? I don't understand how you could send people to catch me. You will never succeed."

"Allah! You are mad. You are my prisoner now."

"No, you will free me. I know it."

"Rather would the devil…"

"Stop! Don't swear, you don't know what you are doing."

"And you are more cunning than a fox. Nobody can trust you. You only pretend that you know everything."

"Would I know that your father was the leader of the group?"

"No. But why did you come to the isle of Hassanieh?"

"To negotiate with you."

"Who told you that I was to be found here?"

"Your father. This is the best proof that I spoke with him."

"What did you want to negotiate?"

"About the freeing of my prisoners."

"How? Did you want a ransom?"

"About that we will talk later."

"I don't understand why you didn't talk about that yesterday."

"I had to tell you who I am and it would be impossible to save the Reis Effendina."

"Did you know that I expected him here?"

"Yes, from your father."

"That is impossible. My father would never tell you such things."

"He did without knowing it."

"I don't understand that."

"If you continue to seek my life, there will be many things you won't understand."

"You are talking proudly, and here you lie helpless before me."

"Helpless? Don't be mistaken. If I am not back at a certain time, all the prisoners including your father and the Fakir el Fakura will be shot as your people were in the Wadi el Berd, where only you escaped on a fast camel."

There was a short pause while Ben Mubarek digested the meaning of these words. "How many of my people escaped?"

"Not one."

"You are lying in spite of the honest face you assume."

"I am telling the truth."

"I can prove that you are lying. Did you see the rider who came to the river bank?"

"Yes."

"It was Oram, who was with my father."

"But not at the time I took your father and his men prisoner. He may have been away on some errand. When he returned and saw his comrades tied up on the ground, he rushed to you."

"May I learn how you managed to catch my people?"

"I don't mind, but I have no desire to tell you myself."

"Then let Abu en Nil tell me."

"He knows nothing. He was not there. Since I helped him to escape, I haven't seen him until he entered your ship."

"Is that true?"

"Don't ask me constantly if what I say is the truth. You will consider that it is an insult to me."

"So! An insult. And who called himself Abd Selad yesterday and turned out to be Poldi Ben Anglesi today? Wasn't that a lie?"

"No, that was a stratagem – a trick of war."

"You unbelievers don't seem to know what one understands to be a lie."

"And you Moslems don't even bother with stratagems, but you'd rather commit murder. And now, let Ben Nil tell you what happened."

The people were pushing each other to come nearer so as not to miss a word of the exciting account. He was clever enough not to mention the place of the event. When he wanted to mention the way Leopold was eavesdropping behind Abd Mubarek and the Fakir el Fakura, Leopold stopped him. The fact that he knew everything, without telling them how he acquired the knowledge, was more impressive. They listened breathlessly until Ben Nil finished. Ben Mubarek then called:

"Is it believable that you alone have killed the lion of El Teitel?"

"You have heard it."

"You didn't know what you dared."

"I risked my life – what else?"

"That is enough. A man can't lose more than his life."

"Oh yes, much more."

"What would that be?"

"Something you have lost long ago, namely your honour, your good name and being agreeable to God and people."

"Poldi Ben Anglesi!" he roared, "don't think that I have suddenly became forbearing. I am your master now and your life is in my hand."

"That's right, but with my life you also hold the lives of your father, the Fakir el Fakura and all your people."

"You have come to negotiate about these people. What are you

64

asking for their freedom?"

"Your oath that you stop hunting and dealing in slaves, and my freedom as well as that of Ben Nil and his grandfather."

"Would my oath suffice?"

"Maybe, maybe not. I may ask for guarantees."

"Why do you assume that I might swear falsely?"

"Because I know several Moslems who swore falsely."

"Then they were not followers of the prophet."

"Well, I have proof that the Fakir el Fakura as well as your father, whom people think is a holy Fakir, swore by Allah and by the beard of the prophet, and they lied."

"Was it you to whom they swore?"

"Yes."

"Then they committed no sin. You are an unbeliever."

"And there you ask I should believe you. You've caught yourself."

"So we have finished?"

"Not yet. I will make you another offer."

"Let's hear it."

"You give the three of us our freedom against the freedom of your father and the Fakir el Fakura. The others I hand to the Reis Effendina."

"What audacity," laughed Ben Mubarek, furious. "This giour is in my hands and talks as if he could give orders. You want me to free three people against two. Is that a reasonable calculation?"

"Yes, Abu en Nil doesn't count. He never did anything against you."

"And how high are you in your estimate?"

"In this deal I am only a number. Two against two. The helmsman goes by the way."

"Is that your last offer?"

"Yes," declared Leopold, decisively.

"How can I free you? Think what you have done to us in the past. And there lies Tara, whom you have murdered."

"Not I. It was you and Tara himself. He will not bring anybody to sing again. That happens if you enjoy torturing people."

"Now I have to hear what Oram, the one who was with my father, will have to tell me. In no case will I free you!"

"So you are prepared to sacrifice your father?"

"Let him die. He has lived long enough. I have long strived to apprehend you without being able to catch you. I will keep you until the last sigh of your breath. Now take these mangy dogs out of my sight, down into the punishment room and put the bolt in place. Also, place a guard there."

They were grabbed and dragged across the deck to the hatch, where they were dropped down the stairs without asking whether they would break anything. From there they were taken into a room. A door was locked and a bolt was pushed. Then they heard the men talk: "Much too much talking. A knife into their flesh would be best. Allah may burn them. Who is staying first guard?"

"I will." The voice sounded familiar to Leopold.

"All right, I will relieve you. There is not much guarding to do. They are tied up and couldn't escape from the ship anyhow."

One of those outside the prison room moved away. After a short silent pause, they heard someone scratching at the door, the oriental way of knocking. But so carefully as only to be heard a few steps away. The prisoners didn't answer. After renewed stronger scratching they heard a subdued voice: "Effendi, can you hear me?"

"Yes," Leopold answered.

"I stayed on purpose as your guard. Do you intend to ruin me?"

"Ruin you? Who are you?"

"Idris, whom you met in Hegasi."

"Ah, thank God," thought Leopold. An unexpected star begins to light up; hardly perceptible, but properly handled, it could become a bright saving star. The man was afraid. He thinks that I will, in despair, forget my promise and betray his loquacity. This worry was opportune. If Ben Mubarek learned what Idris has told me, he could expect severe punishment. Leopold crawled closer to the door and whispered:

"You know what is going to happen to us?"

"You will have to die, most probably."

"Then Abd Mubarek and his people will have to die as well."

"Oh, Ben Mubarek will let his father die, to be able to torture you."

"What are the other men saying to this?"

"Many want you to die; others want to give you freedom to save their comrades."

"Which party is stronger?"

"I can't say that, but I beg you, for Allah's sake, not to tell Ben Mubarek what you have learned from me. He would throw me to the crocodiles."

"Then I am sorry that I cannot spare you."

"Not? Allah kerim! Won't you, a Christian, practise mercy?"

"I am not a Christian, but I like my life no less than a Moslem."

"Oh Allah, oh prophet! So I am lost!"

Idris grew silent, and Leopold wanted to let his threats work on him. He was quiet too. The result was even more favourable than he expected. After a while the scratching started again. "Effendi, if you could escape…"

"That would be good. Also I wouldn't be forced to speak about you."

"Unfortunately, this is impossible. You are tied up and there is a guard in front of your door constantly. And how would you leave the ship?"

"Have you any other consideration?"

"No, these three are enough."

"These three points wouldn't hinder me if I had someone to help me."

"That is dangerous, Effendi."

"Not at all. Nobody would know about this helper."

"What has this man to do?"

"Two things. Firstly, to give me a knife…"

"You will have that as soon as we finish talking," interrupted Idris.

"Secondly, only some information."

"Well, ask. I will answer – be quiet, somebody is coming."

The steps creaked. Somebody came down with a lamp. Leopold could see the light through the crevices of the dried-up wood. His first glance was to look for the bolt. It was in the middle of the door. It covered two boards that stood a little distance apart and could be moved from the inside with a knife. This observation took three seconds. His heart jumped for joy. A man opened the door. It was Ben Mubarek.

"Well, how do you like it here?" asked the slave-hunter mockingly. "Let's see whether your fetters are tight enough."

He was satisfied, because these fetters were unusually tied. He asked: "Will you tell me when you are expected to return?"

"Just when I come back," was the answer.

"That will be an eternity. The dogs which belong to you will never see you again." He turned to the guard: "If these jackals talk to each other take the whip and hit them on their heads." Ben Mubarek spat on Leopold and went. It took Idris a while to announce himself again.

"Effendi, you can ask me now. He is gone."

"Where does the crew sleep?"

"Down here, everywhere."

"That is bad."

"The crew is on land and go to sleep rather late – the same time as yesterday."

"When will we reach the Maijeh es Saratin?"

"Probably before midnight. We made good speed with the extra boat and the twelve oarsmen helping the ship's speed."

"We will have to leave as long as the crew are on land. Do you

67

know a comrade who is vicious and you don't like?

"Yes, why?"

"Could you arrange for such a man to be our guard?"

"That wouldn't be too difficult."

"Now tell me: Where are our weapons?"

"In Ben Mubarek's cabin. He regards them as his booty."

"If you do your task to my satisfaction, I will not betray you but even leave a present for you. Except for our weapons, they haven't taken anything away from us."

"If you want to leave me a present, Effendi, there is no better place than under some old palm mats at the bottom of the stairs. Is there anything else I can do?"

"Yes, I would like to know what Oram, who will meet you at the Maijeh es Saratin, will report to Ben Mubarek. This has to be before the conversation has ended. By that time, we will have to be gone."

"It will be possible to let you know part of what he is saying by pretending that I am informing your guard."

"That is an excellent idea. My present will be bigger, depending how satisfied I am with you. I know enough, and now bring me the knife."

He brought a knife; it was sharp and pointed. What luck, thought Leopold, that Idris had such fear of being betrayed. It was late in the evening when they reached the Maijeh. His successor threatened with the whip whenever they whispered. As Leopold expected, Ben Mubarek came once more to check his fetters. He didn't bother with the others and, of course, didn't notice the knife. It was hidden in the furthest corner with the helmsman. A man, probably Oram, called to throw him the ropes; he would tie them round trees.

"I am going to talk to Oram now, then your fate will be decided. Your torture will begin in a short while." Ben Mubarek grinned.

"You are talking like a child," Leopold scoffed. "You cannot alter my fate. It has been decided already. You'll be unable to do anything to us."

Ben Mubarek broke out into roaring laughter. "Your fear has made you mad. In one hour you will sing differently."

"You have learned today what happens to those who were going to make me sing."

"That can only happen once. It won't happen again." Ben Mubarek bolted the door.

Now was the time to rid themselves of their fetters. It had to happen carefully and noiselessly. They waited for their accomplice. Twenty minutes after they had freed themselves, they heard steps coming down the stairs. They recognised Idris' voice:

"If you could come on land, there is so much news."

"Do you want to annoy me?" growled the guard. "What is new?"

"This unbelieving Effendi had spoken the truth. Our comrades are captives. Ten of them have been killed with rifle butts."

"Allah destroys the breed of the Reis Effendina. Our prisoners have had it, that is for sure. How did Oram escape?"

"The asakers didn't tie him properly. In the morning he managed to sneak away. He even managed to grab a camel. Our comrades will not be brought to Khartoum but to Hegasi, where the asakers expect to meet Poldi Ben Anglesi Effendi."

"They will never see him again and we will receive them properly. If only I could be down there. Wouldn't you take over here? I give you…"

"No, thank you. I have been here for two hours, that's enough."

The steps creaked again. Idris went. The guard went several steps toward Idris during their conversation. Idris was Leopold's enemy, but he had to keep his word. He should not think of him as a cheat. The discussion had another advantage. The moving of the bolt could not be done noiselessly and Leopold managed to shift it while they were talking. He opened the door and went outside in the dark.

When Idris left, the guard turned round and walked towards the prison room. On the way he collided with Leopold, who took him by the neck. With Leopold's iron grip as well as the shock, he broke down almost immediately. The guard was tied up with his own belt. His headgear was used to gag him. Leopold went up the stairs. He could not see the fires on land, but their light was enough to show him that there was no one on deck. He went down again and put a sum of money under the palm mats. His two comrades had come out of the room and waited for his instructions.

He went upstairs again, followed by his friends. They went to Ben Mubarek's cabin to fetch their weapons. They did not go upright for fear of being seen from the land. "What now?" whispered Ben Nil. "We cannot go down on the ladder."

"We would be caught before we reached the ground. I have a better idea. We let ourselves down on a rope into the boat that was used to help the ship's speed. With a bit of luck it will be out of reach of the light from the fires." They went to the far side of the ship and could see the boat, still connected to the ship by rope.

"You, Ben Nil, go first, after you, your grandfather. I will be last," said Leopold. Ben Nil, the rifle on his back, had started to climb down when they heard Ben Mubarek calling: "And bring a jug of raki down with you."

Raki is a strong drink not forbidden to Moslems. These words told Leopold that someone was on his way up. He turned around. In fact, he saw one man coming up and behind him a second. "Quickly, quickly," he whispered to Abu en Nil. "They haven't seen us yet."

Leopold bent down so as not to be seen. The old helmsman had to go over the rail: They had to notice him. A third man came up. The first one saw the old man and subsequently Leopold. He understood the situation at once and shouted: "Come up, men, the prisoners are loose."

He rushed hither, the other two following. When the first one was three steps from Leopold, he sprang toward him and ran his rifle butt into his body to make him bound back against some boxes. The second one stretched his arms to grab Leopold, receiving a blow to his head. The third one was cleverer. He pulled his pistol and shot at Leopold. He didn't hit because Leopold jumped aside. In the next second he was felled too by the rifle butt.

The three had roared with all their might. Now they lay there, motionless. From below came answers. Everybody shouted, everybody came running. Another few moments and it would be too late. Abu en Nil was already in the boat. Leopold jumped on the rail, climbed down the rope, cut it and pushed the boat away from the ship, when Ben Mubarek's roaring voice shouted: "Where are they? They killed our three men. They are probably hiding in the cabins. Search – search."

The oars were still in the boat. "Let's get away out of reach of their eyes," said Leopold. "He can shoot then, I don't mind. Take the oars, but use them quietly and in time." His comrades obeyed. When they were far enough, Leopold asked them to stop. The shouting on board had subsided. It was inexplicable to them where the prisoners could be. They deliberated. Leopold showed a sense of humour. The high, dense wood which surrounded the area made the sound of his voice come from a different position. He held his hands to his mouth like a loudspeaker and called, making his voice come from a different direction. He shouted: "Ben Mubarek, Ben Mubarek – come and get us!"

"There he is, that son of a dog," shouted Ben Mubarek. "There on the right, they are on the water. They must have our boat."

"Yes, we have your boat," answered Leopold in the same way. "Now let me sing."

"Are you listening, are you listening?" roared Mubarek. "They are about seventy yards north. Shoot, shoot all of you."

The shots rang out while the escapers were to the west. Now Leopold turned around, his face to the south, and shouted, laughingly.

"Wrong shooting. Where are you looking for us?"

It sounded from the opposite direction. All of them turned and Ben Mubarek ordered: "They are near the entrance of the side arm: All of you shoot in that direction."

They all shot south without success, of course. Leopold turned north again and laughed mockingly. They immediately turned again and Ben Mubarek shouted: "The giour has the devil, now he is up there again."

Leopold's intention to lead the slave-hunters astray was successful. They could, without worry, continue their flight. "At least they told us where the entrance of the Nil arm is. Let's go south."

The journey down the Nile was helped by a good wind, the flowing of the water, and the strong arms of Ben Nil and Leopold, who let the weaker old helmsman take the rudder. They all were quiet, Ben Nil and Leopold Ellman because of several sleepless nights and Abu en Nil because of other reasons. Leopold saw he was depressed and asked him why.

"The Reis Effendina will recognise and arrest me. Please let me go on land before we reach him."

"But you are alone and without any means. What will you do?"

"Ben Nil, my grandchild, will be with me."

"No," countered the youth. "You are the father of my father and it is Allah's command that I should honour you, but I am the servant of the Effendi now and nothing can persuade me to leave him."

"Son of my son, who would have thought it of you. Will you deny the blood of your veins or the laws which are anchored in everyone?"

"No, my love for you and the loyalty to my Effendi can be united. You don't have to leave the boat. I know Poldi Ben Anglesi Effendi. He will take you under his wing – he will guard you."

"He can't do that!"

"Don't doubt it. He can do anything he wants."

"At least I will do what I can," remarked Leopold. "Abu en Nil, you don't need to be anxious, the Reis Effendina will forgive you your past."

"Oh, Effendi, if that were true. I am not as bad as it seems."

"I know that, that's why I helped you to escape at the time."

"If the Reis Effendina forgives me, I don't have to fear anybody. I could even go home: But if he asks how I managed to escape?"

"Tell him the truth."

"Then he will be angry with you."

"That is not so bad. By the way, your grandchild has served him well and his gratitude will persuade him to forgive."

The old man calmed down.

Chapter 8

A trap is being set

When, finally, they neared Hegasi, they saw a little lamp on a ship. Leopold recognised the contours of the Reis Effendina's vessel. The light came from a lantern which burned at the fore-mast. They steered toward it. Before they had reached it, a voice called: "Boat! Get to the side of the ship!"

For the fun of it, Leopold asked the old man to steer away from it. The voice immediately called: "Stop or I shoot!"

At the same time he sounded the alarm. Within a minute the whole crew would be awake and on board. Leopold did not want to go too far with his fun and ask to steer toward the ship.

"Steer to backboard!" ordered the voice. They obeyed.

A short while and everybody seemed to be on deck. A voice asked: "Who does this boat belong to?" Leopold recognised the voice of the Reis Effendina and whispered to Ben Nil to answer: "To the Lizard."

"Come up immediately," came the excited order. Several lanterns were lit; a rope ladder was let down. Leopold, in jocular mood, asked the helmsman to go first. Abu en Nil obeyed without noticing Leopold's intention. Once on deck, Leopold heard the Reis Effendina: "I know that face. Who are you, tell me where we have met before!"

The old man was shocked by this reception and forgot to answer.

"If I'm not mistaken, your name is Abu en Nil – confess immediately!"

"Yes, Effendi," admitted the helmsman, anxiously.

"Call me Emir. You know very well what to call me. You were the helmsman of a ship that I sequestered."

"Yes, I am he."

"I took you all prisoner, but you escaped. Welcome here. Tie him up and throw him into the prison cabin."

"No, no, Emir, don't tie me up!" called the helmsman. "I am not your enemy, I came voluntarily."

"Voluntarily? That is a lie. The guard had to threaten to shoot. Where is the ship you came from?"

"At the Maijeh es Saratin."

"I don't know it. What did it do there?"

"It was hiding from you."

"It was at the isle of Hassanieh, what did it do there?"

"They wanted to catch you."

"To catch me? Who is the Reis, the captain of that ship?"

"It has no Reis, its master is Ben Mubarek, who gives the orders."

This name caused excitement. "Ben Mubarek, Ben Mubarek!" sounded from all their lips. The Reis Effendina expressed his astonishment: "Do I hear right? Ben Mubarek, the infamous slave-hunter is on the "Lizard'? Now I can see, this son of a dog intended to set a trap for me. Confess immediately!"

"Yes, Emir, you guessed right, he wanted to burn you and your ship."

"Allah kerim! He had caused me to feel mistrust. It was lucky that I went by land and not by ship. I wondered about the barrels. Now bind his legs and give him the bastinado."

"Not the bastinado, Emir, I am completely innocent."

Ben Nil hurried up the ladder now. "You mustn't hit the old man, he is my grandfather and has told you no lies."

"You are here, Ben Nil? In the company of a slave-hunter?"

"My grandfather never was a slave-hunter. He only served a short time as a helmsman on a slave ship. My Effendi will tell you the same."

"Where is your Effendi?"

"I am coming," answered Leopold and jumped over the rail. "Here I am." One could hear a general call of joyous surprise. Achmed Abd el Insaf, the Reis Effendina, took one step back and looked astonished. But only for a moment, then he opened his arms and came toward Leopold.

"Poldi Ben Anglesi, you here! What joy. Arrived from the land of the Fessarah. Come to my heart and let me hug you." His joy was as big as it was genuine. Leopold was honoured and happy. His Lieutenant, the old Onbashi Mustafa and many others came and shook his hand.

"There must have been matters of great importance to make you come here instead to Khartoum. Where are my asakers?" asked the Reis Effendina.

"They are on the way here to bring you a group of slave-hunters belonging to Ben Mubarek which we have taken prisoner."

"So you have again captured some of them. What a lucky man you are. I haven't caught anybody since I met you last."

"If I am not mistaken, you will, by tomorrow, catch Ben Mubarek himself."

"Really? Where is he?"

"In the Maijeh es Saratin, as Abu en Nil already told you."

"And you were there? How is that possible?"

"Oh, I was, before you came to Hegasi and on the isle of Hassanieh.

Ben Mubarek took me prisoner."

"Prison–," the word stuck in his mouth. "Effendi, you are joking?"

"No."

"I thought you were in the western steppe and you are here and engaged yourself with Ben Mubarek, whom I have long chased in vain."

"The matter is simple. I will tell you about it, but order your people to be quiet. It is better for our purpose that no one in Hegasi knows what is happening here and what we are going to decide. Ben Mubarek has spies everywhere. Ibrahim, the resident sheik, is his accomplice."

"You know all that? I am really curious to hear what happened to you since our last success in freeing the Fessarah women and men from Ben Mubarek's slave dealings. The helmsman we will put into our prison."

"No, Emir! He is a good, honest man. I recommend him to you. Leave him with Ben Nil and order some food for them. We haven't eaten anything since yesterday."

"You must be hungry. You will have what your heart desires."

In the dim light of early morning five people left the ship in a boat – the Reis Effendina, Leopold, Ben Nil and two sailors to do the rowing. They rowed up the Nile and Leopold had time to tell the Reis Effendina what had happened since he left him after their last success. Then he explained how he would lure Ben Mubarek into a trap to which there was one alternative, to submit or die in the swamp.

Leopold had asked the Reis Effendina to change his uniform into local attire, because he didn't want him to be recognised by anyone in Hegasi."

"I am going to arrest the sheik," ventured the Reis Effendina.

"No, you will be very friendly with him. Through him we will get Ben Mubarek where we want him. You will tell him that you were falsely informed Ben Mubarek would be here. But you assume now that he went to Khartoum and you will go there to catch him. We know that he will try to free his father and his men. The more so, because I will go to him after you have left Hegasi and tell him what happened to me. I must also tell him who I am because, if I lie, he wouldn't believe what else I have to tell him to lure Ben Mubarek into a trap. So, when I say that I am going to join my prisoners, Ben Mubarek will eagerly try to catch me again."

"And where shall I meet you?" asked the Reis Effendina.

"Do you know the mountain Arash Kol?"

"Yes, I have been there several times."

"There is a side arm of the Nile that ends in a marsh. Next to the swamp is a mountain with a narrow passage. The side of the mountain is vertical. I intend to lure Ben Mubarek to go there."

"How will you do that?"

"I will tell the sheik who I am as I am sure he will be visited by Ben Mubarek or one of his messengers. I will tell him that after what has happened to me, I have decided that all followers of the slave-hunter must die and I will throw them into the swamp. That alone will make him follow me. You will hide in the nearby wood. When you hear the first shot, you will be behind him and his men. We will have them between two fires. They will have no alternative to submitting, unless they want to die in the swamp."

"Ben Mubarek will be there sooner than you. If he puts the same trap on you then you will be between two fires."

"I have been thinking about that. He would be stupid not to try that trap on me. But thinking what he might do, I don't have to fear it. When I know there is a mine, I either avoid it or render it harmless before it explodes. I calculate that I will meet my caravan by tonight."

"No fear," confirmed the Reis Effendina. "I will be there, but you can't meet your caravan tonight: It has to make a journey of five days."

"Normally yes, but since Oram escaped, they will tell themselves he would ride to Ben Mubarek and they will speed up their journey."

Achmed Ben Onsaf, the Reis Effendina, stepped onto land and made his way back on foot to Hegasi and to Ibrahim el Beled, the sheik. The two sailors accompanied him, but when they came nearer to the town, they separated and went back to their ship. Leopold and Ben Nil took the oars and rowed until they could observe the 'Hawk', the Reis Effendina's ship, in the distance.

It took nearly an hour until they saw the erecting of sails and the ship's departure. The main thing now was to reach the Sheik el Beled. Luckily they noticed him at the water, looking curiously at the two rowers and the large boat, which he knew belonged to Ben Mubarek's ship, the 'Lizard'.

When they rowed to the river bank, the sheik walked toward them. "How is it that you are returning. I thought you would go to Fashodah with the 'Lizard'?"

"We were nearly forced to go to Fashodah."

Ibrahim took great care to look unconcerned, but couldn't quite control his strained attention.

"I will tell you, but come away from here. Things were happening, we can only tell you in private."

"You fill my soul with curiosity," said Ibrahim as he followed them.

"What can happen in this little place that could be important?"

"Do you know which ship the 'Lizard' is?"

"A trading ship from Berber," he answered.

"Didn't you ask the name of its owner?"

"Why should I fill my brain with unnecessary knowledge?"

"That is a pity. You could have warned us that we would be in danger of losing our lives."

"Your lives?" asked the sheik, seemingly shocked. "Have you been in such danger?"

"To be sure. The 'Lizard' is the ship of the greatest criminal and slave-hunter there is. Can you think who I mean?"

"The worst of all slave-hunters is Ben Mubarek, whom Allah may condemn. But he wouldn't dare to be seen here."

"He did dare!"

"Had I known this, I would have taken all the men in Hegasi to arrest him and deliver him to the Reis Effendina."

"Do you know the Reis of the Viceroy?"

"It is less than an hour since I spoke to him."

"Was he really here?" asked Leopold, pretending to be surprised.

"Yes, he was here today, yesterday he was on the isle of Hassanieh."

"We had already left. Allah be praised that I have managed to save him. I didn't believe he would be so careless as to come. They wanted to lure him here to kill him."

"Who? Who?"

"Ben Mubarek."

"Is that possible? The shock affects my veins and my blood. My tongue refuses to serve me. Please tell me, Effendi, please tell me!"

"I will tell you, but tell me beforehand – do you know me?"

"No, I haven't seen you, nor do I know your name."

"They call me Poldi Ben Anglesi from Anglia, a friend of the Reis…"

"Allah, Allah," interrupted Ibrahim in uncontrolled shock. "So you are the foreigner who freed many slaves and…"

The sheik stopped. He recognised that he had gone too far. He actually should not know about these matters. But Leopold pretended not to notice.

"So you have heard about me. I am glad. You know that I have helped the Reis Effendina a little in his task."

"Only a little? Effendi, I know you were successful where the Reis Effendina would never have managed."

"You will understand now that Ben Mubarek is to seek revenge."

"An extraordinary revenge. I believe he hates you more than the

Reis Effendina."

Leopold told him as much as seemed to be necessary. The sheik pretended to be shocked and called out when Leopold had finished:

"Oh Allah, oh prophet, should one think these things to be possible? You are an unbeliever, but Allah must favour you, otherwise you wouldn't be able to escape these hyenas."

"We would have been here earlier if we hadn't lost time looking for the Reis Effendina. We thought he would pursue the 'Lizard'."

"The Emir never suspected the 'Lizard'. The Reis Effendina believed himself to be purposely misled by Ben Mubarek to come here, while he was going to do business in Khartoum."

"How do you know all this?"

"The Emir himself told this to me."

"Where is he now?"

"Back in Khartoum."

"Ah! pity. He could have taken the boat I captured."

"You could go with the next ship to Khartoum and fasten the boat to it."

"I can't do that. You forget that my asakers, with the prisoners, are on the way here. I have to ride toward them."

"Then you can leave the boat here. I will send it to Khartoum. I hope you trust me."

"Certainly. You are the head of Hegasi and I would trust you with much more. But you don't have to send the boat to Khartoum, leave it here until the Reis Effendina comes here again."

"Is he coming soon?"

"I don't know that. He would have cause to pursue Ben Mubarek, who probably went on to Fashodah and even further to collect slaves. It would be too difficult to follow him. But when he returns, he would have to share the fate of his father."

"What would be the share?"

"Death. I should have shot these criminals there and then, as the Emir did with their accomplices in Wadi el Berd. I was too good to them, but I changed my mind. I have been given the right over their lives by the Reis Effendina, who has been given the authority from the Khedive."

"You are right, but did you think of the responsibility?"

"Pah! I am also responsible for all the infamous actions which they would do if I would let them escape. Do you feel pity for them?"

"What a question. The sooner they are extirpated, the better for all. I would like to help. Will you judge them in Hegasi?"

"No, they won't see Hegasi at all."

"Where will you judge them? Effendi, I am not asking from pure curiosity, I want to know whether judgement will be executed."

"I love your sense of justice and I will make no secret of the place where justice will be meted out to them. Do you know the Dshebel Arad Kol? And the swamp which is at its foot?"

"Yes, I was there a few times, it is full of crocodiles."

"I know that. There is no better place for my intentions as this swamp."

Leopold saw that the Sheik was shocked. "Oh, Effendi, that will be terrible. But when will this happen?"

"The day after tomorrow, one hour after the morning prayer we will reach the Dshebel Arash Kol and the swamp."

"And that will be the hour of death for these men?"

"Yes."

"And when do you leave Hegasi?"

"Now. I will fetch our camels."

Leopold was fastening his saddle when Ben Nil called: "Effendi, look over there." He pointed to the steppe where a rider on a camel was to be seen. He was at a distance, but Leopold recognised him. It was Oram who had escaped from the asakers. Ben Nil recognised him as well. He raised his finger.

"Attention, Effendi!"

Ibrahim stood there and had heard it. That's why Leopold said:

"Attention? Why? Since you were imprisoned with me, you smell danger everywhere. This is a traveller, nothing else. Mount your camel and let's go. Ben Nil threw an astonished glance at Leopold but obeyed.

They rode in the western direction, while Oram approached from the north. He also stopped when he saw Leopold and Ben Nil, whom he possibly also recognised, but when he saw them ride away, he continued on his way.

"I don't understand you, Effendi," said Ben Nil, "this rider was Oram, why didn't you seize him?"

"Think about what I have told the sheik. Ben Mubarek should learn it from him and will follow us into the trap at the Dshebel Arash Kol."

"I hope we won't miss our asakers."

"Do you see a dark line in the grass?"

"Yes, it is a track."

"It is Oram's track and our asakers will surely follow it. We will meet them for sure. Let us hurry. The sooner we find them, the better."

Chapter 9

At the Dshebel Arash Kol

The camels had had a rest and enjoyed a good run. Leopold's assumption proved right. The sun was near the horizon when they saw a group of people and camels in the distance.

"This is our caravan at the well Es Sāfi," said Ben Nil. "What will Abd Mubarek or the Fakir el Fakura say when they see us? They surely believed that we have found our end, Allah exterminate them."

Now they were near the well. The asakers recognised them and shouted joyously: "Poldi Ben Anglesi, Poldi Ben Anglesi and Ben Nil! They came running and the pair had to dismount. Leopold found it pleasurable. They did not extend such a welcome to their boss, the Reis Effendina. It showed that he, Leopold, was no stranger to their hearts.

Now they were asked to tell. But before that, Leopold wished to know how everything had gone. They sat down and the old askari, Ismael, whom Leopold entrusted with the command, reported the flight of one prisoner with the name of Oram: "He took a camel and..."

"And followed us," interrupted Ben Nil.

"That's right, but how do you know?"

"We have seen him and we will tell you. I don't blame you because I have reason to be glad. He wanted to harm us, but it will turn out to our advantage."

"Is that possible?" The old asaker breathed easier.

"Certainly. We could have caught him today, if we wanted to, but he is more useful to us free."

The old Abd Mubarek broke into a mocking laughter. "You are bragging. You are telling lies to annoy us, but you can't cheat me. If you had seen Oram you would have seized him. The fact that you didn't proves to me that you haven't seen him."

"Your head is full of wisdom, you holy Fakir," countered Leopold.

"If you had seen him, you would have been with my son."

"We have been with Ben Mubarek on his ship and have talked to him."

"Lies! Lies!"

"Take care or you will get the whip. In your situation, you should be more polite."

The Fakir el Fakura rose to a sitting position. "You demand

politeness. Are you treating us in such a manner that we should offer it?"

"I am treating you the way you deserve. I have saved your life and yet you wanted to betray us to Ben Mubarek."

"Prove it!"

"I know it. Your ungratefulness has brought you fetters. If you don't like it, quarrel with yourself – not with us."

"If you don't give me my freedom, I will evoke Allah's curse on you."

"Allah will change your curse into blessing."

"You will soon think and talk differently. When you learn the power given to me, you will beg for mercy."

"For the moment I have the power over you. Over whom you will have power later, over your harem or over your dogs, is indifferent to me. And now be quiet, otherwise you will get the whip as well. I have no intention to be roared at by a man who has so distanced himself from Allah and his commandments that he is able to betray the one who saved his life."

"Good. I will be silent now. The time will come when millions will listen to my voice and you will be the first to crawl in the dust before me." Mohammed Achmed lay down again, but Abd Mubarek was too curious to learn what had happened, as he expected the two would be dead.

"Yes, you will crawl in the dust before me too. You have no idea of the danger of your situation. My son will overcome you and destroy you just as he destroyed the Reis Effendina."

"Yes, he has destroyed him," said Leopold with a woeful expression.

"He has? Hamdulillah," rejoiced Abd Mubarek. "It has succeeded. The enemy is crushed and will never rise again."

It is imaginable what impression this story had on the asakers. They were storming at Leopold with questions. He asked for calm and explained: "The rejoicing of this holy man will not last long. I rode to save the Reis Effendina, and what I undertake, I accomplish. Achmed el Insaf, the Reis Effendina, is alive."

"Allah be thanked," the asakers called out, but Abd Mubarek shouted:

"He is lying, he wants to spoil our rejoicing. Our saviour will be here any moment."

"So wait until your sinning skin bursts with disappointment," Ben Nil entered the conversation. "You will soon hear what our Effendi has to say."

All eyes were on Leopold. Every asaker as well as the prisoners tensely awaited his report. He told them everything, except the new plans he had arranged with the Reis Effendina.

"Why didn't the Reis Effendina send us more asakers?" asked one of them.

"Because, you father of curiosity, there were no camels and we are men enough for these cowardly toads. And now the holy Fakir may continue with the rejoicing he didn't want to interrupt."

Leopold went to sleep. He and Ben Nil had had no sleep last night. The next morning the caravan went south. It was difficult to get the prisoners mounted, they made it as toilsome as possible. Leopold approached the mountain of Arash Kol from a different direction. Ben Mubarek had a hundred men, he only had twenty. Ben Mubarek may have had the idea to attack them before they reached the mountain. When Leopold saw the Dshebel Arash Kol from the distance, he asked the caravan to make camp here for the night. The asakers couldn't understand why they were stopped so early in the day and it was important to let them know the plans without the prisoners hearing it. He led them far enough aside and explained his action and the plan to trap Ben Mubarek and his men.

They were enthusiastic. Every asaker wanted to know what role he had to play. Leopold could not tell them for it was essential to go reconnoitring first, and that couldn't happen before evening. Ben Mubarek, so he reckoned, was at the mountain already and could possibly notice them. The asakers were ordered not to talk to each other about their intention.

Afternoon passed without a human having been seen in the steppe. When the sun went down and the soldiers prayed the Maghreb, Leopold began his way to reconnoitre. It could be expected that this would take hours or even until morning. His task was not easy. He had to find the Reis Effendina but avoid Ben Mubarek's camp. Luckily, the latter, who did not expect the Reis or Leopold, had a large camp-fire which betrayed his whereabouts and could be avoided by reconnoitring.

It took an hour's ride to reach the wood where he expected to find the Reis Effendina. Leopold imitated the sound of a hyena; it is similar to deep laughter. Only after the sixth time he heard a voice calling: "Is it you, Effendi?"

"Yes," Leopold answered and stopped his camel.

A man stepped nearer and looked at him. "Yes, it is you. We have to walk quite a distance to the Emir. He has sent a large chain of sentries to make it easier for you to find us."

"All right, please lead me to the last post near the Emir. He may hold my camel." The Emir received him with a firm pressure of his hand. He was happy to see Leopold, especially as he had been unable to tell for sure that he would come.

"The enemy has already arrived, in the early afternoon. They encamped at the end of the Maijeh."

"Did they make any fires?"

"Six of them. At all events because of the stinging flies. We are happily not plagued by them in the dry wood."

"Do you know anything about Ben Mubarek's plans?"

"No, how could I?"

"I thought you had been there. Didn't you eavesdrop?"

"I did not go near enough to listen. I didn't want to be caught."

"How far is it from here?"

"Nearly half an hour. I have to go there. Will you accompany me?"

"Yes, if you don't ask me to sit next to Ben Mubarek. I almost trust you to do that."

Leopold left his rifle and they both went between bushes and little swamps, which they could avoid because these betrayed their presence by their gleam. After a quarter of an hour, Leopold noticed the first fire. Then another and another until he counted six. They stopped behind a bush, about sixty steps from the first fire, where he saw Ben Mubarek sitting with two of his officers and another two men. He could hear them speak, but couldn't understand the words.

"I have to go there," said Leopold more to himself than to the Reis Effendina. "I must hear what they are discussing."

"Are you mad? You would be lost as soon as they saw you."

"No, I have encountered greater dangers, against which this is child's play."

"And I tell you – I won't take another step!"

"I don't want you to. I am going alone. Between here and the fires are two thick trees. In their broad shadows I will crawl toward them. The second tree has a low branch onto which I will swing myself. There, hidden under leaves, I can hear every word. It is only fifteen steps to the first fire."

"No, Effendi, I cannot permit you to risk your life."

"I risk my life in tomorrow's battle, why not now? Perhaps by listening I may get an idea how to avoid a battle."

"Do you think that is possible?"

"Yes, perhaps I will learn something that will induce me to render a resistance by the enemy fruitless."

Achmed wanted to hold him back, but was not fast enough. Leopold had already ducked into the shadows and crept forward. It was not difficult. To keep the stinging flies away they threw damp branches into the fire, making thick smoke. It took only two minutes for Leopold to sit on a branch with dense leaves, where he could hear and see everything without being seen himself.

He had hardly made himself comfortable when he heard a shout:

"The Sheik el Beled is here. He finally came!"

Truly, there he approached from the last fire, holding his camel by the halter. He was told where to find Ben Mubarek.

Ibrahim let his animal lie down and stepped to the fire, where he was welcomed. Leopold pricked up his ears, as he expected plans would be discussed. "Sit down and report," offered Ben Mubarek. "Did you see our opponents?"

"No, but I know they are coming; I saw their tracks."

"You shouldn't have rested until you saw them."

"It was dark and I couldn't see their tracks any more."

"Pity. We could have attacked them in the steppe. We are a hundred men, they are twenty. There would have been no chance for them."

"The twenty would have shot twenty of our men, not counting Poldi Ben Anglesi, who would have shot more. You would have been the first."

Ah, I was right, thought Leopold. He would have attacked us in the steppe, had we not made a detour.

"I would not be there. I am paying my men enough to do the work for me. This is not cowardice; I owe it to myself to be careful."

"And it is probably good for us. We can now revert to our old plan without losing any lives," continued the sheik.

"Do you mean attacking them from the front and behind on the narrow ledge? That plan is good. There would be no way out for them. The mountain on one side is too steep to climb. The other side is the swamp and certain death. I am going to send forty men. You will lead them and when you hear the first shot, you will prevent them from retreating."

It was clear that there was nothing more of importance to hear. When there was another cloud of smoke, Leopold went back to the Emir.

"Effendi, I almost trembled for you. This daredevilry could have cost your life," said the Reis Effendina.

Leopold told him the plans of the enemy and, once again, his counter move. The Emir was excited and whispered: "They are going into the trap, they are going, but how will you prevent the sheik and his forty men from coming behind you?"

"There is no trick. I have to take them prisoner."

"That is dangerous. It won't go without a battle."

"Not at all. I will occupy the place before them. They will have to surrender or be shot. But I need another forty men to do it."

"You will have them, of course. But when?"

"Go ahead and prepare them. I will follow you shortly."

"Why don't you come with me now?"

"Because I want to fetch the Dshebel-Gerfeh-mare, the fastest camel I have ever seen, the one which Ben Mubarek once used to escape from me."

"Won't you leave it. If they catch you, all is lost."

"Catch me? Pah!"

"But when they miss it, they will know that a thief or people are near."

"They will think the mare was insufficiently tied up and they would find her in the morning. There is another reason for taking this fast animal. Ben Mubarek may keep away from the troop we want to encounter. In which case I would ask you to assign ten men to watch out for him. If I have this fast camel, he will not escape."

Achmed, the Reis Effendina, still opposed Leopold's intention for a while, but then went away. Leopold sneaked back to the fires. The camel he aimed for stood in the dark by a bush, the leaves of which it plucked. It made no sound when he came closer. Ben Mubarek obviously didn't understand how to train an animal. It should have tried to escape or panted loudly. Leopold untied its legs and led it away. It followed willingly as if it belonged to him.

The Reis Effendina awaited him with great tension. The forty soldiers stood already prepared.

"Allah, it has succeeded," said the Reis with astonishment. "You are a dangerous camel thief. One should imprison you for life."

"Pardon me, presenter of Egyptian justice. I only steal from thieves or robbers," Leopold laughed. "Let us move immediately and give the soldiers enough rope. We will have forty prisoners."

"They will have them. We brought along everything needed from the ship."

"Farewell until we meet tomorrow, victorious and joyful."

"Inshallah – if God wills."

"Don't let Ben Mubarek escape," warned Leopold again and moved on with the forty asakers. It took nearly three hours before they reached the north of the swamp. They rode around until they saw the dark mass of the mountain. Another half hour and they reached the basin where they expected the enemy to wait until they heard the first shot. The camels were taken a further stretch and then left with only one guard.

85

Thirty men were ordered to climb the moderately steep hill and ordered to surround the expected enemy and to keep utterly quiet until Leopold started the attack. They were also advised to seek cover behind rocks, in case the surrounded opponents defended themselves. With the rest of the troop, he went back where they climbed the bank of the basin and waited for the sheik and his forty men to arrive.

It was almost morning when they heard the enemy ride past. They climbed quietly down from their height and followed them. They stopped near the entrance to the basin. The slave-hunters believed they were alone and spoke loudly. They proved by their cheerful laughter that they were in a good mood. The sheik was the loudest of them and talked about the distribution of the loot. Then he said he would look out for the sunrise and came through the exit slowly toward the asakers.

"Bend down," whispered Leopold as he bent down himself. When the sheik passed near him, he rose and put both hands around his neck. "Tie his hands but not his legs," he ordered the soldiers. They obeyed.

The sheik's shock was greater than his energy; it was not surprising that he did not resist. "One sound and I will stick this knife into your heart." He was a coward and he only took the leadership of the forty men because he was convinced he would find no resistance. He was led away from the basin. Far enough not to be heard by his people.

Leopold let the sheik feel the point of his knife and asked him: "Do you know me?"

"Yes, you are Poldi – Ben Anglesi – Effendi," he stammered. "Why are you treating me like this? You told me you honour my position."

"And you believed it? Only a brainless person could believe he would deceive me. I looked through you as soon as I saw you. You lent Ben Mubarek your horse. That betrayed you. When you saw me, I had already met the Reis Effendina. He was friendly to you as I was. It was to lure Ben Mubarek into a trap. It succeeded because your stupidity is bigger than your evil. Ben Mubarek is here, so is the Reis Effendina."

Leopold turned to one of the asakers and ordered: "Your comrades with the prisoners are south of the Marjei. Bring them as fast as you can. You can ride the Dshebel-Gerfeh-mare for this purpose. If you go straight south from here, you will see my tracks in about two hours. Follow them and you can't fail to meet them."

He turned to the sheik again. "I listened to the conversation with Ben Mubarek. You wanted to find out where to attack us on the steppe. Are you denying that?"

"Effendi, how many asakers are with you?" asked the coward.

"More than enough to destroy your forty men. We occupied the heights and the entrance to this basin. You, their leader, have already been caught by us. If you ask your men to hand in their weapons, I will use my influence with the Reis Effendina to lighten your punishment."

"Allah! To hand you their weapons, to surrender – forty men."

"Yes, it sounds different from dividing the loot. Answer my question. Say 'yes' and you save your lives; if not, we shoot you all."

At this moment, shots cracked from the basin and a confused shouting was heard. Then it was suddenly calm again.

"Oh Allah, oh Mohammed, it has started already."

"There you have the proof of my words," Leopold warned. "Come, you will serve as my shield. Should somebody shoot at me, you will be hit." They moved ahead. At the entrance stood asakers with rifles in their hands. It was light enough now. Daylight in these areas arrives as quickly as dusk changes to night darkness.

"Why was there shooting?" Leopold asked.

"Some of those in the basin wanted to climb the mountain. We asked them to stop, but they didn't obey – so we started shooting."

"Why is it suddenly so quiet?"

"The slave-hunters went into hiding under the bushes."

"You can see what courage your heroes possess," Leopold remarked to the sheik, grabbed him with his left by the neck and held his right hand with the knife against his body. "Let's go forward and observe the rifles aimed at your people. My men are behind rocks and yours are easy to wipe out. The bushes are no cover."

"The Effendi, the foreign Effendi." The calls came from the bushes.

"I will give you one minute," Leopold continued. "If you don't ask your people to come forward singly and hand in their weapons, my knife will go up to the hilt into your body."

"Will I be pardoned?" The sheik asked, dejectedly.

"I promise mitigation, more you cannot ask. And now decide, the minute is over."

Anxiety made the sheik give the asked for command. His people obeyed. One after the other crawled from under the bushes. In less than a quarter of an hour they were all disarmed and tied up. The first act of today's drama went to Leopold's satisfaction. Next they had to await the arrival of the caravan.

Leopold left the basin and sat down outside it. It took nearly an hour before he saw them. Ben Nil and the messenger rode ahead of the troop. "You didn't return by the morning and we were afraid that something had happened to you. Are the enemies in your hands?"

"Yes. Do your prisoners know anything about it?"

"No, the messenger spoke quietly, but they saw Ben Mubarek's camel. They must deduce that something important has happened.

Where are your prisoners?"

"They are only five minutes behind me in a gorge. We will take your prisoners to ours, but the camels stay here under the supervision of four men." The caravan was here now, the legs of the prisoners were untied and they had to dismount.

Abd Mubarek could not be quiet: "Why do you drag us about in the desert. I demand to be taken to Khartoum."

"This wish will soon be fulfilled," answered Leopold significantly.

"You think you are clever to drag us about? How easily could you encounter my son, then you are unconditionally lost."

"I have come across your son several times, without being lost."

"You were lucky. It won't happen again. You know how many warriors he has. Here, in the steppe, you couldn't overthrow him, he would squash you and your little troop. The prophet cannot possibly allow an unbeliever like you to go on like this unpunished. The sword of revenge flames above you. Who knows how soon it will hit you."

"I will show you above whom it flamed – follow me."

The soldiers took the prisoners between them and led them into the rain basin. One can imagine their shock when they saw their accomplices imprisoned and on the ground. Abd Mubarek shouted with anger and flooded Leopold with insults until Ben Nil quietened him down with the whip. The others were quiet. They were again bound at their feet and put down with their fellow accomplices.

Chapter 10

At the swamp

Leopold could march off now. He left the twenty asakers he had with the Fessarah, to guard the prisoners and the camels. The forty men he received from the Reis Effendina accompanied him. Ben Nil asked to come as well and as there was no reason to fear any surprises, he was permitted to accompany them. Leopold was convinced he had made no mistake, but as it turned out later, he overrated his self-confidence.

It was arranged that he would be at the Dshebel Arash Kol, but it was a bit later. That could not be a disadvantage. The space between the swamp and the mountain was comfortably wide, but it became narrower as the path went higher. After a quarter of an hour it was only wide enough to let two camels walk next to each other. When it became a little broader there were even some trees to be seen. Leonard stopped and said to Ben Nil: "Ben Mubarek wants me alive. He probably gave orders not to shoot at me. I am going thirty yards ahead. When I stop, you do the same. They have probably sent one or two men to announce us."

"I must obey you, but I would have liked to be on your side when the moment of decision comes."

"Not yet. Ben Mubarek will not show himself until we are in the middle of the narrow path."

Leopold went ahead. It was really a place of horror. On the right was the mountain. It was too steep to climb. On the left, only a few yards below the pathway, was the swamp with uncountable crocodiles. Into this swamp they want to push the asakers: For Leopold, they had even worse tortures in mind. It seemed to him, that a proper punishment would be to push the slave-hunters into the swamp. An eye for an eye, a tooth for a tooth, that was the law of the desert, of the prairie and the pampas.

He couldn't finish the thought because an imperious voice, not far from him, called: "Not a step further or we shoot!"

Leopold stopped. There were two trees and some rocks, behind which he expected three people to lie in waiting. An unpleasant situation. He saw three rifles aimed at him. "Who are you?" he asked, pretending he had only to do with one person.

"I am an old acquaintance of yours, do you want to see me?"

"Certainly."

"Remove your weapons, then I will step forward."

"I am not stupid," answered Leopold and jumped behind the next tree, behind which he found cover. The people over there seemed to be in a dilemma. They were here at the right time and expected to hear a shot from the Sheik el Beled. It seemed they were trying to win time by talking. The speaker answered: "We could force you if we wanted to, but you should learn in peace what we ask of you."

"Then say it!"

"Not like that. Put your weapons away and come to the stone between us. I will do the same."

"All right, I am coming, but if I see the smallest knife on you, you will go to hell." Leopold put his rifle at the tree and the knife next to it. The revolver he put in his pocket. Looking back, he saw the asakers had stopped. Since there was a slight bend, Leopold could see them, but the three slave-hunters could not. Ben Nil was nearest, behind a bush.

Leopold stepped from behind the tree to the rock, where he stood still. The man whom he recognised as Ben Mubarek's lieutenant went toward him, stopped a few steps away and asked mockingly: "You didn't expect me?"

"Yes and no," Leopold answered calmly. "Yes, because I knew that you expected me here and no because I expected Ben Mubarek."

"Allah! You knew that we awaited you here?"

"I know even more. You expect a sign from the Sheik el Beled. A shot from his rifle should start the hostility. Isn't that so?"

"Allah knows everything, but how could you know about Sheik Ibrahim and his intentions?"

"You will learn that. Call Ben Mubarek to come here."

"He is not here."

"I know he is."

"You know it? Then your know-all is not significant. If you knew you would not behave so confidently."

These words made Leopold think. He wished he had left Ben Nil with the prisoners. Ben Mubarek didn't trust the sheik with sufficient circumspection to handle any situation. It was very unlikely that he could free the prisoners, but if he had sufficient people with him, the situation could become dangerous. In any case his capture was not as certain as Leopold believed. He did not show his worries and answered with a smile: "Where he is now, you don't have to tell me. He is either with his sixty men here at the Maijeh or with the forty men in the valley of the water basin who should be behind us."

"Allah kerim! He knows about the basin," called the lieutenant. "Who has betrayed that?"

"I know it, that's enough. You are too stupid to deceive me. The situation we are now in was arranged by me."

"You?" laughed the lieutenant sarcastically. "Allah has made you blind. You can see only me, but let me tell you that you and your twenty asakers are locked in. You called us stupid, but I have never met anyone as stupid as you."

"Really? Will you prove that to me, you clever-dick of all clever-dicks?"

"That is easy to prove. Haven't you told the sheik you would throw your prisoners to the crocodiles?"

"That was a stupidity? I want to weep with sympathy." Leopold told the lieutenant that it was calculated to lure them to come here. "And where is the sheik now? Why doesn't he fire the arranged shot? Because we have captured him and his forty men."

"You have only twenty men. Don't rejoice too early. We are more than three times as many and we will…"

"Nothing you think will happen. You think your way back is free. It is not. The Reis Effendina and his asakers are behind you."

"The – Reis Effendina?" he stammered. "You are lying."

"I am speaking the truth and ask you to surrender. If you don't, you will be thrown to the crocodiles."

"Effendi, what are you thinking of? Do you want us to surrender with your lies…"

"Be quiet and don't insult me," Leopold interrupted him. "I want to be merciful and give you proof." He held his hands like a loudspeaker and called: "Reis Effendina – Emir!"

"Here we are," came the reply. Much nearer than Leopold expected.

"Well?" Leopold asked the lieutenant, "Can you hear by the sound that the Emir is less than two hundred steps away from us?"

"Was this the Reis Effendina?"

"Who else? My call told him that I am here and now he will move forward. I advise you to surrender. And if you come a few steps nearer, you will see my people."

Leopold waved back and Ben Nil plus the forty asakers came from behind bushes, rifles in hand and ready for action. They had to walk in a long line, one or two behind each other. The lieutenant was shocked. "Oh Allah! There are nearly a hundred men. I won't let them catch me, I am going, Effendi, I am going." He ran to the trees where he was before, grabbed his rifle and hurried further back, followed by his two comrades. Leopold didn't believe it would come to a battle, but he let his people only move forward to where they could be covered by bushes or rocks. Now he waited for things to happen and for what the

Reis Effendina would do. The lieutenant had received a salutary shock when he saw the long line of asakers, whom he thought were nearly a hundred.

Suddenly, after a quarter of an hour, a shot rang out, then another and then two more. After that it was very quiet. Another quarter of an hour had passed when a man in asaker uniform appeared from around the bend. When he came nearer, Leopold recognised him.

"Did the slave-hunters let you through?" he asked full of hopes.

"Yes, Effendi, they had to. They have surrendered after we shot four of them dead. You should come and help tie the prisoners' hands."

Upon this direction they marched forward. They soon met the first enemies. They all held their rifles in their hands, but did not use them.

"Effendi!" Leopold heard the voice of Reis Achmed calling.

"Here I am," answered Leopold.

"Our opponents have laid down their weapons. Their hands will be bound. Let none of them escape. They will go in a single row to the rain basin."

This arrangement was, with the condition of the way, the only right one. First to go was Leopold and his asakers, then the prisoners and behind them the Reis Effendina and his people. As the road grew wider, the prisoners marched in a double row with asakers at their side. The Reis Effendina came forward and vented his annoyance about the absence of Ben Mubarek. Leopold told him that he knew from their lieutenant that Ben Mubarek went to the sheik in the rain basin and maybe it would be better for him to ride ahead, to see if anything had happened. "Yes, do that and take Ben Nil with you," agreed the Reis.

"Is Ben Mubarek known to your asakers?"

"No, they don't know him by sight."

"So it can be expected that he pretended to be someone else and could do great harm."

"Don't let us speculate and hurry ahead."

Leopold's fear was unfortunately justified. From afar he noticed a group of people next to the camels. They wouldn't be there if everything was in order. When they reached the group, they saw Abdullah and the older Askari Ismael, to whom Leopold gave the command over the others. He saw them embarrassed and asked what had happened. Why were two of their men lying on the ground, motionless?

"They – are – wounded, Effendi," stammered the old fellow.

"By whom?"

"By a stranger."

"These two on the ground are hurt?"

"I think so, Effendi. I hope they are only unconscious. We worked on them for over an hour, but in spite of our efforts, they didn't wake up."

"I believe that. Look at their faces. Those are the features of death. Let me know how that happened."

"Ask Yussuf, he was there." He pointed at a soldier.

"Tell us!" Leopold ordered.

"We three had just relieved the other guards when we saw this stranger. He seemed shocked at first, but came nearer afterwards."

"Did he have any weapons?"

"Yes, he only came closer when I permitted it."

"That was a mistake, either you should not let him go near you or take him prisoner."

"We wanted to, that's why we let him come nearer."

"Did he ask who you were?"

"Yes, there was no reason to be discreet. We told him we are asakers of the Reis Effendina."

"That was an unforgivable stupidity. He could now arrange his answers accordingly. Can't you see that? He was cleverer than you three. Tell me every word that was spoken. What did he ask first?"

"Who we are. He said he was a friend of the Emir."

"And you believed that?"

"Not at once, I was careful and told him that he was lying. He began to speak proudly and said he was an express courier from the governors of Khartoum and had orders for the Reis Effendina."

"The governors cannot give any orders to the Reis Effendina."

"I didn't know that. He said he was a colonel and spoke so imperiously that we believed him."

"Did he ask questions about me?"

"Yes, he did and spoke in a very friendly manner about you. Our mistrust disappeared completely."

"Do you, the son, grandson and great grandson of a grandfather of foolishness know to whom you have betrayed these important things?"

"No."

"It was Ben Mubarek, the leader of our enemies."

"Allah! Is that possible?"

"Certainly, with you everything is possible, even the most impossible brainlessness. What did he do after you gave him all the information he wanted?"

"He asked to speak to the commander of our unit."

"And you went, which saved your life. Three were too many for him, so he sent you away. What happened then?"

"I was hardly gone when I heard two shots. I looked back and saw him ride off on the white camel."

"Did you not try to shoot him?"

"Yes, but my first shot missed and by the second shot he was already too far away."

"I believe that, he had his own camel, the fastest I have seen. Where did he ride to?"

"He disappeared behind the swamp."

"It is your fault that your comrades are dead and the slave-hunter has escaped. I will leave the punishment to the Reis Effendina."

Leopold turned to Ben Nil: "I should follow the escaped fellow, I did once, but there is no chance of reaching him, as long as he is riding his Dshebel-Gerfeh mare. The most likely thing he will do now is to go to his ship, then to Fashodah, where he will hire a new team to continue his gruesome profession."

"And we can do nothing about it?" asked Ben Nil.

"We will consult with the Reis Effendina about the next move. Personally I would like to go to Khartoum before following the slave-hunter. I expect a letter from my mother and my betrothed. My mother, as usual, will be worried and my wife-to-be will be angry because of my love for adventure before marriage."

Chapter 11

Righteous punishment

Leopold and Ben Nil went to the basin. They noticed from afar a brisk movement of people. The new prisoners were united with the old ones. They were surrounded by numerous guards. The asakers where happy. They were victorious without any loss of life – except the two, which they thought was their own fault.

The Reis Effendina sat with his officers at a distance. The prisoners were subdued and threw hateful glances at Leopold. Only Abd Mubarek talked to his neighbour. Leopold heard him say: "We have to thank the mangy giour for all of this, the stinking son of a bitch. May Allah tear him to bits and throw them to the dogs."

Leopold ignored him. The Reis Effendina came toward him. "I learned everything before you came and I am going to punish the guilty."

He pointed to a spot which Leopold had not noticed. There was Yussuf who was so communicative with Ben Mubarek and had let him escape. He was tied up like the prisoners. He continued: "If we had caught Ben Mubarek we would have been saved a lot of trouble and exertion. I mustn't rest until I have this rogue in my power. This man is more dangerous than all his people together. But I shouldn't complain. We have caught one hundred and sixty slave-hunters. There has never been a catch like this."

"I, at least, have never heard of anything like it."

"My name will be known to these rascals and I have to thank you for your powerful assistance. Do you want to help me further? I want to ask a favour of you."

"What kind of favour?"

"When do you have to be home?"

"Within the next six months. I am engaged to be married and promised to be back before my fiancé's eighteenth birthday."

"Good, so you can stay with me until then. If you help me to catch Ben Mubarek, I am prepared to…"

"Stop! No promises," Leopold interrupted him. You have permitted me to call you a friend and there is no bargaining or reward. I have started the game to catch Ben Mubarek and I will stay until it is won."

"I thank you, Effendi. Now I am sure to catch him. Where do you think he is going next?"

Leopold explained his theory as he had before to Ben Nil. "But," he continued, "I don't believe he will use his ship for the journey to Fashodah. He has an incomparable camel that will take him there in a much shorter time. Ben Nil and I have excellent camels too and I suggest we start the pursuance right now."

"I have to go to Khartoum first. I will follow as soon as I can. By the way, Ben Nil does not have to be parted from his grandfather for long. I found him to be an excellent helmsman and engaged him for my ship. But first, I have to dish out some justice."

Leopold felt very uneasy. He remembered Wadi el Berd where the Reis Effendina shot all the captured slave-hunters. "Will you hold judgement here already? Whom will you judge?"

"First comes Yussuf, he deserves to be shot."

"To be shot?" asked Leopold, shocked by the severity of the judgement. "His offence is not so great as to deserve a death sentence."

"He blabbed events to a stranger without permission and his stupidity caused the death of his two comrades. He also let Ben Mubarek escape."

Perhaps he was right, perhaps not, thought Leopold. He begged for mercy until the Reis Effendina gave in. "All right, I will allow him to live. He can go but must never come before my eyes again."

"Hold on, I didn't mean it that way. To chase him away is no complete pardon. You are not a dark monster, although you want to appear to be one. I tell you that obedience with love is worth a thousand times more than obedience by fear or anxiety. I know that your asakers love you in spite of your strictness."

"Is that so? Did you learn that?" He asked mildly and a sunny smile came over his face. So you want me to keep him in my crew?"

"Yes, I beg you to do that!"

Reis Achmed ordered that Yussuf be untied and brought to him. One could see that Yussuf's face expressed fear of a strong punishment. "I intended to shoot you, you son of disobedience, but Poldi Ben Anglesi asked for your pardon and when I granted his wish, he even asked me to keep you on. I also granted him that. Kneel down before him and thank him for saving your life." Yussuf threw himself down and kissed Leopold's hands. When he went back to his comrades, Leopold saw the grateful looks of these rough people towards him. According to his belief, love is the greatest power in heaven and on earth. There are no men whose heart won't open to love – sooner or later.

"I actually enjoy granting your wish," said the Reis Effendina. "But let me tell you that, in spite of my gratitude and friendship to you, as great as they are, they won't induce me to grant you a similar plea. I entreat you, do not embarrass me. Bring me the Fakir el Fakura." He was brought. His hands were tied and he stood between two asakers.

"What is your name?"

"They call me the Fakir el Fakura," answered Mohammed Achmed.

"I asked your name, not what you are called – answer!"

"Fakir el Fakura," he answered defiantly.

"Asis, open his mouth!"

Asis was Reis Effendina's favourite. He knew how to handle the hippopotamus-whip skilfully. He hit the Fakir five or six times on his back before he could make a defensive move. But then he turned and spat Asis in the face and shouted: "Son of a dog, you dare to hit me, the holiest of the holy, the Fakir el Fakura, before whom millions will kneel…"

"Asis," interrupted the Reis with a thunderous voice, "the bastinado!"

Mohammed Achmed turned to him: "The bastinado for me? Has Allah turned away from you that you are capable of hitting his favourite…"

"Asis, gag him," interrupted the Reis Effendina again.

With the help of the two asakers, this order was quickly obeyed. He was put on his stomach, two asakers sat on his back, others lifted his legs upright and took of his shoes. Asis then performed the bastinado on his naked soles.

"Twenty on each sole," was the judgement.

Forty hits were scrupulously counted. When the last ones were done; the soles of the chastised were two swollen, red masses of split flesh. Now they took his gag off. He sat up groaning and looked at his judge with blood-red eyes.

"Now again: What is your name?"

"Mohammed Achmed," he murmured faintly.

"Had you told me that when I asked you first, you would have been spared the bastinado. That you call yourself Fakir el Fakura does not impress me. Poldi Ben Anglesi has saved your life, you rewarded him with ingratitude. You intended to betray my asakers. You deserve a death sentence. I despise you and won't do you the honour of being judged by me. Drag this fellow to the swamp and dump him at the edge of the Maijeh. There he can tell the vermin that are his like about being the Mahdi."

This order was obeyed too. They dragged him to the swamp. What feeling about this episode would he have later, when he really, to a certain extent, became the ruler of the faithful?

The Reis Effendina hadn't finished his judicial proceedings. He ordered Abd Mubarek to be brought to him. He came with a firm step and a defiant expression. Leopold thought about this man who sought to kill him almost every time they met. He had pursued him with devilish hostility. One should honour old age, but a man who with true delight commits the heaviest crime is not respectable but doubly punishable. These may also have been the feelings of the judge.

He looked at the old man with nausea and disgust. "I looked for you for a long time, you holy Fakir. You always escaped me, but this is your judgement day."

"I demand another judge," muttered the old man.

"There is no other who could judge you as you deserve. Your infamous actions are in the hundreds. You have condemned thousands to slavery, death and impoverishment. How many villages have you burned and its people murdered? And you showed the face of a holy man. This role is at its end. I will send you where you belong – into hell."

"You have no right to kill me," shouted the old one.

"Many people have this right and if they neglected to do it they sinned, because they allowed you to commit even more horrible deeds. I must not commit the same sin. I have the holy duty to destroy you, so that your brain cannot think of more bloody deeds. You are a monster and monsters will devour you. You will be thrown to the crocodiles!"

"Oh Allah," cried the old one. "You mustn't do that. Spare me, oh Reis Effendina!"

"Spare you? Think back. Poldi Ben Anglesi spared you, Ben Nil remitted when he could have taken your life. For that, you have sought their lives. You are a devil in whose nature it lies to repay kindness with misdeed. You are being judged by my motto: 'Woe to him, who does woe to others'. It remains – you will be thrown to the crocodiles! Your friend, the Fakir el Fakura, will be witness to how you will be devoured."

When Abd Mubarek saw the iron features of the judge he cried: "That is impossible! That is inhuman!" In his desperation he turned to Leopold: "Effendi, you are a Christian, you mustn't tolerate that I die such a terrible death. Let me be pardoned. I know the Emir listens to you."

"It is true, the Christian religion asks for the almost impossible and rarely adhered to 'love your enemy'. My religion only says 'love your neighbour', but your behaviour does not persuade me to ask the Emir to change his mind."

"And it wouldn't help him if he did," added the Reis Effendina. "Take him away." Abd Mubarek defended himself against this order, with his hands tied up and roaring like a bull.

This scene did not have Leopold's applause. The old fellow deserved to die and he should have his punishment, but to throw him to the crocodiles was not necessary. He had an idea how to avert this. He told the asakers to stop as he wanted another word with him.

They obeyed and Abd Mubarek said: "Thank you, Effendi. That was help at the last moment. Are you determined to beg in my favour?"

"Maybe, but first answer me a few questions."

"Ask, Effendi, I will answer if I can."

"You know Abd Wasak, the Sheik of Maabdeh, where I first met you?"

"Yes, you saw me talking to him."

"Did you know his brother, Hafid Sichar?"

"Yes, I knew him too."

"Do you know his present whereabouts?"

Abd Mubskek looked at him, searchingly. "Why do you ask?"

"I am looking for Hafid Sichar, I want to take him back to his brother."

"Yes, I can tell you where he is. I will tell you if you let me and all the prisoners free."

"Rascal! Are you mad?" called the Reis Effendina. "This condition can only be suggested by an insane."

"I have put this condition up and I stick to it."

The Reis turned to Leopold and asked: "What or who is this Hafid Sichar?"

"He is the brother of the Sheik Ben Wasak, who first helped me to find Ben Mubarek. I promised him I would search for his brother. Hafid Sichar went to Khartoum, where he received a large sum of money from the business man Barjad el Amin. He received the money, but from then on he disappeared. Ben Mubarek worked for Barjad el Amin. He was poor, but after Hafid's disappearance suddenly became rich and started as a slave-hunter."

"So he has killed Hafid Sichar and taken the money from him," said the Reis Effendina.

"No, Hafid Sichar was not murdered," called Abd Mubarek. "I will tell you where he is if you let us go."

"That will not happen, but for the friendship of Poldi Ben Anglesi, I make the following suggestion to you. If you tell us where the lost Hafid Sichar is, I will not throw you to the crocodiles. You will be shot."

Abd Mubarek broke into malicious laughter. "How merciful you are, oh Emir. Do you think that death by a bullet is no death? I want to live! Yes, to live. Should I not live, you will never learn my secret. For the shortening by two seconds of my death you are asking for the freeing of Hafid Sichar, who my son should have killed. This price is too dear."

"Very well, but now take him away finally." The old one's legs were tied together and he was carried away. He was quiet and so was everyone else. Until a pitiful whimper and a death cry was heard. It was over.

Leopold shuddered, but he felt even this punishment was not too hard. The Reis Effendina even gave his opinion, that this punishment was much too fast and Abu Mubarek deserved a longer battle with death. "But we have to leave now. You will be angry that I have not acquiesced to his demand."

"No. What he demanded was insane. And he may have lied as well. But, at least, I have obtained one result. Up to now I had not the slightest trace of the lost one, but from Abd Mubarek's words I know where I can obtain information – namely from Ben Mubarek himself. By the way, do you know the business man Barjad el Amin?"

"Yes, I was quite often with him in Khartoum."

"Is he an honest man?"

"He is honesty itself."

"Well, I will meet him. Unfortunately, not very soon. Are you finished with your judgement for today?"

"Yes, it was only meant for Abd Mubarek. I had to do it here. Firstly because I had the power to do it, secondly because this man had to be rendered harmless, and thirdly because he could have found a judge where he could buy his freedom."

"One should think that in such a case the bribing of a judge is impossible."

"Yes, one should think so. I wouldn't sell my judgement for millions. Did you hear about the Mudir, the head of the town, of Fashodah?"

"Yes, his name is Ali Effendi el Kurdi. He is famous for stopping the military uprising in Kassala."

"There he ruled with too much justice. Later on with less so. In Fashodah the slave dealers went openly into his home. It was said that he received a head-tax for each slave. Fashodah became the focal point of the slave trade. To cut a long story short, with my influence, the Mudir Ali Effendi el Kadir has been removed and a new Mudir replaced him."

"Will he be more righteous than the previous one?"

"Yes, I recommended him. His name is also Ali Effendi but his subjects call him 'Abu Hamsa miah', the 'father of the five hundred'."

"Why is he called that?"

"Because of a praiseworthy habit. He refuses all bribery and whoever he finds guilty is given five hundred lashes. He makes no distinction between rich and poor. He is my friend and I want to give you a letter of recommendation, to give you the necessary support in Fashodah."

The letter was welcome, it would help to make matters easier.

They had worn serious faces during this discussion and the prisoners believed that judgement would continue. In this case, the two officers of the slave-hunters would be next. The captain sent a guard to the Reis Effendina, to ask whether he could have a word. He wanted to give some important information. He was allowed to come. Two asakers brought him. The Reis looked at him questioningly.

"You have executed Abd Mubarek. Are you now going to judge us?"

"Do you expect me to let you go?" answered the Reis.

"No, we are in your hands and don't expect to go unpunished, but we beg you not to throw us to the crocodiles. How can the archangel Gabriel find our bones on the day of resurrection if they have been crushed by the crocodiles?"

"Rascal! Because of fear of death you invoke the Koran. If they rot in the stomach of the crocodile, they don't have to burn in hell."

"Emir, the catching of slaves was allowed for hundreds of years. What has religion to do with the fact that it is now forbidden? I can prove to you that I am not as bad as you think and I don't deserve such a death."

"I would like to know how you, the leader of these mad dogs, will bring me proof."

"I have heard Poldi Ben Anglesi Effendi ask for a man who has disappeared. If I give you information about Hafid Sichar, will you spare me and not throw me to the crocodiles?"

"No, you will bring some lies to save yourself."

"No, Allah knows that I will tell you the truth. Take me with you until you have convinced yourself. If you find that I have lied, then throw me to the crocodiles, or a worse kind of death."

"I can't make any promises, but if you tell the truth I will spare you death by crocodiles. Do you know where Hafid Sichar is?"

"Yes, but the land or the village I don't know."

"You know where he is, but don't know the land or the village? You are talking nonsense!"

"It is really true, Emir."

"Did Ben Mubarek or his father talk to you about their secret?"

"No, but I once heard them talk. They didn't know I was near."

"What did they say about him?"

"I did not hear every single word, but I remember what I heard. Ben Mubarek was poor, but he became rich by robbing Hafid Sichar. He shared with someone else."

"Who is this other person?"

"I don't know that. Ben Mubarek was going to kill Hafid Sichar to put any witness to the theft out of this world, but the other fellow didn't allow it. They sold Hafid Sichar to the leader of a wild tribe in the south."

"What tribe is that?"

"I don't know that either. You have learned all I know. Will you be merciful?"

"Ask Poldi Ben Anglesi. Maybe he will be inclined to plead on your behalf."

The prisoner followed these instructions. Leopold wanted to use the officer's fear of death and pretended to hesitate. "Whether I will plead for you depends on your truthfully answering a few questions. Did you hear about the businessman Barjad el Amin?"

"Yes, he is a businessman in Khartoum. You have already asked Abd Mubarek about him."

"Is Ben Mubarek still connected with him business-wise?"

"No, at least I don't know of any such connection."

"Has Ben Mubarek a lot of money with him?"

"Yes, almost his whole fortune. He intends to undertake a big slave-hunt, but where, he didn't tell anybody. We should learn about it in Fashodah, where he wants to equip his ships with the necessary."

"His ships? Has he got more than one?"

"Yes, but I wasn't told how many."

"Ben Mubarek must have trusted people in Fashodah. Do you know them ?"

"Ben Mubarek is discreet even to his officers, but I know of one. His name is Ibn Mulei, the Colonel of the soldiers which stay in Fashodah."

"I believe you have told the truth. I am satisfied with you."

"I thank you, Effendi. Will you now plead for me?"

"As you didn't lie," the Reis Effendina began his preamble, "I promise not to throw you to the crocodiles. More I can't do."

The officer returned to the others. He was calmed for the moment. Everything was prepared for marching off. The 'Hawk', the ship of the Reis Effendina, was about three hours away on foot. The camels were taken over land to Khartoum by ten asakers. There was no room on the ship. The Reis Effendina went at the front of the column, Leopold went last. His purpose in doing this was to help the Fakir el Fakura.

He put a hose with water on his saddle and went to the swamp where Abd Mubarek's life of crime had ended. Mohammed Achmed lay near the swamp. His hands were still tied. Leopold untied him, put the water hose and food next to him and said: "The Nile is two hours toward east and you will be able to reach it before your provision of food has finished. Have you another wish?" The Fakir el Fakura did not reply.

Leopold mounted his camel. As it started to walk, he heard his thanks: "Allah damn you! Fear the revenge, the revenge!"

Leopold joined the Reis Effendina at the front. As they did not expect anything to happen, they sped up and reached the ship sooner. They went to the Reis' cabin, where he composed the letter of recommendation. Then he put a bag of money into Leopold's hands. "You will have a lot of expenditure for me. I am taking nothing back. The lion's fur was taken to Khartoum to be prepared."

Chapter 12

The Mudir from Dsharabub

Two people alone in the desert. The heat of the sun merciless. The tongue lay heavy in the mouth and nobody wanted to talk. Nothing but sand everywhere. The camels walked like machines. The slightest interruption of such a ride is greeted with pleasure.

A sharp cry woke up Leopold. Ben Nil also reacted and looked up in the air whence the cry came. "Shahin!" He said, pointing upwards, then he sank back into his lethargy. Yes, it was a hawk whose cry they had heard. The appearance of this bird had no significance for Ben Nil. But Leopold warned: "Somebody is coming!"

Ben Nil looked around. He saw nothing but sand. "Has the sun robbed me of my sight? I can see nobody."

"I don't either, but we will meet somebody soon. A hawk only eats live prey. When in the desert where there are no living creatures, he must follow a caravan. Let's pay attention to what it is doing."

They kept the bird in sight. A second bird came from the west. After cruising several times over the two riders they flew back in the direction from which they had come. "They are male and female," mused Ben Nil.

"Yes," remarked Leopold. He stopped his camel and took his telescope to observe the birds. "It is always good to know who is there."

"But you can't know anything until you see it."

"But I have seen things already – the hawks. Now they are circling again. They are moving slightly south. I therefore conclude they are following a slow-moving caravan. I assume there are people on foot among them." Leopold lowered his telescope and saw what he expected. A caravan consisting of camel riders and people on foot.

"How do you know the caravan moves slowly?"

"The hawks are cruising over the caravan. Their speed is the same."

"Effendi, you are deducing things nobody thinks of. Are we going to meet these people?"

"Yes, if we don't avoid them intentionally. Their distance from us is about one hour on foot."

"Allah! How can you know that? Surely the hawks didn't tell you?"

"Who else? One knows how fast the hawk is flying and can calculate the distance easily."

"Would it be possible to observe the caravan without them seeing us?"

"Yes, with the telescope. We will see them in a quarter of an hour."

The lethargy had gone. The cry of the hawks had awoken them fully. They did not want to get too near in case they were seen by the caravan. The ground was even and there was no place to hide. This was to change in the evening, when they would reach the rain basin of Nid en Nile where, as Leopold had heard, there would be water all year round.

Leopold gave the telescope to Ben Nil. "Effendi, you were right. It is a caravan. I wouldn't have guessed it if I had seen many hawks. There are twenty riders and forty-five people on foot. One doesn't go on foot in the desert. Would that be a slave caravan?"

"Hardly likely. Where should they take the slaves from?"

"Which country might they come from?"

"The land of the Takaleh. But wait! Naming this name, I remember that the Takaleh, although Mohammedans, have the detestable custom of selling their children."

"Allah, what a sin and what shame. Are they Negroes?"

"No, they are not completely black. Don't take them for low or useless people. They withstood longest when Egypt conquered the Sudan. They are valiant warriors. They have a king with the right to sell any subjects as slaves."

"Are they a danger?"

"No. We don't have to fear them. We will reach the rain basin before them. Should their aim be the same, we will meet them, but we don't have to join them."

Seeing the caravan removed their lethargy. They rode faster and it was late afternoon when they saw a dark line at the horizon. As there could not be a mountain in this area, it must be a wood, Leopold deduced. When they reached it, they also saw the rain basin. It was large and carried clear water. It was by no means a swamp. They stopped, let the camels drink and tied them to the nearby bushes, where they found nourishment in the juicy twigs. When they gathered dry wood to make a fire to safeguard them from the flies, they saw the caravan approaching.

Among the men who rode in front was a true goliath. They stopped and the giant came forward, observing the two darkly. Then, without greeting, he asked: "What are you doing here?"

In the orient, if somebody at the first meeting does not greet you, it is always a bad sign. This man did not make a trustworthy impression on Leopold. He therefore gave the short answer: "We are taking a rest."

"Will you stay here overnight?"

"That depends whether we like it here and if we are not disturbed."

"Are you alone?"

"Don't ask, use your eyes."

"You don't seem to know the meaning of politeness."

"I know it, but I only use it if somebody is polite to me. You denied us your greeting."

"I don't know you. Who are you?"

"I want to know your name and your position first."

"My position is higher than yours. Actually, you should give me the information first. I am Shedid, the most valiant warrior of the King of Takaleh!"

"And I am the Mudir, the Mayor of Dsharabub. I trust you have heard about this place." This name came to Leopold's tongue quite involuntarily. "The place is known because of the latest famous Mohammedan Order." But there never was a Mudir in this place. Leopold put on this rank to make an impression on the Takaleh. He couldn't tell him the truth for good reasons. He would have played with his and other people's lives.

"I have never heard of this Order," said Shedid, disdainfully.

"Allah may forgive you your ignorance. Did you never hear of Sihdi Senussi?"

"Allah pierce you. How can you insult a pious believer with this question? Everybody on this earth knows that Sihdi Senussi was the greatest prophet. Do you know places called Siwah and Farafrah?"

"Certainly."

"They are lighting stars against other places on earth, because of the university where the students and followers of Sihdi Senussi were educated."

"You know that and yet you don't know Dsharabub which shines even brighter? Sihdi Senussi lived in Dsharabub, in Siwah and Farafrah were his schools. All three places belonged together. My house and Sihdi Senussi's only had one entrance. We lived under one roof. Now tell me who stands higher, you or I? Woe to him who refuses to greet me. He will be like the blasphemer of whom the hundred and fourth 'sure' says: "He will be thrown into hutame! Dshehenna's fire, Allah's, falls on this transgressor. And now continue boasting, you servant of a man."

Shedid made his camel kneel, dismounted and bowed down deeply. "Let the sun of your forgiveness shine over me, oh Mudir. I could not anticipate that you were a friend of the holy Senussi. Your Order will embrace the whole world. Before your might, every man will bow down. How should I address your young companion?"

"His years are not many, but the superiority of his spirit has already made him famous. He is a chatib, a Mohammedan preacher. You may call him Chatib."

Ben Nil, said with dignity: "You have insulted us because you didn't know us. We forgive you."

The Takaleh was embarrassed. He would have liked to encamp right here, but it wouldn't be right to disturb such holy men. "We wanted to rest here until the morning, but we will go to another place. We mustn't dare to be near such holy men."

"Before Allah, all men are equal. I permit you to make camp here."

"I thank you, oh Mudir. My people will listen to your talks devoutly."

"Don't think that we will preach to you. Words must only come from your mouth if the spirit inside is mighty."

Leopold wanted to make an impression, nothing else. To judge by the Takaleh's changed behaviour, it worked. But it was not his intention to act as a Mohammedan preacher.

Shedid waved to his people to come nearer. There were riders and people on foot. Half of those on foot were females of all ages. Males' and females' hands were fastened to a long rope; they were prisoners.

After the riders had led their animals to the water, the prisoners were allowed to drink. Then, still tied, they had to lie down. They obeyed, resigned to their fate.

They sat down, near enough to hear every word, but not so near as to disturb the 'holy two'. They took food from their saddles and ate. The prisoners received nothing. When Leopold asked about this, the Takaleh replied: "It is not my concern if they are hungry. They receive food and drink once a day. Now they should sleep. They have received more than they should, having drunk here."

"Water from the sea, whereas you drank from hoses."

"For slaves, water is water. If it doesn't taste the same, I can't help it."

"Where did you buy these slaves?"

"Buy them? Oh Mudir, how are they who know everything in heaven and earth inexperienced in earthly matters? A Takaleh never buys slaves. He makes them for himself."

"So these are slaves of your own tribe?"

"Certainly."

"What did they do, that you made them slaves?"

"Do? Actually nothing. The King needs money, he therefore sells them. He sells those who were disobedient or whom, for any reason, he doesn't like any more. Every father can sell his children. Every man can sell his wives. Everyone who has people working for him can sell them as slaves."

"What would you say if the King wanted to sell you?"

"I would obey." He added quietly so as to be heard by Leopold only, "I wouldn't suffer it, I would strangle him."

"Have you sold any of your family?"

"Yes, my wife and two daughters are among these slaves."

"Why did you sell them?"

"Because I took another wife and it is better to be paid for daughters than feed them." Shedid said this unfeelingly, as if he had put, not only his own view, but the view of all people.

The sun had reached the horizon. It was the time for Maghreb. Everybody, including the bound prisoners, knelt and all eyes were directed to Leopold. It was customary for the most distinguished to lead the prayers. Leopold had often prayed with Mohammedans, but quietly and not to Allah or his prophets. Ben Nil helped him out of this embarrassment: "Mudir, you always prayed the three daily prayers, the two prayers at evening you left to me. Would you allow this for today?"

"Yes, you lead the prayer, you darling of the prophets," Leopold countered. "Your words go the same way as mine."

After the Maghreb, they ate. The Takaleh turned their faces as it is impolite to observe distinguished and holy men eating. One of them interrupted the silence and pointed to the desert. "A rider; who would he be?" The fact of his coming closer, unhesitatingly, led Leopold to conclude that he must have known who was camping here.

The rider greeted: "Allah may give you a hundred thousand such nights. Permit me to rest with you."

Because Leopold and Ben Nil kept silent, Shedid, the leader of the Takaleh, answered: "Dismount and sit down. You are welcome."

"Allah has led me at the right time to this place. I assume these prisoners belong to the Takaleh. Is my guess right?"

"Yes," confirmed their leader.

"So Shedid, the chief servant of the King, must be here as well."

"I am he. And who are you?"

"I am Amr of the Beggara tribe. I am a friend of Ben Mubarek."

"Has your acquaintance with him something to do with your present ride here?"

"Yes, I am here as a messenger to you."

"How did Ben Mubarek know that I was just at this place?"

"He knows you make this trip twice a year. He also knows the time."

"There must be a special reason."

"Yes, there is a special reason, or actually more of a warning. Don't go, this time, near the Nile and don't bring the slaves directly to Fashodah. Then go to Ibn Mulei, the Colonel and head of the soldiers and tell him where to find them. Because there is a foreign Effendi helping to find slave-dealers and deliver them to the Reis Effendina."

"Allah destroy this son of a dog," Shedid grated.

"To top it all, Poldi Ben Anglesi is an unbeliever."

"Allah may put him into the most terrible corner of hell. Is dealing in slaves his business? I don't care about the laws of the viceroy. I am serving my king and no man can have anything against it. We also have a powerful protector, the Mudir of Fashodah, Ali Effendi el Kurdi, who has snatched away many a catch from the Reis Effendina."

Leopold was glad to learn that they didn't know the old Mudir had been deposed. But he didn't expect the following.

"Ben Mubarek wouldn't have sent me if he weren't convinced it was necessary. This unbeliever is more dangerous than the Reis Effendina."

"Does Ben Mubarek want to insult me? I have never been beaten by anyone."

"He does not want to insult you. Although this giour is very strong, he is also full of tricks. He guesses the most secret matters and whoever puts a trap for him, falls into it himself. Ben Mubarek told me a few things: He didn't have much time, but what he told me is to warn you to take greatest care."

"Will Ben Mubarek come to Fashodah?"

"Yes."

"As all his people are imprisoned, where will he take new ones for his slave-hunt?"

"He will recruit Shilluk and Nuehr. That must happen soon because the Reis Effendina is after him. He has to hide in Fashodah. Now I remember, he asked me to take special care about a man whom he has asked for six months ago."

"You mean Hafid Sichar: There he is, the last one at the rope. But he forgot the main thing. I may not have to fear the strength of this unbeliever, but I could easily fall for his tricks, especially as I do not know him."

"Allah! What kind of a messenger am I," called Amr, hitting his hands on his forehead. "Not he, but I have forgotten . He gave me a good description and he even added the name of his companion, Ben Nil."

Leopold, involuntarily, grabbed at his revolver. The discussion had become dangerous. If this man had an exact description, they were betrayed. Ben Nil had the same thoughts and threw a worried glance at Leopold.

"Ben Nil?" asked Shedid. "Who is that?"

"A young man of about nineteen or twenty, no beard and a slender figure, but considerable bodily strength. Although he is a Moslem, he is on the side of this giour. His eyes are dark and his cheeks are full. The clothing…"

Amr stopped and observed Ben Nil with astounding eyes "What a miracle! The description fits this young man at my side, exactly."

"Nonsense," said Shedid. "The description fits thousands of young men. This young man is from the holy order of Sihdi Senussi."

The messenger crossed his arms on his chest, bowed down and said: "I did not intend to insult him."

Thank God! The least of the danger was overcome. How would it go with the major part of the description? Leopold did not have to wait long, because Shedid asked: "Describe the Effendi now."

Leopold wished it to be a loose description, but unfortunately, it was a careful picture which Amr described in detail. Just as it was with Ben Nil, when it came to describe the clothing, Amr stared perplexedly at Leopold. "Allah is great. The man I should describe is right here. It is him, there is no doubt."

It is not hard to imagine the sensation these words provoked. Leopold looked at Ben Nil. In no way did he looked shocked. His face showed astonishment about such an accident of similarities. Leopold could rely on him. He himself looked questioningly at Amr's exited face and said nothing. He pretended he didn't understand. Shedid looked at Amr and Leopold, but the dignified calm puzzled him.

"What are you saying?" asked the Takaleh. "This man on my right is the Effendi?"

"Yes, it's him. It couldn't be anyone else."

"You are mistaken again. This man is the mighty Mudir of Dsharabub and a trusted friend of Sihdi Senussi."

"Is that true? Can you prove it?"

"I know it from himself."

"From himself, from himself," laughed the Baggara Arab. "If you don't know it from anybody else, your evidence doesn't count. I have told you that the giour puts on a false name quite often."

Shedid looked at Leopold, trust and mistrust struggling. Leopold answered, calm and astonished. "Is this man talking about me?"

"Certainly, he means you. Didn't you understand?"

"If I did, I would have to declare him mad. I would rather think I

110

misunderstood."

"He maintains you are Poldi Ben Anglesi."

"Allah be merciful on him. His spirit is ill. Let him put a cold, wet cloth on his forehead. His fever will subside."

"I am not ill, I know what I am talking about. One description to fit could be mistaken, but two, it is impossible. Ben Mubarek said they were riding on grey hedshihns."

"That is correct," said Shedid. He became more and more suspicious.

He turned to Leopold: "You heard what he said. I am respectful of your dignity, but I have no proof of its genuineness. Please help me to trust you."

"You really mistrust me?" asked Leopold, seeming astonished. I should prove who I am? Tell me where are we now."

"Well, here at the rain basin."

"And where did Ben Mubarek say this Effendi is?"

"On a journey on the Nile."

"Can I be this Poldi Ben Anglesi?"

"What Ben Mubarek has said was only an assumption. If there was only one right description, a mistake is possible. As they fit both of you, your situation is bad. If you are that Effendi, I have to kill you."

"But I am not this person."

"That is not proven, but there is a verse in the Koran that no unbeliever is capable of reciting without stumbling. Do you know it?"

Leopold, who was well versed in all major religions said: "Yes."

"Can you say it without mistakes?"

"Perhaps, if you would say it first, correctly and with good diction."

"All right. I will say it first. By the way, you have betrayed yourself already. A good Senussi, especially a Mudir, should be able to pray this sure without previously listening to it." The Takaleh began: "In the name of the merciful God, say: 'Oh you disbelievers, I do not worship what you worship, and you do not worship what I do not worship, and I will never worship that, which you do not worship, – and you will worship – not worship, what I do not worship. I have – I have not –'…'"

He stopped, he realised that he was in a muddle.

"Well," smiled Leopold. "Are you no Moslem or are you drunk?"

"None of it," said Shedid, annoyed, "This sure is really the most difficult, but you, as a Senussi, must be able to say it without fault."

This is really a tongue-twister, even more so in Arabic. Leopold said it with speed and without fault. "Truly," said Shedid, "he said it with speed and without fault – he can't be a disbeliever."

"But," entered Amr, stubbornly, "Ben Mubarek told me that this giour knows the Koran as if he was born here. Don't judge too soon."

"Do you think so? What else can I try to find out?"

This sounded dangerous. It was advisable not to await any further development. Shedid, whose views were favourable at the moment, could easily swing the other way. Leopold pretended to be angry: "Another test? Do you know what a Mudir of Dsharabub means? I am high above you, but I have consented to be tested. Should I humble myself even more? No! Who insults a Mudir cannot expect to see the face of such a man. We permitted you to stay near us, but now we leave this place…"

"No, you are not allowed to," interrupted Amr. "We won't let you go." Amr stretched out his hands, trying to force Leopold to sit down.

The latter stepped back and thundered: "Stop being imprudent! Should I invoke a curse on you that your body should dry up and your soul pine away? Will you try whether Allah's curse is in our hands or not? I don't mind. But I tell you that your end will be terrible. Who will hold us back? Whose hands dare to touch us?"

Leopold looked around. Everybody was silent. Not so much because of his words, but the tone in which they were spoken. He untied and mounted his camel; Ben Nil did the same. They rode off without being hindered.

Chapter 13

Hafid Sichar

When Leopold could assume he was no longer seen, he turned toward east. Ben Nil, who up to now had been quiet, asked: "Effendi, you are going east, whereas our way is south. Why are you deviating?"

"There are two reasons: Firstly because the trodden grass will erect itself by the morning and the Takaleh will not find our tracks, secondly, I want to free Hafid Sichar."

"Allah! That's another adventure. Effendi, whoever rides with you doesn't have to worry about danger. Why did you lower yourself and let them test you?"

"Because it was the cleverest thing to do. Had Shedid known that I am Poldi Ben Anglesi, he wouldn't go to Fashodah. He would send a messenger to warn Ben Mubarek and the Colonel. Our ride to Fashodah would have failed."

"What will you do with Hafid Sichar?"

"He will have to come with us to Fashodah."

"You will need another camel."

"I will take one from the Takaleh."

"To free Hafid Sichar and use costly time to take a camel is too much for one man."

"I wouldn't mind taking you with me, but where water is, there are rapacious animals."

"Do you believe that I can guard the camels against a lion? If you say yes, I will thank you for your trust, but I wouldn't be able to do it. You know that I am fearless, but to face a lion needs more than that. On your return you would find me and the camels torn to bits. It is in any case better you take me with you."

Ben Nil was right and Leopold decided to grant his wish. He might need assistance. They dismounted, tied their camels to trees and went back on foot. They would have liked to leave their rifles, but took them in case they met wild animals. The way was easy because the moon was shining. Yet Leopold would have preferred a moonless night. Moonlight made his task more difficult.

Near the ford they noticed there was no fire. It pleased them because it was evidence that the Takaleh were asleep. About one hundred steps away, Leopold asked Ben Nil to wait by a tree. He himself started crawling. The moon was low and threw large shadows of the trees, which Leopold found very useful. The Takaleh had a guard for the slaves. He walked up and down the line of prisoners.

In order to reach Hafid Sichar, Leopold had to neutralize the guard. Ten steps away from the prisoners he stopped and listened. They all seemed to sleep. No wonder, as they were badly nourished, not having enough to drink and marching in the burning sun all day. Nothing moved. Only the guard walked the same line to and fro. Leopold moved toward that line as far as he could. After the man had just passed him, he jumped up, took him by the throat from behind and gave him a blow with his right fist at the temple. The guard stretched his arms and fell. There was no conspicuous noise. He had lost consciousness.

Leopold picked him up and carried him to Ben Nil. As he put him down, he noticed to his astonishment that it was not a Takaleh but Amr the Baggara-Arab, the messenger sent by Ben Mubarek.

"Who are you bringing. Is it Hafid Sichar?"

"No, look at him, it is the Baggara who was guarding the prisoners."

"Amr was bad for us, he has to be silenced. Should I kill him?"

"No, we take him with us. Shedid will think he freed the prisoner."

Amr was being tied and gagged. Leopold crept back to the prisoners. Hafid Sichar was the first in line. He, like the others, was tied up and separately tied to the rope. All the prisoners slept as if they were dead – except Hafid Sichar. When Leopold touched him, he whispered: "Effendi, is it you?"

"Yes."

"Allah! I expected you. My heart hammered with worry that you are not the one through whom I hoped to be rescued."

"What is your name?"

"Hafid Sichar."

"You are the one I am seeking. Greetings from your brother."

"Oh heavens, oh Allah, what does…"

"Not so loud," interrupted Leopold. "Do your neighbours sleep?"

"As fast as you could wish."

"Lie still, I am going to cut you loose." They crawled back to Ben Nil where Hafid Sichar intended to say extensive thanks.

"Not now. Later you can talk as much as you like."

Amr had regained consciousness. He tried to tear his fetters and to cry out. He could do neither. Ben Nil put a knife to his chest: "Another sound and I will put this knife into your black heart." This helped. The Baggara remained quiet. "Now we need two camels," Ben Nil ventured.

"We need three," answered Leopold. "We are more people and need a camel to carry more hoses of water."

"Permit me to bring the camels, I know which are the best." Hafid

Sichar rushed away before Leopold could hold him back. He was not in agreement with this arbitrary conduct. He could spoil everything. Luckily, that was not the case. After a quarter of an hour Hafid returned with three of the best camels, three saddles and three hoses.

Leopold offered him the knife and rifle he had taken from Amr. After untying his legs he asked him: "If you promise not to utter a sound I will take off your gag." Amr nodded.

"I warn you. The slightest sound and you will feel Ben Nil's knife."

Amr nodded again. Leopold removed his gag. Amr breathed heavily and said quietly: "Just in time. I nearly suffocated."

They now walked to the two camels, where they had left them. The fears of them being attacked by wild animals were unjustified. They grazed peacefully and willingly fell into a fast trot with the others. The ride to Fashodah had been calculated to take up to four days. The four riders did not make a straight line to their destination. They made a detour, as they did not want the caravan to see their tracks. Through his telescope Leopold saw the caravan in the distance. When he turned slightly, he noticed a few other little points in the desert. They were too far off to be counted or even to guess what they were. But they moved in a direction which would result in meeting with the caravan.

Leopold and Ben Nil had had no sleep the previous night, so they decided to take a rest at the next water hole. Hafid Sichar said: "How can I sleep when life has just been given back to me. I want to enjoy the stars and I will keep watch over our prisoner." Leopold asked him to wake them up before daybreak.

The stars had faded when Hafid Sichar woke them up. Only a short while later they were on their way again. It was an hour after sunrise when Ben Nil pointed forward: "A hyena is sitting there."

"And two others are resting on the ground," added Hafid Sichar.

Leopold shaded his eyes to see better. "These are not hyenas, they are people. I feel a mishap has befallen them. Let's hurry."

They rushed on. The figure which Ben Nil had thought to be a hyena sat there with his back turned towards the little group of riders. He heard them coming and turned around. When he saw the Baggara, his face assumed an expression of shock. "Allah! I am lost. The chief of the Baggara, Amr es Makashef!"

Leopold had heard this name before. The leader of the Baggara was known as a violent warrior. He was a relative of the Mahdi who attacked the town of Sennar in April 1882 with a thousand men, to take it for himself. Amr answered immediately:

"You are mistaken, I am a Baggara but not their sheik."

"Why are you denying yourself? As a trader I have often been with you. I am Sinan and you know me."

Amr's worried glance at Leopold convinced the latter that the trader had spoken the truth. "Look at the sheik," Leopold told the trader. "Haven't you noticed that Amr has no weapons and that his legs are tied under the camel?"

"Allah does miracles. Amr es Makashef is tied up. Did you fight with him?"

"About that later. First let me examine your companions who are lying there as if they were dead."

"My brothers are dead. They were shot. You can see the blood puddle."

"Did they shoot at you?"

"No, they hit me on the head with the butt of their rifle. When I woke up, I saw that my brothers were dead. They robbed us of everything."

"The donkeys are still here. Let me examine your head." It was swollen, but luckily he was not hit with the sharp end of the rifle but with the broad end of the butt. Leopold took the head cloth of the dead brothers, to help with wet poultices.

It helped him. He could rise and spoke with less exertion but still seemed to fear the Baggara. Leopold calmed him: "You are among friends and this sheik cannot harm you. He is a friend of the Takaleh who attacked you. Have you heard of the Reis Effendina?"

"Yes, I have."

"I am his friend and I have taken this prisoner to deliver him to the Reis in Fashodah. You can talk to us freely."

"We were in Dar Famaka where we did good business. We were paid thibr. The Takalehs robbed us and now I am poorer than ever."

The mentioned thibr is gold which was found as dust or grains in the area of which the trader had spoken. It was preferred to the Maria-Theresia-Taler, the second preferred currency. "Did you mention the thibr to them?"

"They were friendly and we had no mistrust. As soon as we mentioned it, their leader, Shedid, asked the caravan to ride ahead. He and four other Takalehs remained behind. We followed more slowly. Until we came to this place, when they suddenly attacked us. The rest you know already."

"You shouldn't have told them about the thibr. The five Thakalehs did not want to share your gold and have sent the others away. They could not take the donkeys as this would have betrayed them."

"You are right, but what is going to happen now? I want to follow these murderers and revenge myself as well as take back the robbed gold."

"You will receive back what they have taken, but you don't have to follow the caravan nor fight with them. In your condition this would not be possible, anyhow. They are on foot whereas we ride. We will be sooner in Fashodah than they. They will be received by the Mudir and the police."

Chapter 14

The father of the 'five hundred'

They buried the dead. The injured trader was put on the camel with the hoses and they rode off. The unloaded donkeys could follow easily. They were about thirty geographical miles away from Fashodah. Under normal circumstances, this would have taken them two days. With an injured person it was much slower, but still quicker than the caravan.

They did not, of course, follow the tracks of the Takalehs, but made a wide circle around them.

On the morning of the fourth day, Fashodah came into sight. It was actually a large village of huts, with the exception of the house of the Mudir and the barracks of soldiers, which were surrounded by stone walls. The streets and lanes, if one may use this expression, were made of holes, dirt puddles, excrement heaps and mud mountains. One had to be a rope dancer not to get stuck.

Fashodah is a place for banishment, but the number of criminals did not rise fast as they were dying of the unhealthy atmospheric conditions.

Leopold and his little group did not enter Fashodah right away. He expected Ben Mubarek to be there as well as other enemies, such as Murad Nassyr and his two sisters, whom he had met while in Cairo. One of the sisters had complained of a steady hair loss. He simply told her to throw away her daily hair conditioner. This simple action would save his life in the near future. She was to marry Ben Mubarek. Murad Nassyr turned out to be a slave-dealer. The Colonel of the soldiers was, as mentioned, a secret accomplice of Ben Mubarek, who had probably heard of Leopold.

They found a place near Fashodah surrounded by trees and bushes, a useful hiding place to rest. Leopold gave Hafid Sichar Reis Effendina's letter of recommendation to the Mudir.

Hafid Sichar returned four hours later bringing with him a man who wore ordinary attire. Leopold expected to see a high official but learned to his surprise that it was the Mudir in person, whose characteristic rudeness showed at the first meeting.

"You had to wait for a long time, Effendi," said Hafid Sichar to Leopold. "This high person is…"

"Silence!" thundered the other person angrily. "I have treated you in a friendly manner because your sad fate was pitiful. But you mustn't

118

think that I am on your level . How do you dare to introduce me to the Effendi and apologise because he had to wait? Am I a dog who has to follow as soon as you whistle, you rascal?"

That's interesting, thought Leopold. How will he behave with criminals when he was even rude to us. Now he observed Leopold with a curious glance but without the slightest friendliness in his face.

"Who are you?" asked Leopold. "Are you Ali Effendi yourself?"

"Ali Effendi?" he asked sharply. "Don't you know how to address a Mudir?"

"I know it and I will do my duty of politeness as soon as I meet a Mudir."

"This is the case now. I am the Mudir of Fashodah."

An oriental person would have crossed his arms and bowed down. Leopold bowed his head slightly, passed his hand politely and said:

"Allah give you a thousand years, O Mudir. I am happy to see the face of a man whose administration will lift the province and clear the town of all rabble."

Ali Effendi hesitated to take Leopold's hand and looked at him curiously. "After what I have heard and read about you, you seem to be a capable man, but you don't seem to be a friend of politeness."

"Everybody has his own way and has to be treated accordingly."

"You unbelievers are peculiar people, but I will take you as you are, very brave and very coarse. Let's sit down."

Leopold smiled to himself. To be called coarse by the embodiment of coarseness. They sat down. The Mudir pulled out a leather bag and laid out a box of matches and some cigarettes. He lit one without offering any to Leopold and started: "You are a servant of the Reis Effendina. Where and how did he get to know you?"

"As to where and how we got to know each other is a difference we will not get busy about right now. But if you think I am his servant, you are mistaken."

"In his letter he calls you his friend, but that surely is only meant as a recommendation. An unbeliever can never be a friend of a Moslem."

"Why not? If I respect somebody, the fact that he is a Moslem, does not hinder me from being his friend. It is of no importance to me whether you believe me or not."

"It is of no importance to you whether the Mudir of Fashodah believes you or not? I have never come across such a man."

"I act according to the phrase: 'How you are to me, so I am to you'."

"That is strong, very strong. If another would have said this, by Allah, I would have let him have five hundred lashes."

"I have heard that you are called Abu Hamsa Miah, the father of five

119

hundred. But I am safe over this gift of love."

"Safe? Don't believe that. If I wanted to give you five hundred, who would stop me?"

"My nationality and my consul."

"I am whistling on them."

"Then this here. I am sure you won't whistle on that." With these words, Leopold put his fist under the Mudir's nose. The Mudir withdrew his face quickly. "Poldi Ben Anglesi, do you want to hit me?"

"No, as long as you won't hit me. But we have joked enough. Let us talk of other things. We are…"

"Who has to decide what we are going to talk about, you or I?" interrupted the Mudir.

"I, because you are with me. If you don't like it, then you can go. I will be able to go alone through the world and this area."

The Mudir stared at Leopold and threw away the rest of his cigarette. "Allah is great, no, he is greater, no, he is the greatest. But you are the coarsest person I ever met. What bliss if I could give you the five hundred. I think I will get round to it yet."

"I hope so too, just to prove to you that my bullet will be in your head before you have finished the order."

"May the devil devour you. I think the best way to get on with you is to be polite." Ali Effendi lit himself another cigarette.

"All right, make a start," smiled Leopold, "by allowing me to take a cigarette." He helped himself, took one and lit it. When he saw that the Mudir became angry, he added: "That was your duty when you lit your first one. You have not done so and demanded politeness from me. What should I think of you? I don't want any favours. I have come to you to help you do your duty. I have talked to higher people than you. They have all treated me with politeness."

The Mudir threw away his cigarette, clenched his fist and intended to get angry again. Then he turned his wrath to Amr el Makashef: "I see you are tied up. Were you the messenger from Ben Mubarek?"

"Yes," admitted the Baggara.

"Dog, you mix with slave-hunters? You will get the five hundred as sure as I have five fingers on each hand. I cannot hang you because you have been only a messenger. Five weeks at a hundred lashes will do to remember your meeting with Abu Hamsa Miah."

With this outburst, his anger seemed to have disappeared. He suddenly had a friendly expression on his face and finally passed Leopold his hand. "Poldi Ben Anglesi Effendi, you must be present when this son of a dog receives his lashes. It will refresh your soul and strengthen your heart. There is no greater bliss than to do justice to our proper laws. To hear them whimper and moan. But now, you must tell me what happened since you met the Reis Effendina."

"Please permit Ben Nil to tell you."

"Why not you yourself?"

"When he finishes, you will know the reason without me telling you."

"All right, let him talk!"

Ben Nil talked. His manner was short but detailed. One could hear his loyalty and devotion to his Effendi. The Mudir learned things of which he had no idea. When Ben Nil finished he grabbed his cigarette bag and emptied it over Leopold and called: "Smoke, Poldi Ben Anglesi Effendi, smoke, you deserve it. Yes, by Allah and the prophet, you deserve it. When you come to me you will get even more, although they are shamefully expensive."

"How much are you paying for them?" asked Leopold, curious about the price of cigarettes that had found their way to the Sudan.

"A whole piaster for each of them."

"That is too dear. Didn't you bargain a bit?"

"I do not bargain. I pay honestly, in full and at once. For every piaster one lash. After twenty lashes he declared himself to be paid and ran away. Smoke, Effendi, you are a devil of a fellow. You unbelievers are not so bad and I will believe that the Reis Effendina regards you as a friend. I am Mudir, and that, by Allah, is nothing low, but I ask you to pardon my straightforwardness. But for that you must do me a favour."

"I don't know whether I will be able to."

"You can do it."

"In this case – yes."

The Mudir pressed both of Leopold's hands. "Hamdulillah! There will be lashes, lashes, five or six thousand or even more. You should catch Ben Mubarek, not for the Reis Effendina, but for me."

"All right!"

"And that fat Turk and his sisters."

"These as well."

"I thank you. That will be a feast as I have never had before. They will all receive five hundred lashes and if they survive they will be hanged."

"You can't hang the girls. They are innocent."

"One of the sisters wanted to marry Ben Mubarek, that's enough!"

"She doesn't want to, she has to. That is only a seal to a business connection."

"Don't tell me what to do. Nobody has to seal anything here but me, and I seal it with five hundred lashes. But you must catch them all –

you promised."

"I will keep my word, but one of them is already in your hands – the Colonel, Ibn Mulei."

"He will receive his five hundred as well…" He stopped. A thought had struck him. He continued: "My people caught a Nuehr-Negro yesterday, who was suspicious to them. They found a letter in his tuft of hair. He tore himself loose and intended to escape. They shot him dead. This morning they brought me the letter. It was from the seribah Aliab at the river Rohl. The receiver should hand it to Ben Mubarek."

"Ah, should this seribah belong to Ben Mubarek?"

"I don't know that. I am only here for a short while."

"I would almost assume that it does. May I see this letter?"

"Of course. I tortured my head as to whom it was directed, but now I believe it was to Ibn Mulei. I have a wonderful idea – he should get this letter."

"The idea is good, but who should take it to him?"

"You."

"I mustn't be seen in Fashodah. Not yet, anyhow."

"Why not? The people who shouldn't see you are not there yet."

"They may arrive at any moment."

"Not possible without me noticing it. There are guards at the river bank day and night. You pretend to be a messenger from the seribah. When Ibn Mulei receives this letter – he is convicted. I will whip him until he confesses and we will learn how to catch the others."

"If the messenger is not described in the letter, I could go as a Greek."

The fact the Mudir showed such trust after the unfriendly greeting clouded Leopold's sagacity. He accepted against his feeling that a conviction could be achieved without the danger.

"Where does Ibn Mulei live?"

"He occupies a whole house next to the barracks."

"I will send Hafid Sichar to collect the letter as I will take on this mission at night."

"He will receive it and I will send fresh food that you can eat."

"Until we reach town we have enough food. More important would be another suit, because this one will have been described to him already. I mustn't take my usual weapons."

"But everybody here is armed."

"Please send me an old rifle, an old knife and an old pistol."

"Your wishes will be fulfilled. The others can stay in my house where you will join them after your visit with Ibn Mulei."

"So I have only to mention the Takaleh. Are you ready to seize them?"

"Allah! What a question. They will be seized, naturally. The slaves will be freed, the others receive their punishment. For the five murderers, death is assured. Think! Everybody receives five hundred. Calculate how many these are. Such joy has not been experienced in Fashodah before. All thanks to you, Effendi. When do you expect the Takaleh to be here?"

"Not before the day after tomorrow, but then they can be expected any time."

"They will be received as is proper. This Baggara, however, will receive his bastinado before their arrival." The Mudir left with Hafid Sichar but came back once more and said: "I take none of the cigarettes with me. The little bag you can keep as a souvenir." He gave the Baggara a kick and left.

Leopold shared the cigarettes with Ben Nil. They sat in silence for a while. The undertaking which he had taken on seemed uncanny now. He regretted letting himself be persuaded to do it. But there was no going back on his word. Amr turned from side to side. The Mudir's kick gave him pain. When he had previously thought that, as a sheik, he would escape punishment, he now realised the inevitability of receiving the 'five hundred'. He was thinking strenuously how to avert this punishment and came to the decision that only Poldi Ben Anglesi could help him.

He turned to Leopold and said: "Effendi, may I talk to you?"

Although Leopold had an idea that what Amr el Makashef was going to say could be of value, he asked him to be quiet. Amr became silent, but after a short while he started again: "You will regret it if you don't let me talk. What I have to say is important to you."

"I don't want to hear it. You want to avoid the five hundred which, of course, is important for your soles."

"But I am offering a lot for it."

"What, for instance?" Leopold began to come round.

"News about the seribah Aliab, of which I heard you talk. I think it would be useful for you to learn about this settlement."

"That is the case. Who does the seribah belong to?"

I have been there and I know everything about it, but you must talk to the Mudir to release me from the punishment."

"I can only promise to ask. Whether it will have any success with the Mudir, I don't know."

"I don't doubt it. I know how much he thinks of you. Your intercession will be successful."

"You are probably wrong, but I promise to put in a good word for you. I must, however, tell you that I won't let myself be cheated. If you think you can escape the five hundred by lying, you are mistaken. What do you know about the seribah?"

"It belongs to Ben Mubarek."

"I thought so. Did you do any deals with him?"

"I did, but please don't tell that to the Mudir."

"I do not believe I can be silent about this, but I promise you that this will not be counted against you. I can understand your position. You, as a Moslem, believe slave trading was permitted."

"That's right, Effendi. The Baggara live from their herds. One epidemic amongst them, and we suffer greatly. Dealing in slaves was the only means for us to live until our herds recovered."

"Who is in command when Ben Mubarek isn't there?"

"A sergeant major, Ben Ifram. A shot caused him to have a stiff leg. He is very loyal to his boss."

"I know enough for now, but may have further questions later."

"Later? I hoped the Mudir would let me go upon your intercession."

"I hoped so too, but it is possible that Ben Mubarek has left Fashodah already. In which case we have to follow him to the seribah Aliab and, as you well know, we need you as a guide."

"May Allah prevent this. What will my people think when I stay away for months and Ben Mubarek is a friend?"

"These are considerations that we don't have to think about yet. I only talked about a possibility. Let's be calm and see how things develop."

"Let's be calm," he sighed, "but I – I – !"

Amr was right. His information was of great importance. Now they knew where to find Ben Mubarek whatever the case. For the moment, Leopold hoped to find him in Fashodah.

After about three hours, Hafid Sichar returned. He was heavily laden. He brought a suit, the weapons asked for, two roasted chickens and a bottle of raki. They ate and the Baggara received his portion. It was afternoon now, two hours before nightfall. Leopold changed clothes. With a sunburned face and hands, he could be taken for a slave-hunter. His features he couldn't change; they could betray him.

It was dark when they reached the house of the Mudir. The group, which included Sinan, the trader, stayed there, whereas Leopold went to the nearby building of the Colonel. He knocked at the door. It was a while until he heard steps, A voice asked: "Who is there?"

"A messenger to the Colonel from the seribah Aliab."

"Come again – he isn't here."

"I am a stranger here. Let me in, I want to wait until he comes."

"Is your message important?"

"Yes, I have a letter."

"All right, give it to me. I am going to open the hatch."

"I cannot do that. I have to hand the letter to the Colonel in person."

"Well, come in."

A heavy iron bolt was pushed back and the door was opened to a small windowless room. The man who opened the door carried two pistols and a knife. He looked at Leopold angrily. "Why can't you come in the day time?"

"Nobody can come sooner until he arrives."

"You are giving clever answers, fellow. I am a soldier here and my knife is never out of reach. Understood? Now follow me."

The soldier led Leopold to a larger room which was sparely lit by a smoking oil lamp hanging from the ceiling. It was also windowless. Under the lamp was a rush-mat on which four wild-looking fellows squatted. They played at dice and eyed Leopold with unfriendly eyes. The soldier who brought Leopold into this room asked him to sit in a corner and wait until the Colonel returned, and to be quiet, otherwise they would shut him up. He then joined the others to continue the game.

It is easy to imagine that Leopold was not delighted with the situation. He was in a spot that was probably the assembly place of all his deadly enemies. He was poorly armed and felt he could, if the need arose, only rely on his strength. He had left all his possessions with Ben Nil. The abysmal coarseness of these people showed with every word they uttered. Their speeches were curses and every game ended in a quarrel. Leopold sat there for three hours until there was a loud knock at the door.

"The Colonel," called the soldier who had opened the door. His comrades rose too, but the dice they left lying on the mat. The Colonel was allowed to see them. When Leopold saw his face, he involuntarily thought of a bull ready to attack, with horns lowered. He threw a short glance at Leopold and ordered: "Come!"

But before going on, he ordered his soldiers to go over the back wall. "There was a fellow listening outside our front door. He ran away when he saw me. Should he come back, arrest him!"

With this he went to a well lit room. He turned round and asked:

"You have a letter for me?"

"Yes, from Sergeant Major Ben Ifram."

"Give it!"

Ibn Mulei received the letter, held it in his hand without looking at it, observed Leopold sharply and asked: "Your name?"

"Iskander Nikopolus."

"A Greek, where from?"

"I was born in Cairo. My parents were Greek."

"What are you doing in the seribah?"

"I am an interpreter. I was a long time with Negroes and understand their different languages."

"That brings you money without having to smell gun powder," he observed, contemptuously. "Let me see what Ben Ifram has to say." Luckily, his curiosity was greater than his caution. He did not notice that the seal was broken and tore the letter open. Leopold felt more at ease. "Do you know the content of this letter?"

"Ben Ifram has not told me."

"He doesn't seem to trust you very much."

"If that were true, he wouldn't have sent me to Fashodah."

"You will be hungry. You will receive some food and tell me about the seribah." He asked Leopold to sit down. Leopold would have preferred him to say goodbye. There was no doubt now that he was connected with the seribah, the sergeant major and Ben Mubarek. But he couldn't walk out without the permission of the Colonel. He had to submit and rely on his luck. He should tell the Colonel about the seribah. He wished now he had let Amr tell him more about it.

The Colonel returned after a short while. With him was a soldier who carried a small board with a large bone on it. It was the rest of a leg of beef with a shred of meat on it; but it looked as if dogs had fought for it. Leopold took his knife and tried his best to cut something off.

The Colonel asked: "How long have you been on the seribah?"

"For about two years," Leopold answered while trying hard to cut a digestible tendon off the bone.

"Who hired you?"

"Ben Mubarek himself; Amr Ben Makashef recommended me."

"The sheik of the Baggara? That speaks for you; he is a reliable acquaintance of ours. How is the sergeant major?"

"Not very well. His leg wound broke open again."

"Allah! He will probably die. Ben Mubarek had been away for months; what have you been doing in the mean time?"

"The men exercised diligently. I wasn't there."

"No? An interpreter belongs to the seribah. Where were you?"

"I have been with the Negro peoples to prepare a good catch. I was quite successful. The sergeant major gave me another task."

"Where did he send you?"

"To the Takaleh."

"Yes, we receive slaves from them, twice a year. Did you dare to go there?"

"Dare? I have been there several times. The King is well disposed to me and his intimate friend Shedid is a good friend of mine."

"You know Shedid the strong and you are his friend? Then you are a useful man indeed. How long are you staying here?"

"I mustn't delay for long. The ship that takes me to the isle of Matenieh leaves before midnight."

"Then you must eat quickly. But beware of the Reis Effendina and especially of the Jewish son of a dog who has done great damage to us."

"I don't fear him and have no reason to avoid him."

"You have a lot of reason to avoid him. You obviously haven't heard of him; let me tell you things about him."

Leopold was glad about the change of subject. He had succeeded in gaining the trust of the Colonel. Up to now, luck favoured him, but suddenly it changed. At the entrance door was a great commotion. A soldier came in and reported catching the fellow who tried to eavesdrop on them. "When we caught him, your friend the fat Turk just came by. He seemed to know him." After this he left. Leopold had the uncomfortable feeling it could be Ben Nil, worried about his being absent for so long.

The door opened and Ben Nil, the poor devil, was brought in. Five soldiers held him in their grip. Four more soldiers and the fat Turk came in as well. With the Colonel there were eleven people Leopold had to overcome in order to escape. There were more soldiers in the other room. Iron doors, his ignorance of the house and the uselessness of his weapons were what he considered in one instant. He had no time to consider further. The Colonel snarled at Ben Nil: "Who are you, son of a dog?"

The so asked had not seen Leopold and thought he could save himself by a simple lie. "I had no wrong intentions. I am a sailor in a ship which arrived here a while ago."

"Liar! Don't believe him!" entered the Turk. "I know him."

"Well then, tell me who he is."

"Colonel, our heart rejoices and you will be amazed. We have caught the friend of our fiercest opponent, whom Allah may curse."

"Which opponent?"

"This youth is Ben Nil, about whom we told you. Poldi Ben Anglesi cannot be far off. Whip him until he tells you where his boss is."

Leopold, who up to now stood unseen in a corner, stepped forward and called: "There is no need. I can tell you where I am."

The impression of this admission was different from what Leopold expected. He thought of surrendering without resisting and calculated better opportunities in the future. He expected that they would throw themselves at him, but the opposite happened. "Poldi Ben Anglesi himself!" shouted the Turk. "He is among us! Allah save us! Oh Allah, Allah." The shocked people stood like icons of marble. Some of them stood with their mouth open. Nobody moved. Leopold felt he must grab the opportunity. He jumped to Ben Nil, tore him loose and threw him out of the door. Now he worked with his fists. The soldiers flew back, left and right. Another jump and he was through the door. Ben Nil was still lying on the floor. Leopold stumbled over him and fell to the ground. Another door was torn open and hit him on the head. For a few seconds he was dazed, enough for the soldiers to grab him and Ben Nil and tie them up.

"Lift them up and put them against the wall," boomed the bass voice of the Colonel. Mocking and at the same time rejoicing, he continued: "What a lucky day! What a surprise. Did I hear right? Yes, he wouldn't have tried to escape if he wasn't the man he was pointed out to be."

"Pah!" countered Leopold, "I admitted myself who I am."

"What cheek, what impudence to admit it. What did you want from me? You didn't call without purpose?"

"Certainly not."

"Well, speak! What was your purpose?"

"Maybe I'll tell you later – not now."

The Colonel turned to the Turk: "This most cursed giour is worse and more dangerous than you described him to me. He told me his name was Iskander Nikopolus and pretended to be an interpreter from the seribah. He brought a letter which he probably wrote himself. What purpose lies behind that?"

"Nothing good, for sure. If he doesn`t tell you, thrash him until his pain makes him admit."

"I will do this right away."

"Then we will take him to Ben Mubarek where his fate, which was predestined, will overtake him."

"Yes," Leopold interrupted. "All my limbs will be torn from my body. But that will take a while yet. To learn what I have to say to you, you don't have to whip me. I came to you to warn you from Ben Mubarek and his people."

"What a warning," mocked the Colonel. "Are you mad?"

"Then the Mudir must be mad too. It is he who sent me to you."

"He? That's a lie, a threefold lie!"

"Ask Ben Nil, my companion. We are staying with the Mudir and he has told me to talk about Ben Mubarek to you."

Leopold noticed the Colonel's shock. He changed colour.

"Son of a dog, tell the truth," he ordered Ben Nil. "Where do you live?"

"In the Mudir's house," replied the youth.

"Did he speak about me?"

"Yes, as Poldi Ben Anglesi has told you already."

"You have conferred with another."

"Think what you like." Leopold said. "But I will tell you one more of my deeds. I have taken Amr el Makashef, the Baggara chief, prisoner. He is in Fashodah's prison now and will receive the five hundred."

"Rascal, what damage you are doing to us! I would like to crush you."

"You won't do that because if I am not back by midnight, the Mudir will arrest you."

"Don't believe him, he is lying to save himself," the Turk warned.

"I will know within minutes whether I can believe him." With these words the Colonel went outside. After he returned he went with the fat Turk to the furthermost corner of the room where they talked quietly but very lively together, until a soldier came in.

"Well?" asked the Colonel loudly.

"The sheik of the Baggara is tied up and in prison," reported the man.

"Put the prisoners on the floor and get out."

Leopold and Ben Nil were put on the ground again while the Colonel and the Turk went into the corner and quarrelled. Ibn Mulei then came to Leopold, spat in his face and said: "You arranged everything very well, but it won't help you. We will never see you again. The devil devour you mangy dogs!" He, the Turk and all the others left the room.

Leopold and Ben Nil were alone. Leopold did not want to reproach Ben Nil, who had been driven by worry to commit the stupidity. It wouldn't help matters as they were now. Ben Nil began himself: "Effendi, I have committed a great stupidity for which you cannot possibly forgive me. Pour out your wrath against me. It is better than your silence!"

"I am not angry with you," Leopold consoled him. "You brought harm to yourself, not me."

"If I had not come, you would be free now."

"You are mistaken. The Turk would have recognised me anyway."

"If that is your view then I am less worried about your anger, but not about what we have to expect. They will surely kill us."

"I still hope. I have no intention of giving up. I have been in more difficult situations without losing my courage. I am sure that nothing will happen to us in Fashodah."

Four men came in, carrying large bast-mats and strings. The prisoners were gagged and rolled up in these mats. The strings were used to wind round the stiff parcels. They were lifted up and carried. They couldn't see where to. When they heard the splashing of water, they knew they were on a boat. "Now away, fast and carefully," they heard a commanding voice say.

Now they heard the sound of rowing. When Fashodah was passed the voices became louder, but there was nothing of significance spoken. Many hours passed. Leopold could not assess how many.

Chapter 15

Judgement in the Sudan

When they reached a ship, they heard a voice asking from above: "Who is there?"

"People from the Colonel. Is Ben Mubarek there?"

"No, come up here."

The prisoners were lifted onto the ship. They could not hear what was spoken but discerned sounds of joyous surprise. They were unrolled from their wrapping and their almost choking gags were removed. There were twenty men on board. Leopold could see their faces in the moonlight. The journey had lasted for many hours. No wonder he had lost count in these conditions.

Nearest to Leopold stood Murad Nassyr, the Turk. Leopold didn't fear him as much as his accomplices, who had more energy. The fat Turk spoke to a man who had brought the prisoners. "Ben Mubarek is expected here any time now. He will bring Dshangeh people he had to hire because the stinking dog here arrested most of his men."

These words proved that Murad Nassyr was not very clever. It was a mistake to talk about Ben Mubarek hiring a band of Dshangeh for a slave-hunt. Now he turned to Leopold to ask a poisoned question: "Do you still remember the threats I uttered when we last parted? You stinking dog! I told you I would crush you if I should see you again. Now I see you. Prepare for death. You are lost. You can expect no mercy here."

Murad Nassyr must have thought Leopold would reply, but he received no answer. He kicked him and asked: "Open your mouth, you dirty toad! Or has fear made you dumb?"

Leopold laughed loudly. "Fear of you? My dear fatty, don't make me laugh. Nobody fears you and I the least. You can devour rice and sheep's flesh, but not me."

"Son of a dog! Are you mocking me as well? I shall double your torture!"

"Leave me alone. Your playing the avenger is ridiculous. You know already that bragging does not impress me. Go to sleep. That is better than your useless attempt to make me fear you."

Murad Nassyr gave Leopold a second kick. "You will pay for that. You know the tortures destined for you. They will now be even more horrible than you know. Don't believe you can escape this time. I will personally guard you until Ben Mubarek returns. Lift these dogs and follow me." His command was obeyed. The prisoners were carried to a room partitioned with a linen canvas. He tested their fetters, gave Leopold another kick and said: "I live in the next room and can hear everything you say. If I don't like it, you will be whipped."

He went into his room. The prisoners heard voices, one of them female. They assumed that it was the Turk's sister, Kumru. They could see the shadows move. After a while of whispering, he stood up and went outside, followed by his kin. Just then the curtain was lifted and the favourite maid servant of Kumru appeared.

"Effendi, where are you?"

"Here," Leopold answered. "Who are you?"

"I am Fatma, you know me."

"What do you want from me?" he asked.

"My mistress sent me. She knows you would be killed and that hurts her."

"Allah bless Kumru for her sympathy!"

"Yes, she is good, she wants to save you."

"Hamdulillah! In which way?"

"Unfortunately, she cannot do much, but what is possible should be done. You saved her hair from falling out. She has not forgotten. She wants to thank you and asked your wishes."

"Where is your mistress?"

"Outside on deck. She persuaded her brother to go there, for me to be able to talk to you."

"If he suddenly returns and sees what you are doing?"

"She will keep him outside until I give her a sign that I have carried out my task."

"That's good. Bring me a sharp knife."

Fatma scurried out and soon brought a knife, including its sheath, and passed it to Leopold. "I can't grasp it, I must ask you to kindly cut me loose."

"Allah, what are you asking of me? My hands are trembling with fear. But I will do it because you are the benefactor of my mistress."

Leopold felt the trembling of her hands when she cut the strings. Then he took the knife and pressed her hand. "I thank you, Fatma, you're delightful. May Allah reward you. Do you know how many men are on board?"

"Twenty and a few. They are lying outside and they are sleeping."

"Where are the people who brought us from Fashodah?"

"They are still here among the others."

"So is their boat still beside the ship?"

"Yes."

"That is what I want to know. You can go and you don't have to give your mistress any sign. She will learn in a few minutes that you have executed your task. We will probably meet again when I will thank you better than I can now." Fatma withdrew.

"What bliss, Effendi!" Ben Nil breathed again. "You were right. One shouldn't give up hope. We are saved if they don't stop us."

"Stop us? If I am in free possession of my limbs and have a knife in my hand, twenty men wouldn't stop me. It is as if we were free already."

After cutting Ben Nil's ties Leopold lifted the canvas a little. Near the ship he saw three trees in the shape of chandeliers. They would serve as a sign to look out for later. On deck were the people asleep, except, of course, the Turk and his sister, who stood at the helm looking down into the flood. The boat that had brought them must be on the water side. The ship was anchored on a metal chain which was near where they were imprisoned.

"We will climb down on these chains and swim to the boat. The water will do us good in these climes." It was easy. While swimming they kept near the ship and avoided the making sound of splashing. To their delight, the oars had been left inside the boat.

"Let's get away quickly," ventured Ben Nil. "Don't let us waste a minute." But they were spotted already.

"The prisoners are loose." shouted Murad Nassyr. "A thousand piaster to whoever brings them back." Confused voices were heard from the deck. Everybody hurried to get into the boat that belonged to the ship. It was at the rear near the helm." Quickly, quickly," Murad Nassyr shouted again. "Two thousand, three thousand piaster when you catch them."

"Ten thousand piaster for the one who catches us," laughed Leopold, answering. Then he dipped his oar into the water. Ben Nil did the same. Both were excellent oarsmen and the boat flew down the flow of the river as an arrow from a bow. After only a short while, they couldn't see the ship. After a quarter of an hour, they relaxed their strenuous efforts. They had no worries they would be overtaken.

Looking at the sky, it was about three o'clock in the morning. According to Leopold's estimate, it was five hours since they had been taken prisoner. They were about an hour on the ship, that would leave a four hour journey up stream. As the journey was now down river, he reckoned to make it back in three hours. That meant they would reach Fashodah about six o'clock in the morning.

They were both in a jubilant mood. And what did they have to thank for their rescue? Simple advice from Leopold to the Turk's sister, Kumru, on how to prevent the falling out of her hair. She was a good and grateful girl, and Leopold decided he would do his utmost to prevent her marrying Ben Mubarek.

At dawn they reached Fashodah. A small sailing boat crossed the river to and fro. There was only one man in it. When he saw Leopold and Ben Nil, he dropped the sail, came nearer and asked: "Where are you coming from?"

"From up there." Leopold pointed backward.

"Who are you?"

"Why do you ask? Are you an official of the Mudir?"

"No, but I am looking for a Poldi Ben Anglesi Effendi and a young man called Ben Nil. They disappeared last night without trace. The Mudir sent people to find them. As you are two whom I don't know and the description fits you, I believe you are the right ones."

"Do you know the Colonel of the soldiers here?"

"I have seen him, but never spoken to him."

"Do you like or hate him?"

"The answer to this question is likely to cause trouble. As I have nothing good or bad to expect from him, I can answer that I neither love nor hate him."

"Well, I will admit that we are the ones the Mudir seeks."

"Hamdulillah! It is I who will earn all the money."

"What money?"

"The hundred piaster the Mudir will pay for you."

"You will have them, although he would have seen us without you."

"He would?" asked the man disappointedly. "Allah! So I won't receive the money."

"The Mudir will give it to you. Only ask him."

"No, I won't. I would receive five hundred lashes instead."

"You will receive the money. I give you my word. If he doesn't give it to you, I will, but I have one condition. Take me to the Mudir without the Colonel or any one of the soldiers seeing us."

The man looked at Leopold wonderingly. "Are the soldiers guilty of your disappearance?"

"I can't tell you that. I don't know you."

"You can trust me. I am Denab, a poor fisherman. Everything I catch goes to the Mudir."

"Where do you live?"

"Here, outside the town. You can see my hut at the bank. Far from the other houses. You will wait there, and I will report your story to the Mudir. He will decide what to do."

"Good, I agree."

"But you mustn't follow me in your boat. I think it is best if I take one of you. The other will wait here at the river bank until I collect him. Two of you together would be too conspicuous."

Leopold jumped into his boat and was taken to the hut. The fisherman's wife received the order not to let anybody in. Then he collected Ben Nil.

It took more than an hour before the fisherman returned. He brought two outfits, one for Leopold as a eunuch, and he had to paint his face black; the other was female attire for Ben Nil. It included a veil.

Ben Nil was amused and chuckled, more about Leopold's face than about himself. They walked for about fifteen minutes without meeting anyone. That was probably because they were all searching for the missing two, hoping to earn the hundred piaster. At the government building, they were expected by a servant, who took them to the Mudir. He had arranged they wouldn't meet anyone.

Ali Effendi, the Mudir, sat on a silken sofa, smoking. When Leopold and Ben Nil entered, his usually serious face changed to a smile. It appeared he was trying not to break out laughing loudly. "Allah does wonders! Whoever saw a eunuch with such a beard." Leopold hadn't shaved for a long time. He really looked odd. The Mudir turned to the fisherman: "Wait outside until I decide whether I will give you the money."

Leopold and Ben Nil sat down next to the Mudir. They lit their pipes and Leopold had to tell him what happened. The Governor listened. His facial expression betrayed no emotion. He kept silent for a while after Leopold had finished. Then he clapped his hands. A servant came in and received the order: "Go to the Colonel and tell him I wish to speak to him. Tell him it is a secret and he shouldn't let anybody know where he is going. Before you go there, send me 'Abu Chabta', the 'father of thrashing'."

The man went. After a short while, a squarely-built fellow entered. He put both hands on his chest and bowed nearly to the ground.

"There will be work for you," said the Mudir. "A dog of all dogs will receive five hundred and will never be seen again."

The 'father of thrashing' grinned, bowed down and left.

When they were alone, the Mudir asked: "Do you know why the Colonel should come secretly?"

"I think it is for your safety."

"Allah! You guessed it," called Ali Effendi, astonished.

"It's not difficult. If they knew you caused the Colonel's death, there would be a revolt."

"Ibn Mulei should receive his punishment without his soldiers knowing it. This son of a dog is a murderer and accomplice of slave-hunters. You will hear what I say to him. Go into the side room when he comes. When I need you, you will enter again at the right moment."

They went into the room to which the Mudir pointed. To his joy, Leopold found all his belongings. There was also what he needed to clean himself of his black colour. He also changed his attire while Ben Nil had to keep his on, because his suit was with the fisherman. The door consisted only of a carpet. They heard the Colonel enter.

"You have called me, O Mudir?

"Yes: Does anybody know you are here?"

"Nobody."

"Did you hear anything about the lost men I am seeking?"

"Nothing has been discovered so far."

"That's bad. I will not rest until I find them."

"I too have done my utmost. All my soldiers have gone to search for them, although they can't understand that I asked them to find the trace of a stinking unbeliever."

"I want to find him. That's enough. Have you searched your own place?"

"Yes, but in vain."

"Strange! Poldi Ben Anglesi went to you, his companions have heard him knocking at your door."

"That is possible, but when the door was opened, there was nobody to be seen. My guards noticed some figures who crept round the house. Who knows what intentions this unbeliever had and why he suddenly disappeared?"

"Poldi Ben Anglesi has told me his intentions. There was no reason for him to vanish, but there are people who have motives to let him disappear."

"I advise you to ask these people."

"I have done so, but they deny knowing anything."

"Give them five hundred and they will confess."

"I will follow your advice and you will be present."

"I thank you, O master. It will be bliss to be present to hear these dogs howl. But now I ask you to please tell me the secret reason why I should come to you."

"It is a secret and you are the man to help me. Do you know a Turk with the name of Murad Nassyr?"

"No, what about him?"

"Do you know a Ben Mubarek or Shedid?"

"I have heard of Ben Mubarek but never met him. The other one I do not know. Why do you ask me about these people?"

"They are, or will shortly be in Fashodah. You will help me to find them."

"If they are here, I will certainly discover them."

"Further, there is a ship, about four hours by boat from here, that belongs to Ben Mubarek."

"Allah, Allah!"

Up to now, the Colonel had spoken unaffectedly. The last exclamation he made in shock. "The ship was observed," the Mudir continued. "A boat with two long parcels was arriving there. These parcels were heaved on board. Do you know what they contained?"

"How could I know that?" answered the Colonel, depressed. "If you want me to find out, I will find that ship. The parcels must still be there."

"They are so important to me, I have thought of a reward for you. The size of which you have no idea."

"Mudir, I am the most loyal of your servants," reassured Ibn Mulei, flattered. "My happiness consists of your kindness and grace."

"Yes, you are the most loyal of all. I have, therefore, selected a most beautiful wife for you. A wife to whom the most beautiful haura of paradise cannot be compared."

"A wife?" called the Colonel, amazed and disappointed.

"Yes, a prototype of beauty and virtue, a sample of loveliness. You should see this angel right now. Enter and unveil your face, to make Ibn Mulei sink to his knees before the sight of your eyes."

The last words were for Ben Nil who, in his female outfit, entered.

"A woman, really a woman! What a surprise. Is she still a girl? What colour is she – black or white?"

"See for yourself. See and be amazed."

Ibn Mulei rose and removed her veil. The result was as expected. Ibn Mulei uttered an unintelligible shriek.

"Well, how do you like the girl? Aren't you delighted?" asked the Mudir, deliberately arranging that the Colonel's back was turned toward an entering Leopold. "You are speechless with bliss," mocked the Mudir. "If the view of one parcel delights you so much, turn around and look at the other one."

Ibn Mulei, who stood speechless, turned around, thoughtlessly. When he saw Leopold, he regained his composure. "Hell and damnation," he shouted, "you have been playing with me. The devil will annihilate the three of you." With that he went for the door. Leopold saw this coming and stood in his way. "Away with you, son of a dog, you revolt me."

137

"Is that the reason why you said we won't see each other again?" said Leopold mockingly. "I was convinced I would meet you again because I have to settle an account with you."

"Away! Or I force my way." Ibn Mulei pulled his knife and lifted his arm for a hit. Leopold punched him from below at his elbow to make him drop the blade, lifted him up and threw him on the ground. For a moment he thought that the Colonel had broken his neck.

"Allah, Allah!" called the Mudir. "The Reis Effendina has told me about your strength. I wouldn't believe it. Is he dead?"

"No," declared Leopold, "Ibn Mulei will soon move to suddenly..."

He couldn't end his sentence. What he expected, happened. The Colonel, suddenly, took a pistol from his belt and aimed it at Leopold. His immobility was a trick. Ben Nil, who stood behind him, seized the hand with the pistol. Leopold, at the same time, kicked him in the stomach to throw him backward and make him drop the weapon. The kick robbed him of the ability to get up. He clenched his fist against Leopold and uttered curses which are impossible to repeat here.

"Leave him!" ordered the Mudir. "The rascal is not worth being touched by your hands." Ali Effendi clapped his hands. Two blacks entered at this sign, grabbed the Colonel and pulled him up. When he saw the men who did the lashing, he roared at the Mudir:

"You are not going to have me beaten?"

"I intend to fulfil your own will. You have given me the excellent advice of the bastinado. And now it will be executed on you."

"Do you know what that means?"

"Nothing other than a dog will get beaten."

"But this dog has teeth! A small sign from me and my soldiers attack you. You don't know me yet."

"I know you well. I have named your friends before; that makes it superfluous to enumerate your sins. If you think I don't know you, I know that you know me. I am called Abu Hamsa Mia. You'll get the five hundred."

"Five – hun – dred!" shouted the Colonel. "That will cost you your life."

"Don't threaten. Beg Allah to lead you safely over the 'Bridge of Death' so that you won't fall into the fire of hell."

"The 'Bridge – of – Hell'. So you – want – to beat me – to death?"

"I have ordered you to receive five hundred and you won't be seen any more. And what I ordered will happen."

"Not yet, not yet! I still have arms and hands to tear you apart." Ibn Mulei intended to throw himself on the Mudir, but the assistants of the 'Father of Five Hundred' had practice. They held him down and, in no time, a leather was strapped over his head and chin. The jaw was tightly pressed against its upper part to stop him shouting. They then carried him out.

"The rogue gets what he deserves," said the pitiless judge. "We will be witnesses."

"Not I," Leopold warded off the invitation. "I renounce my presence at such a scene."

"Do you have weak nerves? An official who wants to go the way of justice must not have them. I will not force you. Wait here for me."

"Stay for a moment, O Mudir, I have something important to tell you."

"What is it?"

"I reckon Ben Mubarek's ship will have sailed away after we escaped, but I expect Shedid and his group to have arrived. They are not likely to come to Fashodah without contacting the Colonel first. Could we move into the Colonel's house to intercept any messenger he is going to send?"

It was late that evening when Leopold, Ben Nil, Sinan the trader and Hafid Sichar moved there. The soldiers, but for a few, were sent to Kuck to collect taxes. Woe to these poor people. They had to pay ordinary taxes plus maintenance for the soldiers, the amount of which the military determined themselves. When these tax-soldiers came, whole families took flight with their possessions, to return only when the soldiers had gone.

It was the next day when the expected messenger arrived. He was led to Leopold and was not a little perplexed to see him instead of Ibn Mulei, the Colonel. It was the threat of the bastinado that made him betray the place where Shedid and the caravan were. Before they went there Leopold reminded the Mudir about the fisherman who still waited for his reward. He was called. The Mudir asked him whether he expected the reward.

"If your kindness permits, I hope so," answered Denab humbly.

"My kindness permits nothing. They would have returned without you. You can, however choose being paid with five hundred lashes."

"I declare being paid," answered the anxious man.

The 'father of five hundred' was a friend of justice, but making payments which were not absolutely necessary was not one of his passions.

The fisherman walked to the door. He turned round and asked Leopold:

"Will you keep your word? I am a poor man."

"What word should you keep?" asked the Mudir.

"I promised Denab that I would pay him the hundred piaster," answered Leopold, pulling out his purse.

"You wanted to give him the hundred piaster? You are my guest and have to pay nothing. Didn't you hear he declared himself paid?"

"I heard it, but I didn't see it. Permit me to give it to him."

"If you insist, he will receive it from me. But money I haven't got. Taxes are paid in animals and fruit and I can only pay in this currency. Let him go to my shepherd and receive three sheep. And now away with him."

The first forty soldiers returning from their task to levy taxes were given to Leopold by the Mudir. The messenger had to walk between Ben Nil and Hafid Sichar, who told him that the tiniest betrayal would be punished with death.

Caution required a detour. Shedid would direct his attention toward Fashodah. They entered the wood from the south instead of the east. Because they came from a different direction, the messenger lost orientation and Leopold went to find the place by himself.

As luck would have it, he quickly found the resting place of the caravan. He observed them from behind trees. The camp lay favourably for Leopold's group. It was enclosed on two sides by bushes which allowed unnoticed approach. Leopold brought his soldiers and placed them behind the shrubbery.

It was in Leopold's adventurous and fun loving nature to make the short walk, approaching the group from the Fashodah direction, by himself. The Takaleh jumped up in surprise when they recognised him.

"The Mudir from Dsharabub!" they shouted.

Leopold was as fearless as if there had never been any discord between them. He went nearer and greeted them.

"You are here in the area of Fashodah. How did you get here?" asked Shedid with a dark expression on his face.

"On my camel."

"What do you want in Fashodah? This is suspicious. Why didn't you tell me that you are going to Fashodah?"

"Because you asked where we were coming from, but not where we were going."

"Did you arrive here today?"

"No, we came earlier. We live in town with the Colonel, or rather in his house."

"You know I know him. I have sent a messenger to him. Is he at home?"

"Not any more. He is in heaven or in hell."

"Allah! So he died?"

"Yes; yesterday."

"What did he die of?"

"He died from the bastinado."

"Oh Allah, oh Mohammed, oh prophet! Do you want to tell me that he was beaten to death?"

"To be sure."

"A Colonel beaten to death. That could only happen by order of the Mudir, and he was his friend."

"Yes, the previous one, but not the present Mudir. He extirpates slave-hunters and slave-dealers."

"Is there a new one now?"

"Yes, the previous Mudir, Ali Effendi el Kurdi, was dismissed because he favoured the slave-trade. The new Mudir's name is also Ali Effendi, but he is known as Abu Hamsa Mia because he gives every slave-dealer five hundred lashes."

"Allah be with us! Our calculations are all wrong. I fear for my messenger. If the Mudir catches him, he will have to tell him why we came to Fashodah."

"That doesn't matter."

"It doesn't matter? You just told us that every slave-dealer receives five hundred lashes and we are here to sell slaves."

"But you didn't catch them. They are owned by your King who sent you to Fashodah. You had to obey. He cannot punish you, but he will forbid you to sell them."

"Allah be thanked. Your words ease my worries. I don't have to be anxious about myself as you are about yourself."

"I, to worry about myself? Why?"

"You are not the man you pretended to be. When you left I thought about various points of your assertions which I found suspicious. The more I thought about it, the more I was sure that you were not from Dsharabub. Now you are in my hands again and you had better tell me the truth. I know ways to get it out of you."

"Pah! What is it to you who I am?"

"I am very concerned, because I have, in my credulity, told you things that shouldn't be known to everybody, especially if you were this damned Poldi Ben Anglesi."

"Hm! That is true, but you can't change it now."

"I can't change it?" asked Shedid, while looking at Leopold in surprise. "What does that mean?"

"It means I am the damned Poldi Ben Anglesi."

"Son of a dog! You dare to tell me that?"

"Why not? I can't see any daring. I want to tell you even more.

141

When we left you, the Baggara and Hafid Sichar disappeared. I freed Hafid Sichar and took Amr, the sheik of the Baggara, prisoner. He is now in Fashodah and awaits five hundred lashes. What you told me about the Colonel was fatal for him. He received the bastinado and died."

"You are guilty of his death and you brag about it? That should be revenged right away. I will crush you with my fists."

"Don't dare to touch me, you may come to harm."

"I? Come to harm? Show me how I may come to harm," shouted Shedid and attacked Leopold.

The latter easily evaded the giant Takaleh, who pressed even more impetuously forward, not paying attention to Leopold's words nor the shouting of his people, who saw the soldiers with Ben Nil surrounding them. Shedid had eyes only for Leopold. While attacking, Shedid stumbled over a root. Leopold grabbed him and held him down while Ben Nil and a few soldiers came and tied him up. The giant grated his teeth with rage; his eyes were suffused with blood.

The Takaleh were quickly subdued. They were not prepared for such an attack. They were disarmed and sat in a group with soldiers with rifles surrounding them. Leopold turned to Shedid: "You are coming with us to Fashodah, I will hand you to the Mudir."

"What should I do there? You assured me that he can have nothing against us for obeying our King."

"He can't do anything to you for your intention to sell slaves, but for robbing and murdering he will punish you."

"What are you talking about?"

Leopold turned to Ben Nil: "Search his belongings, including the saddle-bag of his camel."

"I don't know which camel is his." One of the slaves pointed it out. It contained, among other things, two bags of gold dust.

"Where have you got that from?"

"When I travel, I take my possessions with me."

Sinan the trader, who had kept himself in the background, stepped forward. "Yes, these are two of the six bags he has robbed from us after he killed my brothers."

"This is a lie, fabricated to intimidate me," roared Shedid.

"We will soon find out," said Leopold. He turned to Shedid's companions. "You remember your caravan met three traders. Your leader and four of you then killed and robbed them. Before that he sent you ahead so as not to share with you. In order not to be punished for that, will you point out who the others were."

Shedid tried to prevent them answering, saying: "We are neither

142

robbers nor murderers and none of my people will humble himself to answer to an unbeliever."

There was a movement away from the culprits, but Sinan said: That is not necessary, I know which ones they are. Let's search their saddle-bags."

The soldiers did and four more bags with gold-dust and gold grains were found. The other culprits were immediately tied up. Against such superiority there was no use defending themselves.

Leopold had his reason to sequester the gold on the spot. If it went to Fashodah, the Mudir, most likely, would keep some, if not all, of it. He took Sinan, the trader, aside and asked: "Do you know the families of your murdered companions?"

"Of course, my companions were my brothers."

"I think you are an honest man. I am giving you all the gold. You will give their families the right share."

"May Allah bless you for this, but please take one or two bags for yourself." The happy trader wanted to pass two bags to Leopold.

"I have no right to take any, and I repeat, I won't take any."

"But the Mudir will be very angry with you."

"Let him be. I don't mind, but you should worry that he doesn't catch up with you and take the gold from you. Leave your donkeys, take a camel and make a wide detour to your destination. Go east instead of south. About half an hour from here is a large stretch of stony ground. Anyone following you will lose your tracks. Before the end of this stretch turn in the direction of your home. Go soon and don't mention the gold to anybody you might meet on the way."

"Thank you, thank you. I will go right now. Allah may bless you. You are of a different faith, Effendi. I wish all Moslems were like you." He pressed Leopold's hand to his lips and rushed away.

Marching off was made difficult by Shedid's struggling. He was in fetters but possessed uncanny strength to make trouble, even in this condition. It was only Ben Nil's whip which made it possible to march off.

The caravan created no little sensation when they marched through Fashodah. Old and young ran after them until they disappeared into the government building. When Leopold reported to the Mudir, the first question, as expected, was a request for the gold. He looked at Leopold with angry eyes when he was told to whom Leopold had given the bags of gold-dust. He ranted and walked about with grim gesticulation. He finally stood before Leopold and snorted at him: "I am going to catch this trader. I must have the gold-dust, I must. Do you understand?"

"And if you don't catch him?"

"Then I chase you to the devil! Are you listening?"

"With that, will you get the gold?"

"Unfortunately not, but at least I have a revenge – ah, revenge, that reminds me of the Takaleh who have the robbery and murder on their conscience. If I don't get the gold – they will have to pay for it."

With this, the Mudir's anger was diverted to people who deserved it more than Leopold. Ali Effendi ordered to lock up every person belonging to the caravan. Guilty or not guilty. Then he sent out every soldier to catch Sinan and his gold. Leopold withdrew to his room until, in the evening, he was called to the Mudir. He snarled at Leopold: "Sinan, this son of a dog, is gone, and with him the gold-dust which belongs to the government. No-one knows where he is gone. He didn't even collect his donkeys. I called to bring me the Takalehs. You will come as witness when I hold court over these dogs."

Ali Effendi led Leopold to the court yard where all the Takalehs were assembled and guarded. Many spectators filled the place.

It is superfluous to describe the judicial proceeding. Shedid and his accomplices were to receive the 'five hundred' and no longer be seen. The others, except the slaves because they were part of the slave caravan, were given ten lashes. The work began and was factory-wise executed. Those who received 'only' ten lashes, took them – in the words of the German poet Uhland – 'mit schlichtem Heldentum' – with plain or simple heroism.

Among the 'slaves', not one of them wanted to return home. They feared the possibility of being sold again. They asked Leopold's advice. He told them of the soon expected Reis Effendina who needed people for his forthcoming pursuance of the slave-hunters. The Takaleh men, known as being valiant, would have a good chance. He would probably employ few women. For the majority of females he had, however, no advice.

Chapter 16

Ben Nil's surprising question

A journey on the White Nile is, if you sail up river in daytime, and up to the junction of the Sobat, favoured by a good north wind. When you reach the mentioned river, you can, because of the numerous bends, hardly use the wind. One only uses sails if the Nile and the wind go in the proper direction. Otherwise one has to help oneself with push-rods or ropes to pull the ship.

When the banks are dry, one is happy, because most of them are swampy. In this case, boats have to pull the ship. Even that is not always possible. There are whole stretches with Om Sufah, through which one cannot row. The only things left are push-rods. It sometimes takes a whole day to get through such a field.

The Reis Effendina's arrival and business in Fashodah was quickly accomplished. He praised the Mudir for his effective ways to mete justice. He took on many of the former 'slaves' and sailed away the same day. He was in a hurry to catch Ben Mubarek and his accomplices at the seribah Aliab. Except that nobody actually knew where to find it.

The Reis also brought letters from England, addressed to Leopold Ellman. Leopold opened them with a bad conscience. Latest events prevented him from writing himself. His mother's letter showed the expected worry on the question of his intended time of return. The letter of his fiancé, Sarah, was in similar vein with an added section, mentioning his praise of his companion Ben Nil. It was almost like an advertisement, and her younger sister bought it. She became really interested. When she explained to her that Ben Nil was of a different religion, she answered flippantly, "I thought by his name that he was Jewish. In any case, he could change." Leopold expected Ben Nil to smile when he told him of his chances, but he became serious and answered:

"Do you remember the first few weeks after you engaged me?"

"I do, but what in particular are you referring to?"

"I have persuaded you, on many occasions, to change your religion for what I regarded as the only true one for this life and assuring bliss for the next."

"You say 'I regarded'; does this mean you changed your mind?"

"Let me answer this in my own way: I observed you in your dealings with people, I saw you at prayers, you have answered my many questions matter of factly without ever trying to change my belief. I observed my co-believers – yes, I changed my mind regarding my own religion, but have to know more about yours."

"Our religion has no missionaries. We don't invite anybody to join us. On the contrary, our rabbis warn you not to take on what might prove to demand too much of you."

"Does that mean it is not possible to convert to your religion?"

"No, but the rabbis make sure you have no alternative reasons, such as pecuniary ones, or marriage. They want to make sure your reason for changing is genuine belief."

"So, for the moment, promise me to answer more questions and tell the sister of your betrothed not to give up just yet."

"This promise is easily given, but now let us take a boat and hunt for some food. In this climate, venison rots after two hours." The river was rather wide at the junction of the Rohl. The sun was burning pitilessly and no trees offered shade. There was reed, nothing but reed. The sailors were tired from pushing the ship with rods and it was decided to throw anchor at the spot. Leopold was providing all sorts of meat for the crew.   Sometimes, when he went hunting, he was accompanied by Pulo, a Negro boy whom he had freed, with his sister, from slavery. They belonged to the Dinka tribe. The Reis Effendina took them on his boat where they worked according to their ability.

Pulo slept at the moment and did, of course, not accompany Leopold. It was hot, too hot even for the animals. The whole of nature seemed to be asleep. To endure the heat, they had, from time to time, to moisten their head and chest. After an hour looking in vain for anything to shoot, Ben Nil suggested returning to the ship. Leopold, who did not want to go back empty handed, stood up to see better. Indeed, he noticed something that moved toward them. From the distance he couldn't make out what it was. He saw a light top and a dark lower part. He took it for a large swimming bird. So as not to be seen, he quickly sat down again. He raised his gun for a shot, but when the 'swimming bird' was near enough, he recognised it to be a black man with white head gear.

"A Negro," whispered Ben Nil. "Should we speak to him?"

"Naturally, he might tell us where we could find the seribah Aliab. He rows fast, let's overtake him!"

When the Negro heard the sound of the boat behind him, he was shocked and rowed with all his might. He wants to escape, thought Leopold, this is extremely suspicious. Only when Leopold gave one shot in the air, did the Negro stop rowing. His face expressed fear and malice.

"Which tribe do you belong to?"

"I am a Bongo," he answered.

"Where do you want to go?"

"To Fashodah; I want to become a soldier. I have heard they are looking for soldiers."

"That is true. You will probably be taken."

"Do you believe so? Are you coming from there?"

"Yes, I was there."

"Do you know the Colonel of the soldiers there?"

"Very well,"

"Is Ibn Mulei still alive?"

"Why shouldn't he be alive?"

"Because – because – because…"

He stammered. Leopold took his gun in hand and spoke to him harshly: "You lied! You are no Bongo. They are brown, but you are black. A Bongo never has his forehead tattooed like you. We will get to know you better. Our ship is nearby. Row slowly before us. Any attempt to escape will reward you with a bullet in your head."

The man saw resistance was impossible. He rowed downstream, slowly. When they reached the 'Hawk' the Negro had to tie his boat next to his captors. On entering the ship he made the impression of a man who is aware of his innocence. But Leopold noticed the worried glances as he observed his surroundings. The Reis Effendina asked why Leopold brought him aboard. He thought the man looked harmless.

"There must be a reason why he lied to us. That he wants to be a soldier isn't true. His question about Abu Mulei increased my suspicion. I think somebody has sent him to the Colonel."

"Not Ben Mubarek?"

"Either him or another slave-hunter."

The man was searched. Neither he nor the search of his boat yielded anything. They had no right to retain him. Leopold asked him if he knew where the seribah Aliab was: The man's glance flew over the ship, the Reis Effendina and Leopold and he answered: "Yes, I know it."

His glance spoke volumes. Leopold concluded that the man knew on whose vessel he was and whom he had in front of him. His instruction must have come from somebody. Most likely from Ben Mubarek. Reason enough to take his statements with care. "Well, where is it?"

"Over there," he said and pointed in the direction of Bahr es Dshebel. "About four days' journey from here."

"What kind of people live there?"

"A tribe of the Dshur-people." He gave his answers slowly. One could see and hear that he was thinking about every word. But he didn't possess the necessary self-control to suppress a trait of slyness. He enjoyed internally the hoax he thought he was playing.

Leopold pretended to believe him and continued asking:

"Do you know it well? Have you ever been there?"

"I was there," maintained the Negro, not knowing that the last question was a trap.

"So you know exactly what you say. How is it that the Tuitsh live there, but not the Dshur?"

"The Tuitsh?" He was embarrassed. "They don't live there."

"But they do! They live on the right bank of the Bahr es Dshebel whereas the Kitsh have their huts on the left. The distance is, as you tell us, four days, but I know that, even with a favourable wind, the journey would take twenty-five days. You want to send us in the wrong direction. Your lies were too coarse and therefore transparent."

"I don't lie, Effendi."

"Effendi? You are giving me this title – so you know me?"

The man's embarrassment grew, but he answered quickly. "I call every distinguished white man like this."

"So you think I am a distinguished man, but you still think yourself cleverer than I am. Of everything you have said, only one thing is true; that you know the seribah. You come from there. Tell me: To whom does the seribah belong? As you have been there, you must know!"

"It belongs – it belongs – to a white man whose name I have forgotten."

"Rather say that you don't want to name him. His name is Ben Mubarek – isn't it?"

"Yes," he answered, hesitatingly.

"All right, you know this man. You are one of the Dinkas he recruited at the White Nile. Ben Mubarek has sent you with a message to the Colonel in Fashodah and told you that you might meet the Reis Effendina or me. He has described us and told you how to behave if you meet us. Will you deny that?"

The man's mind could not work out that Leopold had reached these conclusions by a simple way of thinking. He looked perplexed and kept silent. "Answer!" Leopold said brusquely.

"It isn't as you think," assured the Negro. "I am a Bongo and cannot tell you anything else."

This stubbornness would even have embarrassed Leopold if something unexpected had not happened. Pulo, the Negro boy whom, with his sister Dahangeh, Leopold had saved from slavery while in Cairo, had woken up. Pulo walked to the group gathered around the man questioned. He looked at the Negro and stood large-eyed and petrified for a few moments – then he yelled: "Agadi, aba charang!"

These words belong to the dialect of the tribe to which these siblings belonged. Their meaning was 'Agadi, brother of my father', in other words 'uncle'. The so-called had not noticed the children, but when he heard his name, he turned quickly. They rushed to him. His surprise was so great that he allowed them to hug him without resisting. They wept with joy and climbed all over him. His numbness loosened in a shrill cry of rapture. He pressed the children to his chest and danced with them on the deck. He roared words in the Dinka language which Leopold did not understand. He only knew some phrases. Finally, they became quieter and sat down.

They talked for about half an hour without being disturbed. The Reis Effendina and Leopold waited for the result. When the man had learned everything he came with a joyful face to Leopold, bowed deeply and said in the Arabic language: "Effendi, forgive me. I didn't know about these children and what you have done for them. You are a good man and not as bad as I have been told."

" So you did know me?"

"Yes, when I saw the ship, I knew who you were."

"So, as I assumed, we have been described to you."

"Yes, by Ben Mubarek."

"You belong to his warriors?"

"Yes, I belong to the Dinkas whom he recruited. I am their leader."

"You have a message to take to Fashodah?"

"Yes, a letter to Ibn Mulei, the Colonel."

"We didn't find the letter. You must have a good hiding place."

"Effendi, I have given my word to Ben Mubarek that I will deliver it to the Colonel."

"You are an honest man. Ben Mubarek is a rascal who, most probably, wants to cheat you."

"Cheat me? How?"

"You are the leader of the Dinkas. As such he couldn't do without you. Nevertheless, he has sent you away. It has to be assumed that he had no honest intentions. Your people should not be without a leader. Did he not have a white person whom he could send?"

The Dinka was thinking, then he said: "Ben Mubarek told me it was a sign of trust that he sent me. He cannot have any bad intention with my people. He needs them for his slave-hunting."

"That is true, but when he doesn't need them any longer? If he denies them their reward and makes them slaves themselves?"

Agadi looked at Leopold, shocked. He needed time to think of the possibility of such behaviour. Then he flew open. "Effendi, could such a thing really happen?"

"Ben Mubarek is capable of the worst evil. Ask Pulo and Dshangeh, your young relatives, what type of people surround him."

"They have told me already. You have rescued many slaves. You know everything beforehand. Your eyes can see the time that is still to come. Should you have seen right this time? Woe to Ben Mubarek, if I could only learn whether you are right."

"That is easy. It is probably written in the letter. Give it to me."

"But – but…" His honesty did not allow him to hand the letter to strangers. He fought with himself. The worry about himself and his people influenced his decision. "Effendi, a person should not only be honest but clever as well. Should Ben Mubarek have bad things in mind for us, then my honesty doesn't help. The letter is in a little clay vessel fastened below my boat."

The boat, which was lightweight, was taken aboard. The Reis Effendina broke open the little bottle and tried to read the letter. He shook his head and asked: "Can you read Persian, Effendi?"

"Yes, but how would Ben Mubarek know this language? And the Colonel to whom this letter is directed? Show me the letter."

Leopold looked at the writing. He could read words without making any sense of them. Then he thought Ben Mubarek had used precautionary measures in case someone else would read it. The Arabian language is written from right to left. He tried to read it from left to right. It worked. The letter read:

I am sending you Agadi, the leader of the Dinkas. I have told him we are going to the Rohl to make slaves. But my campaign is against the Gohk, a thing he shouldn't know yet, because they belong to the Dinka tribe, which, in other words are his relations. Send me fifty warriors to the seribah Aliab. They should wait until I return. With their help I will be able to enslave the Dinkas. This way I won't have to pay them. I have removed their leader so that they only follow my orders. I am ordering you to see to it that he doesn't return. I have learned that Poldi Ben Anglesi has been with you. I couldn't come because he escaped and we had to rush off. If Agadi should meet him, he has orders to mislead him.

The letter had no signature. The Dinka looked at the letter in disbelief. He, the Negro, the heathen, couldn't understand such depravity. He asked hastily: "Effendi, allow me to leave the ship. I have to return to the seribah immediately to warn my people and to revenge myself on Ben Mubarek." He wanted to rush away but Leopold held him back. "Stay! You are not our prisoner and you are free to go, but I advise you to remain with us. You would be going into certain death."

"I will kill Ben Mubarek but he will not kill me."

"You don't know him – and you wouldn't meet him at the seribah anyway."

"You are right, he wanted to start the ghasua, the slave-hunt, right away. At the seribah I will find out which way he went."

"You are mistaken; they will retain and murder you if you do that. You, on your own, will achieve nothing. With us, you will reach the seribah faster than in your boat. You are safer with us. We will catch Ben Mubarek and all the whites with him. Then your people will be rescued too."

"You are right, Effendi. Who would have thought that? You have been described to me as the enemy of all black peoples and I took my commission joyfully to deceive you. Now the enemies are friends and the old friends are enemies. I will take you to the seribah."

"How far is it from here?"

"We will probably need five or six days."

"What is the area like?"

"The seribah is surrounded by a large wood. Ben Mubarek had trees felled, which are still lying there. Other trees and shrubbery grew up between them creating an impenetrable wall with only a small entrance from the water side."

"In other words, the seribah is a fortress."

"Yes, Ben Mubarek maintains that it could be defended by ten men against several hundred."

"Yes, if the attackers have no skill. How is the inside?"

"It is a large square place with about twenty huts made of reed and mud."

"Are there any guests there?"

"Yes, a fat Turk, his two sisters, two black servants."

"I know him. I rescued your young nephew and niece from him. I can tell you all this while we are sailing. Why waste time?"

"You are right, let's be off!"

Chapter 17

The seribah Aliab

The anchor was weighed, sails were set and the 'Hawk' was steered into the river Rohl. This side arm of the Nile had enough water to carry even bigger ships than theirs. The journey took only four days. It was evening when Agadi informed Leopold that the seribah was near.

Now the question was whether to land there openly in the morning. It wasn't advisable as the entrance was easily defended. It was about nine o'clock; the stars shone brightly when Leopold decided to take three men experienced on water, Agadi, Ben Nil and his grandfather, in a boat to reconnoitre. Agadi also joined them. There was good visibility. Then Agadi whispered. "Here is the mishra, we have to land here."

A mishra is a place to land, but Leopold decided it was too dangerous to land there. A guard could easily notice them. He reversed the boat about thirty metres where he saw a tree half in the water and half on land. Agadi stood up to tie the boat onto this tree. He didn't see the roots, and the boat nearly capsized. Agadi lost his equilibrium and, with a loud cry, fell into the water. He knew that this stretch of water was infested with crocodiles. A dark streak quickly came nearer. "A crocodile, a crocodile," shouted the man. "Help me quickly!"

Leopold rose from the rudder and, together with Ben Nil heaved him into the boat. But the weight was too much; the boat rocked, its rim below water when the crocodile hit it with its head and straightened it up again. Ben Nil hit it on the snout with an oar; it disappeared.

After tying the boat to the tree, they sat there for ten minutes to listen for whether Agadi's cry had been heard. Leopold left the boat, when Ben Nil whispered, "Don't go alone, take me with you."

After the noise they had created, Leopold found it better to go in twos. He gave him the permission to come along. Once off the boat they listened again, but there was no suspicious sound. They reached the entrance. There were strong stakes connected with a network of thorns. There should be a more comfortable way and Leopold bent down to investigate when he heard a cry from Ben Nil.

Leopold turned round quickly but a hit on the head rendered him unconscious. When he came to, he was tied up like an Egyptian mummy. He found himself lying in a mud hut in which a fire burned. The smoke went out through an opening at the top. Ben Nil lay next to him.

When he saw Leopold open his eyes, he breathed deeply and said: "Allah be thanked. I thought you were dead."

"My head hurts. What happened? Did they hit you as well?"

"No. Just when you bent down four strong fellows grabbed me from the back. One of them swung an oar behind you. I cried out to warn you, unfortunately too late, but I cried loud enough for my grandfather to hear. I hope he rushed back to the Reis Effendina to report what has happened. Do you think we will be able to escape again?"

"I always hope. This time it may be the Reis will rescue us."

"If they don't kill us beforehand!"

"Quite possible. We have escaped from them too often and they might think it better to finish us at once. I am only surprised we have been left alone. But silence now, I hear someone coming."

A mat constituted the entrance. Two people entered. Murad Nassyr, the fat Turk and the sergeant, Ben Ifram. The fat one stood before Leopold and stroked his beard, at ease. He said mockingly: "Are you here again? I hope you will extend your visit a bit longer, or do you intend to disappear again?"

Leopold didn't answer and Murad Nassyr turned to the sergeant: "This is the unbelieving dog about whom we talked. This damned fellow even followed us here. It will be the last journey he makes in his life. I swear by Allah he won't get away from here. He and his comrade have to die."

"I don't mind," smiled the sergeant. "Should we take them out and shoot them?"

"Shoot them? That would be far too quick a death. They should die slowly and suffer several ways of dying. It is night now and I want to observe their torture, their howling, screaming faces. That can only happen in daylight."

"Should they stay here until then?"

"No, we will throw them into the Dshura el dshasa, which is deep and secure. We don't have to guard them and we can continue our fishing. Our meat is all gone now. We have to have fish. Did you secure the boat of these dogs?"

"Yes, we can use it for fishing. Five of us to each boat."

"That's good. It will yield twice the amount of fish and we will only leave two to guard the seribah and the prisoners, which, by the way, is unnecessary. They are tied up and nobody can escape from the Dshura el dshasa, the punishment pits."

"On the contrary, it is very necessary; think of the Reis Effendina!"

"I will ask Poldi Ben Anglesi. Woe to him if he doesn't answer or tells me an untruth."

Murad Nassyr turned to Leopold, pulled his knife and kicked him. "Every question not answered costs you a finger. I am not joking. Did you come here on your own or is the Reis Effendina following you?"

Leopold saw no reason to be silent. Neither did he want to tell him the truth. There was, however, one thing he couldn't explain to himself. They had found the boat but not Abu en Nil nor Agadi. Where were they? Did they want to rescue them? He didn't trust the helmsman to make such a manly decision. It would have been better to return to the ship and alert the Reis Effendina during the night.

"I am only here with Ben Nil," he answered.

"Where is the Rei Effendina?"

Leopold pretended to hold back. The fat Turk took hold of his thumb, put the knife to it and threatened: "Answer or I cut. Where is he?"

"Reis Achmed went to the Bahr es Dshebel. He seeks you there."

"Why are you not with him?"

"Because I didn't believe the seribah was there."

"Who told you that the seribah is there?"

"Your Bongo-warrior with the name of Agadi."

"Ah, you believed that. Where did he want to go?"

"The Reis Effendina believed him, not I. He himself wanted to go to Fashodah to become a soldier."

"Did you take him on board and search him?"

"Yes, but we didn't find anything."

"You are sons and grandchildren of stupidity. You think yourselves clever but are such fools, one should have mercy with you. Do you know who this Bongo really is?"

"Well?"

The Turk spoke in a superior tone. He believed he had outwitted the Reis Effendina and Leopold. It was doing him good. He, whom Allah did not endow with excessive reason. "He is no Bongo but the leader of the Dinkas whom we have recruited."

"Mashallah!" Leopold called, pretending to be surprised.

"Yes," laughed Murad. "You fell into a splendid trap. Agadi had an important letter with him. If you had discovered it, we would have been in dire trouble. But you are too stupid to discover it. Agadi was employed to mislead you and has sent you to the Bahr el Dshebel."

"The others, but not me."

"Which is of no use to you. Tomorrow, you will be executed. The Reis Effendina will take more than a month until he discovers his mistake. Ben Mubarek will be back and we will receive him suitably."

"Allah, Allah," Leopold pretended consternation. "This Dinka is a big rascal."

"He is a clever fellow. Ten times cleverer than all of you. Now tell me, how was it possible for you to escape from the ship near Fashodah?"

Leopold didn't want to betray Murad's sister. "I had two knives," he lied. "One fell out of my belt and you didn't find it."

"That's how it was. Well; we will take better care today. I will personally make sure of that. You will be thrown into the Dshura el dshasa, which you will leave in the morning to walk to your death."

The Dshura el dshasa was near the river, and deep. It was damp and muddy. All sorts of rubbish got thrown into it and there would be no shortage of vermin. After thorough examination they would be transported to the punishment pit. A long ladder lay there. Its length betrayed the unusual depth of the hole. The ladder was put into the pit and the prisoners had to let themselves down.

"Sleep well! May Allah give you pleasant dreams," called the Turk mockingly.

The slave-hunters went away. The stars shone on them. They believed no-one was guarding them when, after a while, a voice came from above: "How do you like it there, you mangy dogs. Have you made friends with the rats and scorpions already?"

They didn't answer. It was nonsense to guard them. Even if they were without fetters, it would be impossible to climb the walls. After only a few minutes they heard him speaking again. "Who comes there?" He received an answer, but the words couldn't be understood by those imprisoned. Then the guard asked again: "Have you dressed differently? Stop or... oh Allah, Allah!" This call suffocated in a rattle. The prisoners heard stamping, then all went quiet.

A subdued voice called: "Effendi, are you down there?"

"Yes," answered Leopold. "Who is there?"

"The helmsman, Abu en Nil. Is my grandson with you?"

"Yes, let the ladder down and come to cut our fetters."

"At once, at once." The old fellow let himself down. The prisoners were in possession of their freedom within a few seconds. "Are you surprised to see us here? We are..."

"Don't tell us now," interrupted Leopold. "I feel no safety until I am out of this hole."

Leopold went up. Grandfather and grandchild followed. Up there he saw the guard lying on the floor with the Dinka's hands around his neck.

"Is he dead? asked Leopold.

"No, he still moves his legs," answered the Negro.

"Don't suffocate him. We need him to give us information," added the helmsman.

Agadi took his hands from the guard's throat and Leopold took his arm to prevent him from jumping up suddenly and running away. He started to breathe properly, opened his eyes and looked at Leopold.

"I know that all except two of you went fishing. Where is the other one?"

"At the entrance. If I whistle, he will come."

"Where are the things taken from us?"

"In the Turk's hut. The second on your right."

"Are the men who went fishing armed?"

"No, they only have their knives and fishing lances with them. Their rifles and pistols are in the first hut on your left."

Leopold did not warn the man to speak the truth. He answered with such fear, one could hear he spoke with verity. Leopold now ordered: "Whistle for your comrade!" A whistle came back from the entrance.

"And now quickly down with you into the pit. If you make a sound you will be shot." Before Leopold could pull up the ladder, the other guard came near. He saw the end of the ladder, which distracted him from the differently-dressed Leopold. He was still fifteen steps away and shouted: "Why is the ladder in there; do you want the prisoners to escape? Out with it!" He came running and grabbed the thing which he thought would help the prisoners to escape. Leopold jumped at him and took him by the throat. "Silence! Not a sound or you are dead."

The man's shock was too great. He didn't move. When Leopold took his hands away, he stared at him. "The Effendi! Oh Allah, Allah!"

Leopold's comrades, who had hidden behind one of the huts, came back and forced the second guard down into the Dshura el dshasa. Then they pulled up the ladder. They went to the hut which the ten soldiers occupied when they were in the seribah. There, hanging on the wall were ten rifles and ten pistols – all loaded. They took them away and Leopold went to the Turk's hut. When he entered the first part, it was dark, but from the second chamber he could see some light. When he entered the second section, he saw the 'ladies' drinking coffee. In the middle, on a carpet, sat Kumru with her sister and two servant girls. They all stared at him, shocked. Leopold, who was usually considerate towards ladies, was now utterly regardless, which, however, did not disturb him. Firstly he came unannounced, secondly he had entered a harem, which was forbidden, and thirdly, his appearance was not gentlemanlike. His attire had suffered during the last few weeks and his ordeal in the muddy pit did the rest. He also carried three rifles. All in all, he looked like a robber-chief in clay. Nevertheless, he crossed his hands over his chest, bowed and said: "Mohammed, the prophet of prophets, may give you the pleasing odour of paradise. I am thirsty. May I ask you for a cup of this delicious drink?"

At this, Kumru recognised him. "Poldi Ben Anglesi!" she shouted and jumped up. "I thought you were imprisoned in the hole!"

"As you see, this is no longer the case."

"I intended – intended – to free you, but I didn't know how."

"I thank you, you loveliest of the maidens. You have helped me before. I couldn't count on you this time, but I have to ask you for another favour: Do not leave the harem until I allow you to do so."

"Why?"

"A bullet might hit you or one of your servants."

"Allah, a bullet! Who will you fight?"

"The sergeant and his soldiers."

"With my brother as well?"

"Yes, if he fights too."

"Allah, Allah! You are a strong and hardy man. You will kill him!"

"No, my gratitude forbids me to grieve you. I will spare Murad. But I can only do that if you stay here and keep quiet."

"We will do that, Effendi, I promise you."

Kumru lifted her hands in asseveration and forgot that her face was unveiled. Leopold had the 'bliss' of seeing her face for the second time. Those curiously creased features that reminded him of a market woman at home. He then took a lamp to light the front part of the hut. To his joy, he found everything that had been taken from him and Ben Nil. He took it all and returned the lamp.

"Everything has gone well up to now. The question now is, how to get the ten people outside into our hands without endangering ourselves," ventured Ben Nil.

"The best thing is to shoot them all. We have enough weapons," said his grandfather.

"We will do that only in case of need. You know I hate spilling blood. Let's go to the entrance and observe the situation."

They saw two boats, including their own, connected by branches on which stones had been put and on which a fire burned to throw its light wide over the waters, to lure the fishes. The fish would then be speared.

"We have time to think," said Leopold. You can tell us how you managed to free us. Did you hear Ben Nil shouting?"

"More than that. The moon was shining and we saw it all. Agadi remembered a secret entrance. We went through it and saw you being pushed into the punishment hole. When the ten soldiers went fishing, the Dinka took your guard by the throat – the rest you know. Didn't we do it right, Effendi?"

"You did and I won't forget it." They sat behind a bush and observed the fishing. The Turk had no talent for it. He missed constantly. He gave up and walked toward the entrance.

"Run to the hole quickly, Ben Nil. The ropes we were tied up with are still there. There are more in the soldier's huts. You others, step aside so Murad Nassyr won't see you when he pushes his head through the opening of the entrance." They obeyed. Leopold put his rifle away as it would hinder him when grabbing the Turk. Murad Nassyr came though the small opening. He could only do so by bending down. Before he came through completely, Leopold had grabbed him and pulled him inside. He then put a knife to his chest and threatened to kill him if he uttered a sound. The terrified Turk stared at him and took a deep breath once Leopold let go of his throat.

Ben Nil returned and the prisoner was tied up. Leopold told him nothing would happen to him if he kept quiet, but at the slightest noise he would find himself in hell. This had hardly happened when they heard steps again. A short glance outside taught them that two soldiers with an earthen vessel came nearer. These receptacle contained their catch so far. It should be emptied in the seribah. The task was to get hold of the two without them making a noise.

That wasn't easy. The entrance was too small to let two of them come through at the same time. Leopold grabbed his rifle and stood aside. He asked Ben Nil to stand nearby and pull him through once Leopold had hit him. The first soldier came in backward, pulling the vessel. Leopold hit him on the head with the rifle butt. He dropped down and Ben Nil pulled him away. Leopold grabbed the handle of the container and pulled it in. The second soldier who was pushing the vessel was also hit on the head the moment his head came through. Both were unconscious. They were tied up and put next to the Turk.

"Are we going to catch the others in the same way?" ventured Ben Nil. "We might not be as lucky as up to now."

"You are right, but let's wait and see."

They had time and didn't have to hurry. The two soldiers were expected back. They heard the sergeant order two more soldiers to take the second vessel and see why the others tarried. Once more they were lucky enough to overcome the second two soldiers as easily and soundlessly as the first.

Leopold wondered what the others would do. They expected the soldiers back. Ben Ifram, the sergeant, put his fingers in his mouth and whistled. As there was no reply, he left his boat and came to the seribah, limping and grumbling. His head had hardly came through when he was taken by the neck. Ben Nil and his grandfather had become efficient in their task. It was a pleasure to watch them at work.

"That went as easily and orderly as the rolling up of a rope," laughed the helmsman. "Now there are only four of them."

"With them we will make it short," declared Leopold. "I am going outside to stand in the dark while you call for them to come in."

"They will hear a foreign voice, Effendi."

"No matter – they will come. You three will take your rifles in hand. They have to submit."

"If the first one who sees us warns the others?"

"That's why I am going outside. I will not allow them to withdraw."

Leopold stood where the soldiers who caught them were standing. The grandfather now called the other soldiers to come in. He didn't have to repeat calling them. The fact that six people didn't return told them that something must have happened. They jumped off their boats and rushed past Leopold. The first one crept in, the second came at once after him. A cry was heard. The third one wanted to return but was pushed inside by the fourth. Another warning call and the fourth wanted to return, but was driven in by Leopold's warning that he would get a bullet in his head.

"Heavens! The Effendi!" he called.

"Yes, the Effendi. Forward if you like your life!" Once inside Leopold saw his friends with rifles at the ready and the soldiers with such sad deportment, he had to laugh out loud. His friends followed him. Ben Nil asked them to throw away their knives. They obeyed and their hands were tied at the back. The four hit by Leopold were conscious but didn't move. They all, except Murad Nassyr, had to walk to the punishment pit, where they were let down.

Leopold stepped to Murad Nassyr, pulled his knife and said: "Murad Nassyr, not answering my questions truthfully will cost you a finger. I like to pay with the same currency. Answer quickly: When did Ben Mubarek leave the seribah?"

"Five days ago." The answer came in a hurry. "He had two hundred people with him."

"Do you know the Dinka who is next to me?"

"Yes, he is Agadi."

"Maybe it has dawned on you that we weren't so stupid as to be cheated by him. We also read your betrayal letter, and the Reis Effendina will be here in the morning. Tomorrow you will be judged and die full of anguish as no other human ever died."

"Mercy, have mercy, Effendi, you are a Christian," he cried out.

"A Christian dog, you called me. I am neither Christian nor a dog. I have nothing to do with you. You are finished."

"Effendi, think of my sisters. What will become of them if you kill me?"

"Their lot will be better than you prepared for them. To become Ben Mubarek's wife is the worst fate I can think of. Throw him down, I have nothing more to do with him."

It was not hardheartedness nor revenge that made him talk this way. He wanted Murad Nassyr to spend a few hours in fear of death. Hopefully he would come to see the error of his ways.

Chapter 18

The end of the seribah

Now they had all twelve men in the punishment pit. Ben Nil reminded Leopold about a supposed carelessness: "Did you forget that the first two soldiers we have put into the pit were not tied up? They will free the others, who could then leave the hole by climbing three on top of each other."

"We have a guard there. Any head who would dare to show above the cave, will get a bullet." It was time to send for the Reis Effendina. Leopold asked Abd en Nil, the grandfather, to do it. He then went back to Kumru, who received him unveiled, as before.

"What have you done with him? asked the kind maiden. "Why doesn't he come? Did you fight with him?"

"Yes, he is our prisoner now and, with the others, down in the Dshura el dshasa, the punishment pit. He will sleep there."

"My brother in the Dshura el dshasa? Is that a place for a distinguished, high ranking man?"

"Do you think I am a common man?"

"No Effendi, if you were not an unbeliever, you would be even more distinguished than my brother."

"But Murad threw me there and didn't ask such questions. I act in the name of law. Your brother is a criminal."

"Is trading in slaves really such a crime?"

"One of the worst."

"I didn't know that. I always believed it to be the right of a white man to sell black slaves. Can my brother be punished for that?"

"Murad has to be punished."

"Allah, Allah, perhaps he will have to die? I know that Reis Effendina wants to catch him and that you are his friend. Is this horrible man here?"

"Achmed el Insaf will be here tomorrow morning."

"Tell me one thing. I heard that he kills all slave-dealers. Is that true?"

"I can't deny that I was present when he ordered a group of slave-hunters to be shot."

"Oh, what a shock. He won't kill my brother as well?"

"I fear he has that intention."

"You have to rescue him, Effendi. I have rescued you once."

"Yes, you helped me once, and I am not ungrateful. I shall ask the Reis Effendina to let your brother live."

"Then everything is all right. I shall prepare coffee again."

"Make it a large potful. My colleagues like it too."

Leopold went. An unadulterated daughter of the orient, he thought. Whatever happened to her brother is immaterial, as long as he stays alive. As they sat, drinking coffee and smoking the Turk's tobacco, the hours of the night went fast. The morning wind would help Reis Effendina to arrive soon.

Leopold and Ben Nil inspected the other huts. They found a few rifles and other weapons. They also found some suits that were an improvement on those they were wearing at present. The change was effected immediately.

Agadi was left to guard the prisoners. Leopold had it in mind to speak to the Turk once more. Maybe he would learn something of importance. As he looked down, he saw that the prisoners had freed themselves of their ties, but they hadn't tried to escape and they didn't sleep. The Turk looked up and saw Leopold. Murad Nassyr implored him to let him come up, he had to talk to him. "You are not worth it, but all right, come up."

The ladder was let down and the Turk came up. He was affected, probably more from the inside than the outside; he had to sit down. "You gave me a bad time," he sighed, putting his elbow on his knee and his head on his hand.

"It is your own fault. We have a phrase. 'Do no wrong and no wrong will befall you!'"

"But I haven't done anything which warrants my death!"

"I have done nothing bad but you decided my death."

"That is over now. I know now that it was my greatest stupidity to come here. How I would like to go back!"

"To start dealing in slaves again?"

"No, there are other goods one can buy and sell. Effendi, let me go away from here and I swear by Allah, his prophets as well as by all my descendants, that I will never sell a slave again."

"This promise is not enough. It is no atonement for what I have to approach you with."

"What else are you asking for?"

"Actually, nothing else but your life."

Murad put his face in his hands, kept silent for a while and then looked up at Leopold. "All right, make it short and shoot me right now."

What a face! The man seemed ten, fifteen years older. Leopold spoke to him less sharply: "Murad Nassyr, we were friends when I was in Cairo, you invited me and I liked you. I was prepared to travel to Khartoum with you. We became friends until I learned that you were a slave-dealer. We had to part. Actually we were finished with one another. But you threw hatred and revenge on me. You became a grim enemy of mine. That wasn't very clever. You knew me as a man who, beside God, fears no-one. I haven't forgotten that we were friends and would like to give you a helping hand. But it is the Reis Effendina who would demand your elimination. If I ask for your life to be spared, I have to offer him more than your promise."

"Tell me, what else are you asking for?"

"A clear proof that it is your intention to stop dealing in slaves. Break with the satan Ben Mubarek. That is the proof I ask for."

"Is that what you are asking? Nothing else?" asked the Turk, as his eyes shone again. "Nothing easier than that. I understand now that this man is my wicked demon. Why did he ask for my sister? Why doesn't he take her when I bring her to him? Why does he lure me deeper and deeper into the wilderness? What is his purpose?"

"A bad one in any case."

"At first he wanted the marriage in Khartoum, then in Fashodah and then here on the seribah. When I arrived he had gone."

"And you haven't the sagacity to look through this devil. Think about the intended betrayal of his accomplice, Agadi. After the Dinkas have helped and spilled their blood, he wants to make them slaves instead of paying them. He sold Hafid Sichar to get at his fortune. You are rich, Ben Mubarek has lost almost everything – he needs money. Do I have to say more?"

"Effendi!" shouted the Turk, "do you mean what I think?"

"Yes, nothing else."

"You are probably right. The more I think about it, the more it seems that your sagacity has it right."

"Turn around. Do you know where Ben Mubarek is?"

"He went to the Gohk."

"Can you describe the way he went?"

"I have sworn not to divulge it."

"Such an oath is a sin. We intend to help threatened Negroes. Your oath was incautious and will be criminal if you keep it."

"Please think, Effendi, I have sworn by the beard of the prophet!"

"Nonsense!" called Leopold angrily. "Your prophet had no beard!"

"How? What? No beard? Mohammed – had – no…"

The word stuck in his mouth. He looked at Leopold absent-mindedly.

"Now, calm down – perhaps he had one."

"Perhaps? Effendi, you know so much, others don't, and you maintained he had no – oh heavens!"

"Those words only slipped out in anger," Leopold said to calm him.

"So our prophet had a beard?"

"Probably."

"Allah be praised. I have never met anybody who doubted it."

"Well, no one has seen it; at least no one alive. If you have sworn on a doubtful matter like this, so your oath has no value in my eyes. You have given it too rashly. Take it back; it is best for you."

"Can you give me time to think it over?"

"I don't mind, but only a short time. The Reis Effendina arrives here any moment."

"Actually, I've told you enough by divulging that he is moving to the Gohk."

"I knew this from his letter. The Gohk belong to the Dinka-people. They are widespread and have many villages. You know Ben Mubarek's way. It is important for our success."

"Yes, I have studied the maps of the Upper Nile with him."

"So you are able to give us the best information. If you refuse you cannot expect any indulgence from the Reis Effendina. Now you will return to the pit."

"One more thing, Effendi. Are you treating my sisters as enemies?"

"No, you can be calm about this. As long as they enjoy their coffee, heaven will not fall." Murad Nassyr went back to the punishment pit and the ladder was pulled up again.

Leopold went outside the seribah. He had only been there for a few minutes when he saw the ship. At the bow stood the Reis Effendina, who saw Leopold and shouted: "Holla! There stands our world conqueror smoking the pipe of victory. Imprisonment did not do you much harm."

"It was short," smiled Leopold. "It entertained me more than it troubled me."

"I have heard it. The old Abu en Nil has told me everything, but I want to hear it from you now. I am coming down." The Reis came down the landing-stage and shook Leopold's hands. "Four men conquering a large seribah after being imprisoned – that is something to be proud of. I congratulate you, but now these dogs have to face death – all of them."

"Slowly, slowly. I don't want to have this said for sure."

"What," he asked, frowning. "Are you interfering again with your humanity?" His previously cheerful face had changed. He continued almost harshly: "Nothing will come of that. The matter is determined already. This brood has to be exterminated. They have no right to live. Come into the seribah."

They went into the seribah via the slip-hole. Leopold showed him about without entering a hut. Then he sat down on a felled tree and asked the Reis Effendina to sit next to him. He wanted to tell him everything. "All right," said the Reis, "but let me tell you first. This Ben Mubarek understands how to erect a seribah. The twelve people here could have defended this fortress against all my asakers."

"Yes, and they had sufficient weapons and gun-powder."

"I would have to leave here unsuccessfully. You have conquered without a single shot. Effendi, you have enormous luck. Take good care it shouldn't leave you. Don't dare as much in the future. Now tell me what happened."

Leopold could make it short. The Reis knew most of it from the report of the old helmsman. The main thing for Leopold was to make the Reis friendlier disposed to the Turk. He brought all possible arguments to excuse the prisoner. The 'servant of justice' listened without interrupting once. He looked darkly and wordlessly for a while.

"I am beholden to you," he then said. "You have a way to use that for your false humanity. I will allow only for one thing. He, the Turk, was a slave-dealer and not a slave-hunter. One is as bad as another, but we would have his sister around our neck. We can't throw her and her maid-servants into the Nile."

"No," Leopold answered, entering his present mood. "Leaving him with the women is punishment enough."

"Oho! Should he go without punishment? And there are other considerations. The ten other slave-hunters and the sergeant have to be punished."

"That is for you to decide."

"You cannot slither out of that. Surely they must be punished. But how can I do that if we let Murad Nassyr go? You can see your plea is very uncomfortable for me. If only the Turk would be sincere. If he misleads us it would be too late – Ben Mubarek would be gone."

"There is a splendid way to avoid this – we take him with us."

"So we have to take the women too!"

"Not necessarily. We can leave them on the ship. We cannot reach our goal on the water."

"That is true. We take Murad with us and if he lied, he gets the bullet."

"I am of the opinion we can already test his assertion. I have maps on the ship which show the exact area where Ben Mubarek used to hunt. If the assertions of the Turk are in accordance with the maps, we can trust him."

"True again. So you will have a merciful judgement on him?"

"Not so fast! You have almost talked me into it, but I would like to listen to what he has to say. My judgement will be accordingly. Now let's bring in my asakers and take over the weapons."

Once inside, the soldiers stood in a circle around the punishment pit. A ladder was let down and the prisoners were brought up. They were shocked to see the soldiers of the Viceroy. They knew their fate would be certain death. The fear showed in their faces. Murad Nassyr stood with them, not daring to lift his eyes.

Achmed Abd el Insaf, the Reis Effendina, observed the Turk for a few moments, then he asked: "Do you know who I am?"

Murad Nassyr bowed deeply but kept silent.

"And you are a slave-flayer whose skin I should cut from his body. Poisonous vermin who should be trodden on and exterminated. Confess! You deal in slaves?"

"Until now – yes."

"You were connected with Ben Mubarek?"

"Yes."

"With this, you pronounce your death sentence."

"Emir, I didn't know him well," stammered the shocked Turk.

"The worse for you. One does not follow a person one doesn't know deep into the Sudan. Where is he now?"

"On his way to the Gohk."

"Which way did he take?"

"First with the ship up river toward Aguda," he answered quickly. Murad Nassyr had forgotten his oath and the beard of the prophet. He was shaking with fear. The tone in which the strict judge talked allowed no resistance – no hesitation. He replied straight away. Leopold pulled out the maps which were brought to him from the ship and compared them with Murad's declaration.

"Which place is he going to attack?"

"Wagunda."

"Why this place?"

"The ruler of Wagunda has considerable amounts of ivory and his subjects have large herds. The men in this area are strong."

"When does Ben Mubarek arrive there. Did he calculate that?"

"We have calculated everything. He believes he will be twenty days on the march."

Achmed threw a questioning glance at Leopold, who affirmed by nodding that Murad Nassyr had spoken the truth. The effect was that the judge became milder. "I am going to believe you. You answered clearly and that saves you. The Effendi has asked for mercy for you and I will try to allow his plea. Do you know the straight and short way to the Gohk?"

"Yes, one goes by ship to the Maijeh Semkat. From there one has to go on land to the west."

"Do you know the way there? Can you lead us?"

"Unfortunately not. I have never been there."

A young prisoner called out: "Be merciful, O Achmed Abd el Insaf and allow me to talk. I have been there making maps for Ben Mubarek." The youth was useful. Leopold gave the Reis a nod. He understood, but his speech was interrupted by Kumru, with a veil over her face. She came with a pot of water to offer coffee for everybody. Her sister and servants followed her. Fatma her favourite, brought ground coffee beans and another brought porcelain cups, pipes and tobacco. However, the pot was too hot for poor Kumru. She didn't have what the Arabs call a Tand-sharaya; in English, oven-gloves. She staggered and wobbled, but had to drop the pot holding hot water, unfortunately over the Reis' legs, which, luckily, were covered by high boots.

Leopold bit his lips. It was too funny a situation. The Reis Effendina saw it and broke out in hearty laughter. Leopold, Ben Nil and his grandfather joined in, and then the asakers. It was impossible to reassume the previous sternness. The water had broken the ice.

The Reis announced his judgement in a loud voice: "In the name and by order of the Viceroy, whom Allah may give a thousand years! This seribah has been a place of crime and has to be destroyed. All huts and fences will be burned. Murad Nassyr, the former slave-dealer, will swear to renounce his trade for ever. He will come with us to Wagunda. If he has told us the truth, he will be forgiven. If not, he will get a bullet in his head. During his absence, his sister and her servants will live on our ship. The other eleven slave-hunters deserve to die, but Poldi Ben Anglesi has asked for their lives to be spared. They are coming with us. If they fight on our side, valiantly, they will be forgiven. If just one of them shows disobedience – they will all be shot. So they'd better watch one another."

There was a silence that lasted almost a minute. The old sergeant jumped forward, swung his arms in the air and shouted: "Allah bless the Reis Effendina, today and for ever!"

"IlyTm, dâ'iman, δbδdi!" repeated every voice present.

The Turk went to the Reis Effendina, bowed to him and performed the requested oath. Then he went to Leopold, gave him his hand and said: "I have to thank you for this. I swear you will not regret your intercession."

The women appeared again. Kumru carried another pot of hot water. This time her hands were covered by her small slippers. Sometimes need is a jocular teacher.

A lively performance went on in the seribah. The previous enemies were now friends and helped diligently with the work. The huts had to be emptied and burned. So had the fence; they had to take care the fire would not affect the surrounding wood.

Up to now, they had been victorious. The curtain of the final act started to lift. Would luck stay with them? Would Leopold's fiancé wait that long?

Chapter 19

Executed by rope

Their next aim was the Maijeh Semkat. In English it would be 'the swamp of fish'. The name told them they could expect plenty of nourishment. It was three days until they reached it. From there, they had to negotiate their way on land. But how? By marching? That would be strenuous and slow in this swampy area. Well, riding then! But on what kind of animal? There were no horses or camels in this stretch of land. They would perish there, soon. The answer was oxen. These animals thrive excellently in the swampy Upper Nile. They are strong, fast, teachable and good natured. They were also good carrying animals.

If they could get such animals, the game was won. Ben Mubarek calculated when he would reach Wagunda. He was five days on the road. That would leave two weeks to go. With oxen, they could make it in nine days. That would leave plenty of time to prepare for a good reception.

Leopold knew that the Bor dwelled in this area; they were related to the Dinkas. He consulted with Agadi, who agreed his plans and offered to help search for their village. Off they went. It took less than an hour's walk to reach an open space that probably owed its existence to a windfall.

There were a number of huts of such light construction, meant to last for a short time. They were probably there for a hunting group. In front of each hut was a big fire. There were no women to be seen. The men were busy roasting meat. Agadi, sucking air through his nose, smacked his tongue and said: "They are roasting hippopotamus meat. They must have killed one this morning. We will eat with them. Should we simply go to them?"

"No, we will go near enough for them to see us, then you, who can speak their language, go forward to speak to their chief. If you notice they are unfriendly, withdraw quickly."

But it was different from what they expected. The moment they were seen in the light of the fires, every single one of them disappeared into one of their huts. Agadi went forward to speak to them. He went to the hut, which, by its appearance, belonged to the chief. There he stood talking for ten minutes. Then he turned round and came back to Leopold. "They believe that I am a traitor and you are Ben Mubarek. In the end I asked if any one of them had seen Ben Mubarek. It turned out the chief had; so I offered for you to step into the light properly for him to see you."

"Nothing easier than that," said Leopold, as he stepped forward into the light of the fires which were burning high enough. As a result, the chief came out, with a friendly face, apologised and said: "No, you are not Ben Mubarek." He then invited them to partake of their interrupted meal.

He used the language of his tribe; Agadi was the interpreter.

"Do you know Ben Mubarek in person?" asked Leopold.

"Yes, I have seen him once at the Mokren el Bohur." (The lake No.)

"So you can see that I am not the rascal Ben Mubarek."

"Where you stood before, I couldn't see your face properly. I know that Ben Mubarek is on a slave-hunt. But now I believe Agadi, who told me that you are after him – can I be of help?"

"Yes, we need oxen to ride and for our luggage."

"So it is true that Ben Mubarek is marching toward our friends and relations, the Gohk? It is our duty to help."

"Yes, he is on his way already. We need about two hundred oxen. Will you be able to bring that many – and quickly?"

"If you want you can have a thousand by tomorrow noon. Anyway, two hundred won't be enough."

With these words, Woat looked smiling at Leopold as if he had some friendly reservations. "Why?" asked Leopold expectantly.

"Because two hundred oxen will be unable to take all the warriors. If foreign warriors are subjecting themselves to the dangers, we cannot stay back. I will give you two hundred of my best men to help you."

Nothing could have been more welcome. Leopold answered: "We don't fear Ben Mubarek, but one can never have too much power. How long will it take you to gather the men and the oxen?"

"You will have everything by tomorrow afternoon."

The Bor had eaten before, but they ate of the hippopotamus roast joint as if they had not eaten for days. Leopold was astonished at the amounts these people could devour. He asked Ben Nil to bring the fly-nets from the boat and to tell the Reis Effendina about the new friends. While the Bor went into their huts, Leopold preferred to sleep in the open.

The bird's cries awoke him early next morning. He left Agadi to explain his early return to the ship. The Reis Effendina received him with the words: "You are surely blessed by Allah. Everything you attempt turns out better than expected. I would like to have only part of your luck. I have you to thank for every single one of my successes."

Leopold thanked him for the compliment. It sounded a bit envious to him. There was plenty of time before the chief of the Bor would assemble his contribution. Leopold decided to shoot a few birds, which he had been assured to find at the other side of the river because there were no people there. He asked Ben Nil to accompany him. This was overheard by a man who had been in Leopold's service before Ben Nil, and who he was glad to be rid of, leaving him on the ship of the Reis Effendina. He was an impossible bragger, an unlucky person, but never aware of it. His name was Selim; he approached Leopold and asked:

"Effendi, please take me along, I also want to shoot birds."

"I cannot use you," said Leopold, remembering the difficulties this man had brought him.

"Why?" asked Selim astounded.

"Because of your silly actions."

Selim clapped his long arms over his head. "Silly actions? I, the most famous warrior and hunter of the universe – silly actions? You are insulting my soul and troubling the feeling of my heart. No one can resist me, and you only want to shoot birds."

Leopold was unmoved by this rhetoric, but Ben Nil didn't mind taking this swaggerer along. He even asked Leopold to take him. "Don't stop him coming with us. You have heard we are safe there. Nothing can happen to us."

"So he will scare away the birds. I am sure he will do something stupid."

"Well, let's see whether he behaves reasonably for once."

They took the ship's small boat. It had room enough for three people. Ben Nil and Selim took the oars and Leopold did the steering.

They went up the river for about a quarter of an hour. When they reached a small creek, Leopold steered into it. "Here we will find what we are looking for," said Selim. He pulled the oar in without waiting for Leopold to agree. They were still a few metres away from the river bank. There was a gathering of swamp-grass which Selim took for firm ground and… "Stop!" called Leopold, when he saw Selim's attempt to alight. "You will break through!" But too late. Selim had made the jump and disappeared below the treacherous green grass.

"I am drowning! – Help. Help!" he shouted, and held himself on the deeply inclined edge of the boat.

"Pull up your legs and swim!" called Leopold, "otherwise the boat will tip over."

"I want to get inside, I want to get into the boat," he cried loudly. "The crocodiles are coming, the crocodiles. Lift me in, quickly, they will devour me." There was no crocodile in sight, but the coward held on with horror.

Leopold tried to keep the boat upright and asked Ben Nil to go to the other end, otherwise they would capsize. Ben Nil intended to obey, but this increased Selim's fear even more.

"Don't go, pull me up – they are coming, they are coming!"

Selim, in fear of crocodiles of which there were none at this place, pulled himself up and grabbed Ben Nil. This was too much for the light vessel. It took in water and overturned. Selim disappeared again under water, so did Ben Nil and their rifles. Leopold did not go under. He stretched his arms and swam. Ben Nil came up quickly.

"Where is Selim?" he asked."

"Below, let's go down quickly, otherwise he will drown."

Leopold went below and was grabbed immediately by his legs. Selim held onto Leopold's legs even when he was already on dry land. Half on land and half in the water, he kept his eyes shut and didn't move. Leopold had to use strength to free himself from the cramping grip.

"Is he dead?" asked Ben Nil, who was also on dry land by now.

"No, nobody drowns that fast."

"But unconscious. I will try to find out if he hears me. Selim, Selim, open your eyes." Selim obeyed, immediately came on land completely and shouted: "Where are the crocodiles, where? Quickly, away from here."

He wanted to run, but Leopold held him. "Stay, coward. No crocodile is stupid enough to think that you are a good meal. You are completely safe here. There are no crocodiles near this place, but we can't hunt any more. I knew by taking you, there would be some stupidity of yours."

With these words, Selim became himself. He saw that there was no more danger. Enough reason to adapt a dignified posture. Playing the insulted, he answered: "Don't say that, Effendi. Who was stupid? You or I? Who steered us into the grass when I thought it was firm bank? It was you!"

"No," answered Leopold, "I intended to pass it, but you pulled in the oar without my order to do so, and the boat took a wrong direction. We should have let you drown, then we would have no more annoyance with such a blockhead."

"Blockhead? You couldn't possibly mean me, Effendi. And I, drown? Let me tell you that I am safe in all waters, and could drown easier on dry land."

"If that is true, will you collect our boat and in the first place our rifles?" Selim scratched himself behind the ears and stayed silent.

Leopold didn't really mean his invitation. He knew he had to do it himself. He and Ben Nil emptied their pockets and went into the water. It was not difficult to find the rifles. Ben Nil had to swim a bit further to retrieve the upside down boat. As they were cleaning their rifles and talking loudly, they were wrongly informed about the presence of people in the vicinity.

There were people – and what kind of people!

Leopold had just finished with his rifle and reached for his revolver to check how much it had suffered from the water, when he heard a voice from behind the nearby bushes: "Go ahead, fellows. Hold them down and tie them up!" He was grabbed from behind by four wild-looking fellows. He tried to defend himself, managed several times to get up, but the four had the better of him. They tied his arms at the back. Ben Nil only had three fellows against him, but suffered the same fate. Selim, 'the biggest hero of the universe', was overcome by one man. Once they were rendered harmless, the leader came out from behind the bushes.

"You here at the Maijeh Semkat? You sons of dogs. That was divine providence. Allah has given you into my hands and you will certainly do no more harm to us."

To Leopold's astonishment, he recognised him as one of the two officers he had met on Ben Mubarek's ship. Nubar's face expressed great joy as he stepped close to his prisoners. "The devil has helped you repeatedly to escape from us. This time his help will be of no use to you as you will have no time to do anything. As soon as we reach our camp – you will be hanged. Unfortunately, this death is far too quick for you. You were to be tortured slowly. But that could still happen if you refuse to tell me the truth. If you want to be spared the pain, speak the truth. Where have you come from?"

The man spoke of a camp. Should Ben Mubarek still be here? Unlikely. Not to answer would be stupid, Neither would he tell the truth.

"We came up the river," answered Leopold.

"Only the three of you?"

"Yes."

"Don't lie, giour. The boat betrays you. Such boats do not exist round here. The boat belongs to a ship which is probably the one of the Reis Effendina's. Confess, you son of a dog. Where is this boat from?"

Leopold decided to tell the truth to make the officer believe the following. "Yes, we have it from the Reis Effendina."

"I thought so. Where is his ship?"

"Further down the river; about one day's journey from here."

"And I should believe that? Why are you not there as well?"

"Because the Reis has sent us to establish hippopotamus traps, for our soldiers to have meat when they arrive here."

"What do you want up here?"

"We are seeking Ben Mubarek."

"Ah! Don't you know his seribah?"

"No, but we will find it."

"You will find nothing. Before the sun is down, you will be in hell. Didn't you enter any seribah on your journey?"

"We stopped at the seribah Aliab."

"Who did it belong to?"

"To a lame old man, who is trading with people near the seribah."

"Dealing in slaves?"

"No, he is an honest man: He sells only legal goods."

Ben Mubarek's lieutenant laughed, mockingly. "Only an unbeliever, a giour, can be that stupid. Stranger, what does your brain consist of? This seribah belongs to Ben Mubarek and the old man is his sergeant."

"Zounds!" said Leopold, pretending to be astonished.

"Yes, that's it. You want to catch Ben Mubarek? Ridiculous. He is long gone from where you are looking for him."

"Where is he, then?" asked Leopold with intended simplicity.

"Where he is? Do you think I am telling you that?" He laughed, but was quickly serious again and said: "Yes I will tell you, just to show you that we don't fear you any longer. He went with more than two hundred warriors to Wagunda, to make slaves of the Gohks."

"Why are you not with him? Are you afraid?"

"Afraid? I? I should write the answer on your face. I am here to build some light huts. Ben Mubarek, when he returns with new slaves, will pass here. We will build a seribah where he will place the prisoners until he finds a suitable buyer. We are going there and you will see it."

Nubar, the officer, had nine men with him. Two at a time were for Ben Nil and Selim, the other five had to guard Leopold. The boat was tied to a tree, to be collected later. It was a short walk through a small wood. They soon reached a large grass plain where several temporary huts had already been built. There were three more men on this would-be seribah.

They said they would hang him before nightfall. Leopold naturally planned to escape. His arms were tied to his body with a headscarf. As the slave-hunters stood together, discussing the torture for their prisoners, Leopold whispered to his comrades: "When I cut you loose, run for the boat. I will join you a little later."

"How will you cut us loose, you are tied up and have no knife."

174

"I will free myself."

"Will we escape? They will all be behind us."

"Not behind you. I will take another direction and they will be behind me. But wait at the boat until I come, otherwise they might catch me."

Leopold moved his arms. Not secretly, he wanted it to be seen, Nubar saw it and stepped towards him. "Son of a dog, you want to free yourself. You won't succeed. Ah, the cloth has been loosened already. I will make it tighter." Nubar forgot he had to open the knot, if only for a moment. But this was enough for Leopold to free his arms and tear the knife from Nubar's belt. With the other hand he knocked Nubar on the head, so that he fell down backwards. A few quick cuts and Ben Nil and Selim were free. They ran as fast as they could. All this happened quickly, but not fast enough. Nubar jumped on Leopold. In order not to kill him, Leopold hit him with the back of the knife, which knocked him unconscious. But only for a few seconds. Leopold went in a different direction from his colleagues. As he thought, everybody was behind him. He ran into the steppe toward two oxen. He jumped on one of them and put his heels strongly into the animal's flanks, so that it stormed off immediately. Leopold soon felt it obey the reins.

The slave-hunters were behind him. Nubar, recovered now, jumped on the second ox. Nobody ran after Ben Nil and Selim, and he had such a start, he did not fear to be overtaken. Unfortunately, this confidence was unfounded. His ox stepped into a hole and somersaulted. Leopold flew in a wide bow to the ground. He was dazed and stayed there for a few moments. The ox had broken a leg and Leopold had to rely on his own legs. Nubar was two hundred feet behind him and uttered cries of jubilation. He swung a pistol in his right hand. Further behind were the others, on foot. Leopold didn't fear them. The more dangerous was Nubar; he would definitely catch up with him. It was probably better to receive him while standing still. Nubar had weapons and Leopold none, but he relied on his sharp vision and on his luck.

Nubar raced nearer. When he was about one hundred steps from Leopold, he shouted: "Die, son of a dog! You want to avoid the rope, so you will get my bullet." Nubar pressed the trigger and shot. Whoever wants to hit from such a distance, sitting on an ox, needs better weapons and to be a better marksman. He missed and drew his second pistol with the same result.

"Now he is mine," said Leopold to himself. Nubar, angry about missing his aim, lost his judgement in stopping his animal at the right time. He shot past Leopold.

While Nubar reined the ox to stop, Leopold jumped on behind him and pressed his arms tightly around his body. The shocked ox ran on.

"Son of a dog!" shouted Nubar, "let go or we will break our necks."

"I won't break anything," laughed Leopold, "but if you don't drop the knife, I will crush all your ribs." It worked. Nubar, who held the reins with both hands, holding his knife in his right, dropped it.

"You are holding the reins; steer the ox more to the left." Leopold accompanied his words by more pressure and Nubar obeyed. His people were still far behind and didn't have to be feared. Leopold's companions were nearing the boat and out of danger. He pressed Nubar's ribs again and asked for the ox to go further left. Nubar obeyed without saying a word. The ox stormed full speed over the steppe. The pursuers, far behind, shouted like men possessed; this did not worry Leopold in the slightest.

They reached the boat. "Hamdulillah!" shouted Ben Nil, "we were worried about you, Effendi, but who are you carrying?"

"It is Nubar, Ben Mubarek's first officer. He wanted to catch us and now we have caught him."

"What a neat trick! How did you manage that?"

"About that later. Now we have to rush off – the pursuers will be here soon." Leopold laid the now tied officer on the floor and sat down to steer the boat. They rowed near the bank under trees, so as not to be seen by the following slave-hunters. It was dark when they crossed the river.

The Reis Effendina was astonished when he heard what had happened. He walked the prisoner to the fire and asked: "Do you know who I am?"

Nubar answered defiantly: "You are the Reis Effendina."

"Do you know what that means?"

"I don't have to fear you. If you are righteous, you will have to let me go. I haven't done anything to you."

"Whether you fear me or not is a matter for you. You are a slave-hunter and as such I have to use my powers of justice."

"Prove it; bring me one slave I have caught."

"Bark, dog, bark, you soon will whimper. Didn't you seek the life of Poldi Ben Anglesi?"

"He lies. And even if it were true he wouldn't have to turn to you but to his Consul."

"You are mistaken. You are a subject of the Viceroy whom I represent here. All your misdeeds are known to me. The Effendi had indulgence with you – several times. But I knew that the moment I caught you, you would be lost. Now I have got you, consequently you are finished."

"Bring me proof. I don't care what others say. I can bring witnesses that I am falsely accused."

"Your witnesses have no validity. I believe your accusers. My law is of the desert: Equal with equal. Woe to him who does woes. Asis, the rope!"

Asis, as is known, was his favourite and executer of the Reis Effendina's judgement. He hurried to bring the requested braiding.

When he brought it. Nubar called out: "Reis Effendina, you are not being earnest. Think of your responsibility. The Viceroy will demand a justification for my death."

"Up with you onto a high branch!" Three soldiers held him while Asis put the rope around his neck and threw the other end to two other soldiers who had climbed a tree. The condemned man tried to defend himself. He cried and called out his innocence. Leopold couldn't neglect to ask the stern judge for mercy, but as expected, received an angry answer.

"Be quiet! I have too often given in to your request for mercy. Had I not done so, we would have finished a long time ago with these sons of dogs. With your requests of weakness and want of judgement, you annoy me so much that I don't want to know you. Go away if you cannot endure the hanging of such a rascal."

That was explicit enough. No 'friend' had ever talked to Leopold like this. He refused to give an answer and turned away. It was repugnant to him to witness the execution. By no means was it a weakness to ask for mercy. After the execution, Achmed, the Reis Effendina, came to Leopold. His anger had gone as quickly as it had come. "Effendi, justice is satisfied, but not completely. We have to get the others. I hope you will not deny us your help."

"Why this question?"

"Because of your humanity. I have to sincerely say, I will not listen to any more pleas from you. If you don't like it, let Ben Nil lead us to the new seribah. You can stay here, so you will not have to reproach yourself with your tender conscience."

"My conscience is as strong as yours. If I am the person sinned against, I must put in a good word for him. If it doesn't work, I have done my duty and don't have to reproach myself."

"So you are coming with us to lead us? I prefer that. You are a better leader and counsellor than Ben Nil. Don't you fear they have escaped already? They have to think you will return."

"No, I have told them you are a day's journey away from them. They believed it and feel safe for the day. They have taken our weapons so I would have to wait for you."

"So we will catch them. When do we start?"

"As soon as possible. We borrow one more boat from the Bor and we will be enough men for the people we want to overcome."

"But we have to come from a different direction. They should not notice our arrival."

"Certainly! They know we escaped in a westerly direction and, if they will be watching at all, it will be in this region. We have to come from the east. Take twenty men besides me and Ben Nil. That should be enough."

Leopold and Ben Nil took the small boat they had before. The others followed in larger vessels. When the moon appeared, Leopold saw they were at their destination. It was only a short march to the seribah. Leopold went twenty paces ahead. He had not reached the end of the wood when he saw the light of a fire and heard loud voices. He let the soldiers stop and went ahead by himself. He was determined to overpower the slave-hunters without shedding blood. He turned around and collected his people. The men of the seribah were clearly visible and Leopold intended to give his views on how to advance to the Reis. But the Reis Effendina took him by the arm and led him to the side. Leopold had no idea why.

"Come here, I don't want you to be hit by any bullets."

"But they sit there without their rifles."

At this point Ben Nil came running and told Leopold the Reis Effendina had given the order to shoot. "Be quiet," said the Reis angrily.

He pointed in the direction of the slave-hunters and shouted: "Fire." Before Leopold could say or do anything, twenty shots rang out. He hurried to the fire to look after the fallen. Nine were hit by several bullets and were dead. Three were heavily wounded. Leopold had wanted no bloodshed.

The Reis Effendina stood nearby and observed him. Leopold went to him and asked excitedly: "Was that necessary? Why didn't you tell me beforehand? Did they all have to be murdered?"

"Murdered?" asked the Egyptian, exasperated. "I forgive you this questioning because you are excited. Could I leave them to continue their business?"

"I wouldn't ask for that, but couldn't you take them into your service as you did before?

"I did that because of your plea. If I conformed to your wishes constantly, I would soon have more of them than of my own soldiers. They would eventually force me to become a slave-hunter. You have seen the executed. Are there still any alive?"

"Three of them are, but they are badly wounded. They can't get up."

The Reis Effendina went to his soldiers and gave some orders which Leopold couldn't hear, but he could see three of them rushing to the wounded. Three more shots told him what kind of order this was. They went into the officer's hut where they found Leopold's and Ben Nil's weapons. The other contents of these huts were given to the Bor. They were delighted. They would collect them in the morning and burn the huts.

Chapter 20

The village of the Gohk

On the sixth day after the evening of the merciless execution, their train went like an endless snail through a big wood. Its giant trees were a roof of leaves, through which even a sunbeam couldn't pass. They were in constant twilight, which was welcome. It saved them from the glowing heat which destroyed all life in this waterless area. The floor of this tract of land was equally, if not more, dangerous. It was a swamp in which it seemed inexplicable that such trees could exist without sinking. The ground was pulpy: It seemed that it would swallow anything that moved on it. Leopold was constantly worried that the man in front of him would disappear below this pulp. It slapped and snapped, but no one was sucked under. He couldn't find an answer.

They were all riding. In front were the Bor, then the soldiers, behind them the loaded oxen. Behind Leopold was another troop of Bors. It was lucky, thought Leopold, that the Blacks had joined them. Without them they would never have reached their destination. Like all people, they knew the paths of their homeland. Their trained eyes easily distinguished the places one could trust. But two next to each other did not dare to ride.

Leopold admired the people and got to know the oxen, whose legs almost disappeared with every step. And yet they trod on, untiring.

This went on for three days. They all were fed up by now when, in front, there could be heard a long-drawn-out cry, which was immediately repeated by all the Bors. Agadi explained this was a cry of a happy incident. After only a few minutes, Leopold saw sunlight coming through the trees, sparser now, and he felt fresh air entering his lungs. The swamp was at its end. Behind Leopold was the rattling voice of Selim: "Hamdulillah! The big pulp has been overcome. It opened its jaws to swallow us, but we went over it like heroes, not fearing dragons. Now it closed its big mouth and disappeared with annoyance and shame that it could not devour Selim, heroic victor over all the swamps and mires of the universe."

The old braggart left no opportunity to show off. Victor over all the swamps and mires surpassed everything Leopold had heard from him.

They reached Wagunda by nightfall. A messenger had prepared the inhabitants for their reason for coming. When he returned, the whole village followed him. Everyone was in their best finery. An old grey haired man, the chief of the village, only wore a loincloth and a plaited wattling on his head. It was covered with feathers. From now on, they were to move forward. In front came the leaders, the Reis Effendina, Leopold and Woat, the chief of the Bor. The rest behind. They had to make much noise and shoot their rifles as often as possible.

Luckily, the terrain was favourable to such exercise. When they were near the village, the Gohk lined up in two rows, then, with weapons swinging and much shouting they ran towards their guests, their leader in front of them. They were on foot. Their weapons were spears, sabres, knives, clubs, bows and arrows. There were three rifles among them. The Reis Effendina and his group moved forward too. The Gohks ran through between the lines of their guests. The guests did the same. The main thing was the noise. They all shouted like mad. Leopold had a raw throat for a few days afterwards. Who travels like him has to be able to sing with the nightingales and howl with the wolves.

This performance of vocal activity lasted for a quarter of an hour, then the mock attack stopped as on command. The chief of the Gohks came toward the Reis Effendina. With many bows, hands and body twisting, he held a speech for another quarter of an hour. Luckily it was too long to be translated. At its end the Gohks broke out in a wild clamour of jubilation, in which the guests joined with all their might.

Now came the moment in which the Reis Effendina was going to answer. He cleared his throat and spoke a few noble sentences. He made a short pause to leave Agadi time to translate. The Reis continued with another few sentences and paused until he realised that his rhetoric was at its end. He then raised his hand in expectation of the same vocal approval as the chief before him. Unfortunately, he inspired nobody and the result was total silence. The guests were unsure how to react. How should this painful impression which caused the silence be wiped away? How could this be remedied? Agadi spoke to the chief and pointed at Leopold. He should give them a speech.

A speech? Yes, the Gohk were to see and listen to him. The madder he appeared, the better impression it would produce. He drove his ox to a frenzied speed, rode ten times around the chief of the Gohk, reciting Hamlet's soliloquy, 'to be or not to be', with the loudest voice he could master. Then, jumping off his animal at full speed, he performed several cart-wheels and somersaults, while still reciting poems. He then ran to his ox and made it run another five times around the chief while he uttered the war cries of the Apaches. He then returned to his place.

What followed was indescribable. At first there was total silence, then Agadi started to shout with enthusiasm, in which all the others joined. And what shouting! Everybody danced and shouted as if he had a hundred voices. If hell had broken loose, against this noise it would have crept away in shame. Except Leopold, only the Reis Effendina kept quiet. He came to Leopold and said: "Effendi, I almost thought your brain had cracked. You, the calmest of us all, behaved as if you had lost your mind. I felt like running away."

"In other words, you disliked my performance," Leopold laughed.

"No, I didn't like it at all. You deprived us of our dignity. I am the representative of the Viceroy, whose authority must suffer with this madness," said the Reis Effendina.

"I had not thought about the authority of the Viceroy, but I intended to gain authority with these people. I don't believe the Viceroy will lose his throne because of my behaviour. Test the matter before you reproach."

"But you must admit that my speech was more dignified than yours."

"For me, yours was the more dignified. But did you address me?"

"No, the Gohk."

"So it is up to them to decide. With their applause and behaviour they have given the answer."

This answer was followed by the chief of the Gohk. He had danced and applauded like all the others. Now he, holding a banner made of a rod with a monkey skin on top, came over. It was the sign for assembly. Everybody went back to their place. The leader of the Gohk held a short consultation with a few men, who in our terms would be called councillors. Then he addressed the Reis Effendina and Leopold via an interpreter:

"Sir, I have heard you have come to rescue us from a great danger. You are a favourite of the Viceroy. We are not his subjects, but you are respected by us. Be our guest and stay as long as you like here." Then he turned to Leopold. "Effendi, the leader of the Bor, who are our brothers, has told me of your deeds. You come from a country which is full of famous people. You are blowing your enemies away like dust and nobody can vanquish you. I have heard and seen you speak as I never saw or heard anyone before. Whoever hears your voice is intoxicated as if from alcohol. Your body movements show the truth of your words. You are the man to save us. I will put my people under your command. Tell me whether you want to be their leader."

This was exaggerated and Leopold felt he could almost take the word of the braggart Selim for himself: To be the 'greatest hero of the universe'. They wanted him as a general. He felt no reason to decline. In this position he would at least be sure that no mistakes were made.

He declared to the chief that he accepted the offer.

When he told his people Poldi's answer, they gave cries of joy, and anybody with legs danced around their new General. After about ten minutes of this carry-on, they were invited to the village, where they were finally offered a meal. By this time, everybody was hungry. On the way, Leopold observed that the village was built on a hill whose other three sides were too steep to climb and could only be reached the way they came up. Defence possibilities of this place were good. The village was surrounded by a wall of thorny plants with only a small entrance. It could be defended easily, but for one disadvantage; there was no water up there and a siege could be fatal. While the others kept eating, Leopold went to reconnoitre the terrain. The matter was not urgent because Ben Mubarek was not expected for a few days. The enemy was expected to come from the south-east. They had to cross the water and there was only one place they could use as a ford. He intended to have one detachment hidden on the far side of the water and another to receive the enemy on the nearside. Ben Mubarek would have no way out. It was life or death. He would have to surrender.

Leopold was happy with his plan and hurried to explain it to the various chiefs. They were all sitting in the Reis Effendina's tent, but looked away when he entered. Something was wrong. Leopold asked the Reis what had happened.

The Reis asked: "Are you an officer?"

"No," answered Leopold.

"Well, I am and as Reis Effendina, a high-ranking one. You will agree, therefore, that it is I who have to make a plan. The leader of the Gohk gave you command over his people. He can do that, but do you think I would renounce the command over all the others?"

Achmed spoke in a downright, unfriendly way. He had become jealous and felt insulted. Leopold had done him good service and it was he who should feel insulted. He didn't, but answered in his usual calm manner: "How did you come to ask this question? Did I ask you to renounce your rights? When the chief of the Gohk asked me to be their leader, you were quiet upon my answer. I assumed that you were in agreement with this decision. Now, when I hear that is not the case, I am prepared to withdraw. But I will be allowed to partake in the battle?"

"Yes, as long as you obey my command."

Leopold turned round: "Allah may protect you." He left the hut.

Outside waited Ben Nil. He expected to see Leopold coming out annoyed. "Your calm face tells me they have not been stupid enough to take away your command."

"Who told you they were going to do that?"

"The interpreter. The Reis Effendina threatened them to withdraw and leave Wagunda to its fate, if he were not the one to take over the command. Such ingratitude must annoy you."

"It is insulting but doesn't annoy me. I am allowed to partake in the battle, providing I obey."

"You, obey?" Ben Nil was astounded. "Wait here until I return. I have to go inside and tell them what they are against you."

Ben Nil wanted to leave, but Leopold grabbed him by his arm. "Stay, they won't listen to you. They will be taught by events."

"What are you going to do? Allow them to treat you as a normal soldier, or put you among the Negroes, like one of them?"

"No. Go to your hut, collect your belongings and come back to my hut."

Ben Nil returned soon. They left the village, walked down the hill to the other side of the sea, to stay and sleep at the edge of the wood. But Leopold couldn't fall asleep. The worry about the fate of those he had left behind did not let him rest. After a while an idea hit him; it didn't bring him sleep, but he calmed down somewhat.

Ben Nil, whose sleep was also restless, woke up. "What now, Effendi, do we go back to the village?"

"No, we are going to Foguda."

"To Foguda? The village of the Gohk of which the interpreter told us when he described the surrounding area? What do we want there?"

"To get help for Wagunda."

"Should we not leave these ungrateful people to their fate?"

"No. I know they will run into bad luck if I don't help them. As they reject my help, I have to force them to accept."

"How will you tell them, as you don't speak their language?"

I trust my luck. Perhaps there will be someone who can speak a little Arabic. If not, there is sign-language and a few words I remember."

"And you believe the Foguda warriors will accompany you?"

"I am convinced. They belong to the same tribe."

"All right, you always have the best ideas. Let's go. We have no animals to ride on and Foguda is three days away. What will we live on?"

"Fruit, and we will shoot birds or animals. By the way, I ate so much yesterday, I don't need anything today."

They had just walked ten minutes when they heard panting behind them. It sounded like a dog who had lost its master and followed his track anxiously. They were being pursued, but they soon saw there was nothing to fear. It was Selim who came running. "Stop, Effendi, where are you going?"

"Tell us first where you are going."

"With you," he answered, breathing heavily.

"In Allah's name, remain here, we don't need you."

"You don't need me, the most valiant of heroes?"

"I don't need you, the bringer of mischief. Every time I took you with me, you brought bad luck."

"Allah, Allah, don't say that, Effendi. All my steps are followed by happiness and blessing. Why don't you stay? Why did you leave the village last night?"

"Because I found ingratitude."

"I have heard it. The soldiers regret it; they like you. They hope you will return. When I rose and looked for you, because I am your natural guardian and protector, I took my weapons and left the village to find you."

"To return immediately."

"No, Effendi, I am coming with you."

"And I order you to return to the Reis Effendina. We are heading toward danger and we don't need you."

"That's what you think. If you really chase me away, I will follow you from the distance."

Ben Nil stood by him and pleaded for him. What should Leopold do? Selim was loyal but brought bad luck, again and again; whenever he took him along. Against his better judgement he decided to take him along.

"I know you will bring us bad luck, but I will try it again if you promise to follow my orders precisely."

"All your orders," Selim asserted with his hands on his heart. "You can demand everything from me, only don't ask me to leave you."

Chapter 21

In the powers of the deadly enemy

The three walked on. They walked fast. Selim had the longest legs and followed easily, but complained of stomach trouble. No wonder after his performance in eating.

The previous day they had gone through the ford on oxen. Today they had to wade through it, whereby the waters reached up to their chest. Now they turned slightly south, away from the direction where Ben Mubarek was expected. Leopold relied less on the description of the route given by the interpreter, but went according to his compass. He knew the direction of their destination. They did not come across any swamps, but through a wood that seemed to be without an end. The trees stood far apart, but close enough to give them pleasing shade. The ground was dry and the wandering was easy. When they reached a large pool with water, Leopold shot a few birds which they roasted in the evening.

The next day was not as lucky as the one before. They encountered swamps where they had to be careful and deviated their direction. There was no sign of life and the evening came without their having seen an animal which they could hunt. They had to lie down without having eaten anything from early in the morning. Selim complained and Leopold had to calm him by asserting that they would have better luck the next day.

The next day started with Selim's grumbling. If Leopold had let him grumble, a lot of misery would have been avoided. But Selim was an insatiable eater. Hunger hurts and Leopold felt sorry for him. Ben Nil also looked exhausted.

As if in answer to their needs, they heard bird voices south of them. Leopold swerved to the left and took his rifle in his hands. Ben Nil saw it and asked whether he would be allowed to come along. Leopold didn't mind, he knew Ben Nil was a good shot. Selim also wanted to come along.

"From my bullet, every bird trembles."

"And flies away unhurt," added Leopold. "You wait here by the bushes. You, bad luck bringer, would scare away every bird or animal. Stay here at the edge of the bushes, so we can find you afterwards. Don't run away."

"All right, I will stay here. I have promised to do everything you demand. Only bring something to eat." Selim sat down. The others whisked along the edge of the wood toward the point of the swamp. They pressed carefully into the reed until they saw two cranes standing in the water. They seemed a bit old, but hunger is the best cook. Two shots and they had their breakfast, when suddenly a flock of peewits flew over them.

"What is that?" asked Leopold, "These birds are scared by somebody."

"They were scared by us," ventured Ben Nil.

"Oh no," whispered Leopold, "we are covered by the reed. If it was us, the wouldn't fly over us."

"They have seen Selim, then."

"That is possible. Let's go back." They both carried one bird in their hand. "Now we have something to eat," Ben Nil laughed, satisfied, "Selim will stop moaning."

When they reached the edge of the wood, they couldn't see him. "He will have gone and tried to shoot something. It is Selim who has scared the peewits," said Ben Nil.

"That is quite possible, even probable." The otherwise careful Leopold did not feel disquieted and went to the place where they had left Selim.

"He went into the wood, but why?" asked Leopold.

He had hardly finished that question when he received an unexpected answer. Several figures came from behind the bushes. With rifles lifted for a hit, they pressed onto Leopold and Ben Nil. Leopold tried to jump back, but too late. One hit his head and he lost consciousness.

Some hours later, when he awoke, his eyes were looking at a peculiar fog behind which sat several figures. His head hurt horribly. He wanted to touch it, but he couldn't. His arms were tightly bound against his body.

"The son of a dog has his eyes open." It sounded near him. "He is still alive. What a joy for us."

The voice came to Leopold as through a thick cloud, or a wall. It sounded familiar, but he thought and thought in vain: His senses were half-paralyzed from the attack.

"If you had, against my order, killed him," Leopold heard the voice again, "we would have lost great enjoyment. As he is alive, he will finally taste the torture I have often threatened in vein. This time, he won't escape again."

Now he knew who the speaker was. It was Ben Mubarek, his deadly enemy. Leopold closed his eyes, but not because of horror. For him, no situation existed where a person had to despair. But, before everything else, he needed a rest. A rest for his senses to be fully awake. When he awoke the second time, his head still hurt, but he felt strong again externally and internally clear, as if nothing had happened.

Leopold raised his eyelids a little, to look around, furtively. What he saw was not comforting. It was still daytime. He lay where he had been felled. Right and left were Ben Nil and Selim, equally tied hand and foot. In front of him sat Ben Mubarek, his eyes looking at Leopold with hatred. Behind him his nearest subordinates. Further on the Dinkas, who were busy loading oxen with forked branches. These were for the prospective slaves who had to carry them around their necks, plus a whole amount of ropes and chains.

"Open your eyes, you son of a dog," snarled Ben Mubarek. "Do you think I can't see you looking through your lids?"

It served no purpose to irritate Ben Mubarek. Leopold opened his eyes. Nevertheless, he received a crack with a hippopotamus-whip.

"Allah finally listened to my prayer and gave you into my hands. Do you know what to expect?"

"Yes," Leopold answered calmly, "freedom."

"Son of a dog, you dare to mock me?" shouted the slave-hunter and gave him a few more lashes with the whip. "The torture you can expect, I have told you several times. You were lucky to escape. This time, you will not be able to run away. First, I will cut off your eyelids. You will die slowly by not being able to sleep."

"You will die before me and Allah will torture your soul with whatever you have decided to do to me and will be unable to execute."

Leopold said this because an inner voice assured him that he would be able to escape this time too. He did not despair, he trusted in God, his sagacity, his strength and his luck. He also knew that Ben Mubarek would not do anything now, as any injury or illness would delay his task in hand, to attack Foguda. It was his intention to save him for longer torture.

"Unable to execute?" Mubarek shouted. "It only needs a wink from me and my order will be executed. But I have neither the time nor the mind for that now. First I will torment you by seeing those you wanted to save. Their pains will make you suffer as well. Don't believe that you will be freed by anybody. I know what you hope for, but it will come to nothing."

"You don't know everything," maintained Leopold, in order to trick him to say more."

"Everything," mocked Ben Mubarek. "You have taken my messenger prisoner and learned of my plans."

"Is that all you know?" countered Leopold.

"Then you went to my seribah and destroyed it. Then to the Gohks in Wagunda to warn them."

"You are dreaming," Leopold laughed, mocking him to keep him talking.

"I don't dream, my informant is sure. Your clever Selim told me everything. You have broken with the Reis Effendina and went to Foguda to get help. Luckily I have changed my plans and arrived here earlier than you expected. I had the good idea to take Foguda before Wagunda. If all the men under the Reis Effendina are as clever as your Selim, I will have an easy victory. I threatened him with death and he told me everything I wanted to know. You are lost. We will now go to Foguda and you will see a slave-hunt. It will give you a foretaste of what you can expect."

Ben Mubarek rose and gave a sign to start the march to Foguda.

Nobody attended the prisoners, and Leopold took the opportunity to ask Selim: "Did you really see Ben Mubarek before he took you prisoner?"

"Yes, Effendi, I saw him with five of his asakers."

"And you still stayed seated?"

"Certainly, Effendi. Did you forget asking me to stay put? And I promised to obey all your orders."

Leopold was overcome by anger. "You stupid donkey of all donkeys. How could I know that Ben Mubarek would come? If you had jumped into the bushes and warned us, he would be our prisoner now. And how is it that you gave him such complete information?"

"You have heard it from him. He threatened me with death."

"You sheepshead. If I can't rescue you, you will be killed in spite of the complete information you gave."

"Do you think you will be able to rescue us, dear Effendi?" Selim asked dejectedly.

"I have not lost hope. Pray to Allah that..." He was interrupted. Several white asakers told them to prepare for the march. Ben Mubarek seemed to try to stop his prisoners being in touch with black asakers or with any of the Dinkas. He was afraid they would betray the fact that their leader, Agadi, was their friend. Leopold had to rise and received a heavy shebah. A shebah is a heavy forked branch of a tree, into which the neck of the slave will be put. Another piece of wood across the back of the neck would prevent him from escaping. The slave's hands were then untied because he had to carry the shebah. As it seemed, the heaviest shebah was selected for Leopold. That was seemingly not enough. Two metal handcuffs connected by a chain were put on his hands. He tricked the asakers by pressing his elbows tightly against his body and clenching his fingers together as hard as he could. By doing this, his wrist became thicker and the asakers had to use a bigger pair of cuffs. He hoped this would enable him to escape from his fetters. From the shebah he hoped he would be freed after the march.

The march began. A rope was fastened at the point of Leopold's shebah, the other end of which was attached to Ben Mubarek's saddle. With the shebah around his neck, he had to stagger along like a slave. Ben Nil's and Selim's shebahs where lighter, but also tied to other riders.

Leopold thought: If the Dinkas knew the real state of affairs, they would probably rebel or even free the prisoners. He intended to use the first opportunity to risk talking to them. When one of their spies came back to report to Ben Mubarek, he searched his brain for the few words he knew in their language. When the Dinka had finished his report and turned to leave, Leopold shouted: "Ben Mubarek is a bad fellow, he wanted to kill your sheik. Your sheik is with us. He is our friend now..."

He got no further. Ben Mubarek tore on the rope which tied his shebah and made him to fall down: "Silence, you son of a dog, your miserable liar. Shall I stop your mouth with this whip?"

He hit Leopold several times while he was trying to get up, and told the Dinka to go. The man obeyed and Leopold had the impression that his words didn't have the wanted effect. "If you talk to a Dinka again I will gag you."

To be gagged for a day or even longer is no pleasure. Leopold decided not to irritate Ben Mubarek again.

They reached a dense wood. It took them two hours to get through. It was nearly dark when they entered open land again. It was dark and about eight o'clock when they met their spies, who had waited for them. The stars were not out, but Leopold noticed they had taken a rest between bushes, a good hiding place for the slave-hunters. The three prisoners were untied from the saddles but bound at their feet.

That meant they had to lie down, which was rather uncomfortable because no one thought of taking off their shebahs. Three men were ordered to sit near and guard them.

There were no fires, but the sound of chains and weapons told Leopold they prepared for an attack. Maybe the village was near and a warning cry would be heard. He knew this might cost his life, but it would be worth it to save many others. If he only knew that such a warning would have success, he would gladly risk his life. But there were other deliberations as well. He intended to save the Gohk in

190

Wagunda, the Reis Effendina and his people. But that wouldn't be possible if he were murdered here.

These thoughts tortured him. The Dinkas and the asakers moved on, leaving only a few men to guard the oxen and the prisoners. Time was pressing and Leopold's fear for the threatened village grew from minute to minute. He tried hard to free at least one hand, but the heat of the day had made them swell. He tried in vain. A quarter of an hour after the slave-hunters had left, his disquiet had reached such a pitch that he could no longer restrain himself. He put his fettered hands at his mouth, took a deep breath and shouted as some peoples do when attacking. He did it two or three times without the guards interfering. One of them even laughed.

"Sheepshead! Do you think Ben Mubarek didn't expect that? He calculated that you would warn the black dogs. From here to the village is an hour's walk. In the name of Allah, shout as much as you like, if it gives you pleasure. It is the last pleasure you will have in this life."

Leopold was almost ashamed, but he was glad to have done what he could and without any harm to himself. Foguda could not be saved. Leopold lay there as with fever. One quarter of an hour went after the other. Leopold calculated by the stars that it was between ten and eleven o'clock when the sky in the south reddened. "Hamdulillah! It has started," continued the last speaker. "The rats will be fumigated."

"Do you want to scorch them?" Leopold asked, horrified.

"Scorch them?" he laughed. "You don't seem to know how a slave-hunt works."

"I am not a slave-hunter."

"I will describe it to you."

"Be quiet, I don't want to hear it."

"You must hear it, you can't order me. If I want to speak – I speak. And, as I know it torments you, I will tell you how we make slaves."

Leopold did not reply and the guard continued: "You know that all Negro villages are surrounded by thorn-hedges. These are mostly dried out and burn easily. They are put on fire at several places. In a few minutes the whole fence is ablaze. Sparks fall on their huts, which are mostly made of reed and burn immediately. The blacks awake and want to save themselves. The old ones and the small children are too weak. The strong ones, and it is those we want, run for the entrance. Outside it is dark. They are blinded and don't see who and what is in front of them. They will be grabbed and tied up. Whoever defends himself will be shot or slain."

"Stop your description. You are devils," said Ben Nil.

"You are right," laughed the other. "We are devils, and you soon

191

will find we are worse. You will be treated worse than the Negroes." The man continued: "Old women and children who manage to reach the entrance are driven back. This saves powder."

The rascal carried on talking. Leopold was unable to stop him. The sky in the south grew lighter – the village burned. A few hours passed again. It was past midnight when two asakers arrived to tell the guards to show the imprisoned dogs what they had caught. The ties were taken off the prisoner's feet to enable them to walk to Foguda. After half an hour they passed fields whose owners were unable to bring home the harvest. Then they reached the village. It was no longer burning.

Outside the burned thorn-fence there were several fires where the slave-hunters surrounded their loot. This consisted of human beings and animals. The herds of the Negro villages were usually kept outside and were more valued than humans. A cow was twice the value of a young strong slave.

Between two large fires lay the unlucky people who, unsuspectingly, slept calmly in their huts. They were lying in long rows next to each other. They were separated from women and children. The guards went to and fro among these rows, whipping anybody who moved. Leopold, Ben Nil and Selim turned away from this picture of horror.

Ben Mubarek stood with the children. He noticed the prisoners turning away and ordered them to be tied to trees in the direction of this ghastly scene. "These sons of dogs don't want to see. If they close their eyes, whip them until they obey."

On their right, they saw the village whose ashes still smouldered. Between and on these ashes they saw remnants of burned bodies. Ben Mubarek returned to the children. All those he found strong enough to withstand the hardship of the march remained. The others were taken away. Leopold thought they would be freed from their fetters and left to simply run away. But he was mistaken. As soon as the tests were ended he heard Ben Mubarek's order. A number of his people went to the separated children. The knives of these monsters flashed. Leopold cried out and closed his eyes. Several strokes with the whip forced him to open them again. When he looked at the separated children – they were all dead. The mothers and fathers cried and howled with pain. They pranced in their fetters. They wanted to revenge the death of their children. Poor people. They were silenced with the whip. Some of them, when this treatment didn't help, were simply shot.

Leopold's anger was indescribable. His limbs trembled. Not because of weakness, but from inner fury. How often had he spared Ben Mubarek or his accomplices. He regretted it now. But it wasn't finished yet. Ben Mubarek tested the adults now. Those who didn't pass his examination were not removed, but killed on the spot. Now the shebahs and metal chains were brought. The 'slaves' kept quiet now, realising that opposition could only worsen their plight.

After Ben Mubarek finished his work, he came to Leopold and grinned mockingly. "Well, how do you like it? Don't you think we made a good catch and an excellent business?"

Leopold supressed his indignation and replied calmly: "Your catch is splendid. I estimate there are at least two hundred slaves. Even if a quarter will perish on the way, you will have profit for a hundred and fifty of them. In addition you have their herd – I envy you."

If this scene had been different, Leopold would have laughed at Mubarek's face. He looked amazed. "You envy me? Allah does wonders. Another spirit must have come to you."

"That is the case, and I think you will get to know it soon."

"Do you want to become a slave-hunter?"

"No, not that. I am not after slaves, but there are a few people I intend to catch, I hope soon."

"Who are they?"

"I could keep that a secret, but I will tell you so as not to allow you to think I am a coward or in despair. It is you I am going to catch, you and all your white asakers!" Ben Mubarek broke out in a resounding laughter.

"Me and my asakers? Why not my black soldiers?"

"Because they were cheated and lied to. That's why the punishment you can expect will hit you and your asakers as well," Ben Mubarek stared into Leopold's face for a minute. Then he stepped towards him and tested his shebah and his handcuffs. When he found them in order he said: "I almost believed that you were rid of your fetters and hoped to be free again. But this isn't the case, so I assume you have gone mad."

"I have all my senses and I know what I am talking about."

"Is that so? I will show you how I treat such..." He stopped and looked at Leopold with anger and contempt. Leopold took this calmly. Ben Mubarek had pulled his knife intending to push it into Leopold's chest; but he thought it over, grinned and returned the knife to his belt. "No, you will not excite me. You know you are lost and want a quick death. To escape torture you tried to excite me, but you are mistaken. I will spare you until I have attacked Wagunda. Then I will have your beloved friend, the Reis Effendina as well, and you will outbid each other with your cries of pain."

Ben Mubarek put his hands with mocking friendliness on Leopold's shoulders. "You see how superior my position is? No Allah or devil can rescue you, you are lost. Perhaps you expect help from the Reis Effendina. I will tell you we are marching to Wagunda tonight. The Reis does not expect us so soon; we will surprise him. The three of you will eat now, to be strong enough to bear the journey." Ben Mubarek turned away. Leopold had achieved his intention and was happy with Mubarek's information. He would, for the moment, do nothing against his life.

Chapter 22

The end of the slave-hunters

The prisoners were fed by hand. They received enough until they were satiated. The march then began. The train had the following order. In front the two guides, who had an excellent knowledge of the terrain, then the 'slaves' with their shebahs and chains, then the stolen herds and the three white captives, also with a shebah each and in chains. Then came a troop of ten of Ben Mubarek's asakers, after which came the boss himself. Two straps were attached to his saddle. One of them was fastened to the point of Leopold's shebah, the other was wound around Ben Nil's body. This way they were forced to ride behind their tormenter. Another strap led from Leopold's saddle to Selim's ox. This arrangement was another design of torture. Every wrong step of their animals would pull Leopold's shebah out of position and cause him terrible pain. Ben Mubarek turned around and said:

"I want to keep you alive until after the attack on Wagunda. You will ride, but with the shebah. Ben Nil and Selim will ride too, in chains, but without the added shebah. I trust you will be grateful for that."

These mocking words told Leopold there was a difficult ride ahead. He took it calmly because he couldn't do anything to save himself at the moment. His only hope was based on water. On water? Why?

When they first put handcuffs on him, he managed to get large ones, which, with a possible loss of some skin or even pieces of flesh, he would be able to prise off. But he didn't calculate the heat. His hands were swollen and sweating, constantly. It was impossible, even with the greatest effort, to strip off the fetters. To remedy this he needed cold water.

Behind Selim were all the others. After five minutes, Leopold noticed they had given him the worst of the oxen, which, from time to time tried to throw off its rider. Also from time to time Ben Mubarek pulled on the strap, causing more pain. The asakers behind Selim hit his ox, which became obstinate and pulled to the side, thereby tugging Leopold backwards. It was such a ride that Leopold had never before and never again wished to have. To judge by the stars, it was about three o'clock in the morning. The only right left to them was that they were allowed to talk to each other. Or was this also a calculation? Should they be allowed to make plans for their freedom in order to perceive more and more the difficulties and the impossibility of escaping?

"Effendi," Ben Nil sighed in an undertone, "this time we are finished."

"As long I am alive, there is no such thing."

"How can you still hope with a shebah, an invention of hell, round your neck?"

"Don't let's talk about it. You never know who can hear us."

At daybreak Leopold could no longer feel his arms. His legs were bloody and yet they kept going until noon. The oxen needed a rest. They were at a place with grass and water. The three prisoners were untied from their animals. When Leopold's feet touched the ground, they couldn't carry him. He sank to the ground.

"Are you that far already?" Ben Mubarek laughed. "Are you still going to boast about your strength?" .

"When did I ever boast about my strength?" countered Leopold. "Do you think I am suffering? On the contrary, I enjoy myself because I know you won't reach Wagunda in time."

"I won't? Why?"

"Because I will prevent you from doing so."

Ben Mubarek looked down, thinking. Then he turned away. Leopold hoped to have reached what he wanted, a little less cruel treatment. His trouser-legs were stiff with blood, but he soon realised that his weakness was only temporary. But he wouldn't allow anybody to notice it and pretended to be weaker than he actually was. His method would not be without success.

They received meat and water. After two hours' rest, Leopold's shebah would be taken off him and he received a better ox to ride on. Toward evening he felt his strength had returned. Only his limbs felt a little stiff.

Again they received their meal. A large fire was lit in order to keep the stinging flies away. Ben Nil and Selim had to lay down there, because the light of the fire would make it easier to guard them. Ben Mubarek came to Leopold, tested the shebah and the handcuffs and told him: "You, I will not leave outside. You will sleep in my tent where I can be sure of you."

Leopold was put in the back of Ben Mubarek's tent. His feet were tied with straps, the point of his shebah was tied to the tent-rod. He could move neither his head nor his body. It was more than an uncomfortable situation. Ben Mubarek's encampment was made with soft blankets and a jug of water was placed near him. This water could save Leopold, but it was outside his reach.

When Ben Mubarek was lying down he remarked: "Don't even think about escaping. If you just move, the tent will shake or even collapse. Besides, there are guards outside the tent."

The man was right, but if the water were reachable, he would have tried in spite of all that. Ben Mubarek closed the curtain and went to sleep without further remarks. Leopold did not speak either. He could not sleep and tortured his brain to come up with alternative ideas for his rescue, but in vain. Sometimes he fell into a half-slumber, but when morning came, he was more tired than the night before. His feet were untied and his shebah loosened from the tent-rod. He was fed again. After this his shebah was removed and he was tied onto his ox. Ben Nil and Selim as well. One of the guides was missing. Leopold learned later that he had been sent in advance to spy out the situation.

While he and Ben Nil did not complain about their condition in the saddle, Selim started to moan. It was clear he could not take the exertion. Although he was partly responsible for the present situation, Leopold felt sorry for him. To comfort him, Leopold threw a few consoling remarks, but Selim was ungrateful. "Be silent, Effendi. Everything I suffer is your fault."

"My fault? Why?" Leopold asked, astonished.

"If you had stayed in Wagunda, I wouldn't have run after you. My limbs are like paper, my soul cries more than it can rain in one year and this ox is my death."

"How is that? I always believed you were such a good rider."

"That I am. I am the most daring and the most dexterous rider in the world, I break in the wildest horses; but which true believer ever had to ride on an ox?"

Selim could not stop bragging, even in their present position.

Ben Nil came closer to Leopold. "When do you think we will reach Wagunda?"

"Probably tonight. In any case sooner than the Reis Effendina expects Ben Mubarek and his people."

"So our friends are lost as well."

"Not yet. Until then a lot of things can happen. Don't despair."

There were enough reasons to deny any hopes. It must be assumed that Ben Mubarek would attack tonight, if he found the village unprepared. If people were asleep and, as in Foguda, fires lit around the village, their friends could be assumed lost.

In short, the final decision was fast approaching If no saving idea came in time, there would be no further need for it.

"Do you think," asked Ben Nil, "the Reis Effendina would be on his guard?"

"I doubt that," replied Leopold. "If he were, it wouldn't be of use for the three of us. If Ben Mubarek saw he would be lost, he would simply kill us."

"Allah! This is true."

"We have to be free before the battle starts."

"That is impossible. I will never see my people again, but I have one consolation. I will die on your side, my dear Effendi."

"I hope you will live a long and happy life. You deserve it. I beg you not to doubt the help of Allah."

Ben Nil didn't answer and Leopold was not quite as confident as he appeared. Secretly he tried to turn the chain on his hands, but it was in vain. Even if he had succeeded, he was still tied with straps and he had no weapons.

The morning passed. When the sun stood at its highest, they stopped to give the exhausted animals a rest. One could see they would endure the speed only till evening. The prisoners received dried meat, of which Ben Mubarek had plenty. After two hours they were off again. Toward evening they had reached the ford, when the spy emerged from behind the bushes. Leopold rode behind and could hear the report.

"Well," asked Ben Mubarek, "have you been lucky?"

"Yes, master," answered the spy, "luckier than I could have hoped."

"How is that?"

"I managed to eavesdrop on two men."

"Blacks from Wagunda?"

"No, white asakers of the Reis Effendina who went into the wood to shoot game. They found none and they just talked."

"What did you hear?"

"That you are expected in four or five days."

"So they are not prepared yet?"

"They want to send spies toward you and will let you come to the sea below the village. There you would be driven into the sea by superior powers."

"That is not new to me. I have heard it from Selim, one of our prisoners. Who is their leader, the Reis Effendina?"

"Yes, but they have not much trust in him. The men said, they would have preferred Poldi Ben Anglesi. The Gohks would have preferred him too."

At that, Ben Mubarek turned around. "Did you hear that praise? I hope you won't disappoint them."

"I will do my utmost," replied Leopold calmly.

"Your possibilities are at an end now," ventured Ben Mubarek, laughing maliciously, then he turned to the spy again: "What else did you hear?"

"Nothing more. They believe the three prisoners went back the way they came."

"So they don't know they went to Foguda?"

"No, they think Poldi Ben Anglesi has been insulted by the Reis Effendina and that he has withdrawn."

"I am satisfied with what you have learned. How deep is the ford?"

"A rider will get wet to his knees."

"Do you know a place near the village where we will not be discovered?"

"Yes. Half-way between here and the village there is a place. If we don't burn a fire, it would not be possible to be seen from Wagunda."

"Well, take us there. We will stay there only a short time, because the attack will take place before midnight."

"Permit me to bring to your attention the fact that the inhabitants of the village have guests. Where there are visitors, people go to bed later."

"That is true. People sleep deepest between midnight and sunrise. We will attack later. Later, I will send another spy there. Now, let's go on."

They went through the ford. Half an hour later the man leading the group turned toward a wood. He declared this to be the nearest and best hiding place. The trees were strong and tall. They stood far apart.

They had reached this place at the right time. They dismounted and the shebahs were immediately put back on the prisoners. It began to get dark. Some men were busy putting up their leader's tent. As the captives had the shebah and handcuffs put on them, they were paid less attention and could speak together undisturbed.

"The situation is bad, Effendi," said Ben Nil. "At first, Selim and I were tied only with straps. Now they put us in iron too. That is a bad sign. We are lost."

"Oh no, something must and will happen to save us."

"What could that be? I can't do anything, neither can Selim and you will be tied to the tent."

"If nothing else occurs, one thing will happen. I will attack Ben Mubarek."

"Impossible, you will be tied to the tent-rod."

"Yes, if I rise, the tent collapses, and I will be surprised if I couldn't grab Ben Mubarek."

"How could that help us?"

"Very much. Once I have him in my hands, I won't let go."

"So they will kill us."

"Maybe not. He will be our hostage and we can get our freedom against his."

"But you are tied and without weapons, while he carries his knife even when asleep. If you, in spite of your handcuffs are able to grab him, he will simply stab you to death."

"I will grab him in such a way he won't be able to reach for his knife."

"One thing is sure. Should we ever get out of this deadly situation, I will come with you to England and change my religion."

"I don't know which religion you want to change to. If it is the Jewish one, it won't be easy. It takes a long time and you would have to learn a lot. And what will you live on? I cannot keep you on once we are there."

"Haven't I told you about the bag of gold the grateful trader whose brothers were murdered had left in my saddle bag?"

"Yes, I remember, but now is not the time to talk about this. Of one thing I am sure, I have not encouraged you to take on my religion."

"No, not with words, but by your actions."

"Why not change to another religion?"

"From what I know, to me the Jewish religion makes the most sense. I cannot see that other religions have done anything good to the world."

They had to break off their conversation because people came and took them near the tent. They were fed again and Leopold was once more put into the tent, where he was tied to a tent-rod as the night before. Ben Mubarek sat in front. Leopold could hear that he sent two spies to the village and ordered water because his jug was nearly empty. It took nearly an hour before the man who was sent for water returned. Ben Mubarek drank and put the jug behind him in the tent.

The two spies returned and reported a lot of activities in the village. It was unlikely they would go to sleep soon. Ben Mubarek seemed to think. Then he said: "All right, we will attack after midnight. We will have a rest until then. Bring the blankets for my bed!"

Leopold listened attentively to every word and, with bated breath, paid attention to Ben Mubarek's movements. The latter took the blankets and prepared his own berth. The jug was in his way. He put it aside so as not to knock it over and spill its contents. Leopold almost trembled with excitement about whether he would take the water away again. When Ben Mubarek finished his activity, he came once more to Leopold to check his fetters.

"Son of a dog, today is your last good day. Tomorrow, the Reis Effendina will be in my hands, then you both will howl so that they will hear you in Khartoum."

He then went to his berth and stretched himself out. He had left the water near Leopold, who breathed deeply with relief and waited until he could assume that Ben Mubarek was asleep. Then he stretched his tied legs toward the jug. With the point of his feet behind the vessel, he slowly, very slowly, managed to pull it toward himself. The opening of the jug was happily wide enough for him to put one hand inside. The left hand which is usually a bit smaller than the right, was put in first. The water was cool. The time, for him, was difficult to estimate. It took another hour before he withdrew it. When he felt it with his right hand, he noticed the skin had little wrinkles. The hand had shrunk. With his right hand he turned the cuffs. He nearly shouted with joy when he managed to free it with losing only a little blood and none of his skin. Quickly, now he reached the point of his neck where the cross-bar of the shebah had held his head in position. He removed it. Now to untie his legs, after which he found himself in possession of all his limbs. The handcuffs were still hanging on his right hand, but they could now be used as a weapon.

He crept to Ben Mubarek on his belly, slowly. Ben Mubarek's breath was regular, he slept. A blow on his temple – a half expiring rattle in his throat – the man was Leopold's.

Now to get out. Leopold took the knife and the pistol away from his prisoner. In front of the tent were the guards; behind and on its left were bushes. He took the knife and cut a big slit in the right side of the tent. He then pushed Ben Mubarek out, crawled out after that and put him on his own right shoulder. He managed to get out of the wood into the plain with only a few shrubs and trees and where he knew the terrain.

Ben Mubarek was heavy and Leopold did not fancy carrying him for half an hour to the village. He still had the straps that were tied on his legs. He bound his prisoner to a tree, used Ben Mubarek's belt and long turban cloth, which were also sufficient for a gag. Then he ran to the lake where he could see the settlement. Everything was dark. Against the supposition of the spies, everyone had gone to sleep. He went on and had nearly reached the village, when he heard voices.

It turned out that, what happened in the western culture also happened in Africa. A pair of lovers had a rendezvous. As luck would have it, it was one of the interpreters, who was not shocked but overjoyed to be surprised by Leopold, or Poldi Ben Anglesi Effendi, as he called him.

"We all missed you very much, Effendi. Even the Reis Effendina's asakers have more trust in you and regretted your departure."

Leopold asked him to call Agadi. The interpreter happily agreed. "Do it without anybody else noticing," Leopold instructed him.

It took only ten minutes for him to reappear. Leopold took Agadi to his people, the Dinkas, who were presently under Ben Mubarek's rule. Agadi woke two of them and told them of Ben Mubarek's betrayal and of his intention to make them slaves after completion of their tasks. It took only minutes for them all to be told of Agadi's presence and Ben Mubarek's treachery.

Ben Mubarek's people were sleeping, Leopold's escape had not been noticed yet. Agadi turned to Leopold. "Please return to your tent. We are three times as many as Ben Mubarek's asakers. We will overpower them. You don't have to help us."

Leopold was happy. It was not easy to reach the tent unnoticed, but he succeeded. His eyes were used to the dark and, looking through the small opening at the entrance, he saw Ben Nil and Selim nearby. Two of the guards were awake but with their backs turned toward the tent. This opportunity had to be taken. With Mubarek's heavy pistol, one blow on the guards' heads was sufficient. He then rushed to Ben Nil, who was awake and recognised Leopold immediately. "Effendi," he whispered, "you are free?"

"Yes, be quiet, don't wake anybody."

Leopold removed his shebah and his leg ties. Unfortunately, he had to leave him with his handcuffs. "Here, on the right are our rifles. Give one to me, I can use it despite my fetters."

"No, come with me into the tent, the Dinkas might mistake you for an asaker."

"The Dinkas? What about them? How can they…"

Leopold did not let him finish his sentence and pushed him into the tent. He had just time to free Selim when the Dinkas attacked. With a threefold superiority it was over in minutes. None of the asakers escaped. Tied up and lying on the ground, it was almost laughable to see their faces when they saw the prisoners free and in friendly association with their former accomplices. They shouted and cursed in vain. The effect of their coarseness was that they were put in the chains and shebahs that Ben Mubarek had brought for the people of Wagunda.

Leopold sent Ben Nil and Selim to collect Ben Mubarek. They brought him after putting him in Leopold's heavy shebah and in handcuffs. Leopold wanted not to talk to him but to show him his contempt. But Ben Mubarek stepped in front of him, looked at him with hateful eyes and treated him to unrepeatable curses.

Leopold became angry: "Be quiet, you miserable wretch. A few hours ago you asked me not to let my people down. I told you I would do my utmost. I have kept my word and it is you whose possibilities are at an end. I have proved to you that good is stronger than evil. I am finished with you. You are now at the Reis Effendina's mercy."

How the few hours till daybreak passed is easy to imagine. The most lively of all was Selim, who forced everybody to listen to his heroic deeds and to convince them that he was the greatest hero in the world.

Daylight arrived and the whole group, including the new prisoners, journeyed slowly toward Wagunda. Leopold had an idea for a bit of fun. As they were walking along the lake, they were seen by early risers of the village. They were thought to be the expected enemy. Their war-cries brought out all the warriors who, at the command of the Reis Effendina, came down in separate divisions to drive the enemy into the lake. Leopold sent Selim on an ox toward them. The greatest hero of the world was best suited for this job. He went, saw and conquered as usual. They had hardly recognised him and heard his words when their masses disintegrated. Everybody ran down the hill to gaze at the miracle of the morning. Everybody wanted to talk to Leopold, who was busy guarding Ben Mubarek, who otherwise would have been torn to bits by the mob. The asaker, on his command, made a dense circle around the slave-hunter, to escort him into the village. The Dinkas followed, then the male and female inhabitants of Wagunda. Everybody shouted with enthusiasm. Nobody seemed to observe Leopold, who was left alone at the lake. He sauntered slowly up the hill.

Selim had time to put their – or rather his – heroics to the crowd and to convince everybody that he was the greatest. The Reis Effendina came toward him with outstretched hands. "Effendi; I was unjust toward you. Nobody believes Selim, but from what we have heard from Ben Nil I realise we were in great danger last night. We were asleep – all of us."

"Not all of you," countered Leopold. "There were two hearts awake for whom the village was too crowded. If not for them…" He couldn't continue. A band of Gohks stormed toward him. He was grabbed, crushed and whirled from hut to hut, through the whole village. It almost seemed to Leopold that riding the ox from Foguda was less horrible than the triumphal procession through Wagunda. In the afternoon there was a procession of a different kind. Ben Mubarek and his slave-hunters were taken around in the village. They wore, without exception, a shebah around their necks and handcuffs. Ben Mubarek carried the heavy forked branch that he made Leopold carry on the journey from Foguda. They were led to the side of the hill which was too steep to climb. Ben Mubarek saw all his soldiers being shot and falling down the abyss before he was hanged on a tree. Although the punishment was just, Leopold found no reason to see the execution. But he breathed easier with the thought that the terrible threats to him and his friends were no longer to be feared. The Dinkas were pardoned. From them they learned that twenty of the slave-hunters and forty Dinkas were assigned to join Ben Mubarek later. They were in charge of the large herd which was their loot.

After the excitement had died down, Leopold, Ben Nil, forty Dinkas and the freed slaves went to recapture the herds. They reached them after two days. It was as expected. The Dinkas who were with the loot saw their leader Agadi with the group of freed Bors, and went over to them immediately. The twenty slave-hunters saw their fate and defended themselves. They were shot dead – all of them.

Leopold felt sorry for the freed slaves. They had regained their freedom and their herds, but they went home to a burned-out village with the loss of all their families. Some people say they feel less pain than the white race; it is too outrageous to be mentioned.

Chapter 23

Home

It was time for the journey home. The arranged year prior to his marriage was nearly over. His task was fulfilled and he hoped to have eliminated if not every slave-hunter, at least the cruellest. Ben Nil insisted on paying his own fare to England. Leopold calculated that the gold would last for several years and he would acclimatise himself long before his means ran out. Selim wanted to come too, but had to see it was impossible. He made Leopold promise to employ him again should he visit the country.

A telegram informed Leopold's family of their arrival. His beloved Sarah, now eighteen years old, had intended to be sulky, but changed her mind immediately on his arrival. Leopold was young, tanned and handsome. He took her in his arms and his kisses melted all her intentions of sulkiness. When he introduced Ben Nil, now his friend, to his family, he was welcomed immediately. With Leopold's betrothed's sister, Emily, it was love at first sight – on both sides. Ben Nil's English, of which he had acquired a smattering, improved fast. In less than a year he spoke it fluently. He also studied and acquired enough knowledge to be accepted into the Jewish faith.

About the time Leopold and Sarah had their first baby son, called Jonathan after his grandfather, Ben Nil and Emily were married. Many a time the family sat together and listened breathlessly to Ben Nil's account of their adventure in the Sudan. When Jonathan grew bigger, his favourite story was that of his father's encounter with a lion.

Also by the same author

The Rescue of the Murdered Consul's Children

Breathe Deeply, My Son: The Survivor's Story

The Exchanged Heir

The Curse of the War Chest: Late Retribution

Lightning Source UK Ltd.
Milton Keynes UK
UKOW04f0408300114

225485UK00001B/5/P